BLOOD REBEL

BLOOD REBEL

THE DIVINE VAMPIRE HEIRS, BOOK TWO

by

GINNA MORAN

Cover design by Silver Starlight Designs
Cover images copyright Depositphotos

For Inquiries Contact:
Sunny Palms Press
9663 Santa Monica Blvd Suite 1158
Beverly Hills, CA 90210, USA
www.sunnypalmspress.com
www.GinnaMoran.com

To those who share my love of vampires and asked me to write about them. It was about time, right?

PERMANENT BLOOD MATCH

A BEAD OF SWEAT DRIPS down my forehead, and I swipe it away, wishing my body would chill the hell out already. Kicking off my crystal-encrusted heels, I toe them under the plush chair and bounce my bare feet on the cold tiles. Twenty minutes have passed according to the clock on the wall screen, and I want to know what's taking my guys so long.

"Everything all right, Ms. Divine?" Pedro, the Divinity Estate's head of security, asks from his spot a few feet away. He repositions his giant-ass gun on his shoulder to meet my gaze. "Would you like me to call someone on staff to bring you something more to eat?"

I raise an eyebrow and flick my gaze to the mini-buffet on the coffee table in front of me. "No, I think I'm good. Thanks."

He nods in response.

My stomach bunches in knots, refusing to allow me to bring even one of the amazing frosted cupcakes to my mouth. I'm too nervous and uncomfortable as all get out, wearing the same white dress I wore thirty days ago. *Thirty days.* I almost don't believe it. I can't believe it. Tonight is the night I'm supposed to decide who I want to permanently Blood Match with between Diego, Kingston, and Austin. A decision I already decided I'd never make. And my guys don't want me to no matter the stupid contract and rules.

They're my perfect matches—Austin my blood, Kingston my body, and Diego my mind. With them, I've never felt so complete. What we have works no matter what the world would think—and it's something we can't tell them. If we do, it'll declare a flaw in the Blood Match Program. It's supposed to be one perfect donor to one vampire—not three.

If it were any other way, most vampires wouldn't pay the ridiculous price that helps keep humans in the program safe. The money also pays to create factions of exempt human heirs. Vampires don't exactly like to share, especially because one human can't provide enough blood for more than one vampire. Without the program, things would be worse off, and I refuse to jeopardize the only real possibility of freedom humanity has left.

And not only could my inability to choose a permanent Blood Match mess up life for many, but it also puts me in more danger than ever. Because I'm certain Donor Life Corp will make me choose, and if I don't, they'll do so for me. Kingston, Diego, and Austin might revolt if that happens. Making two of them hide their love will be impossible. I won't let Donor Life Corp force me to break any of their hearts. They're my perfect matches, and I'm theirs. No one can tell us otherwise. If this wasn't fate for me, then my body wouldn't have adapted.

Something changed me over the last few weeks, and my body remains in what could possibly be a permanent transitional stage between human and vampire. My super hearing and fast regenerating blood never returned to normal after getting poisoned with vampire venom from one of my guys'—and now my—many enemies. I don't heal or move quickly like a vampire, and I don't need blood to survive, but I'm stronger now. Which is a good thing. Being the Blood Match of the heirs of Donor Life Corp comes with a risk my guys are totally worth.

But it's not like I can shout out that I, a donor from The Boxes in Dark Terrace Ranch, am no longer an average human. That I can safely sustain the blood needs of my three perfect vampires even if they are okay with drinking blood from the general population. The consequences of being discovered for what I am now—something yet to be determined—could land me in a cage or lab. It could redefine our entire society. Something I'm not so sure I'm prepared for.

I have too much else to worry about—like the blood debt I'm supposedly going to inherit from my dad that could also threaten my relationship with my guys. Or how my sister's sudden personality change toward me leaves me hurt and on edge.

And I don't even want to consider the state of my best friend, now Blood Matched to the vampire who imprisoned my dad. Just the thought of Brayla being in the care of the unpredictable, most definitely creepy, vampire for the last few weeks makes being here hard. Because it was the Blood Match Program that made it possible and it's the program that makes it difficult for my guys to get a lead on Brayla.

I shift in my seat, trying my best to suppress my out-of-control, wandering thoughts. Without the presences of my guys to distract me, it's too easy to lose myself in every facet of my life I can't control.

I glance at the clock again. *Twenty-five minutes.* Shit. What if something happened? My relationship with my guys and everything we have together is the one thing I feel like I have a semblance of control over. I can't lose it. I won't lose it.

Just when I start to panic, drawing Pedro's attention to me, I hear the rumble of the elevator. I should've spent my time alone distracting myself with one of Diego's favorite movies or Kingston's favorite music playlist. I should've at least tried to crack open the book Austin thought I might like. I should've done anything other than psyching myself out. Because now I'm nervous as hell, and for what happens next, I need to keep myself calm. This is it.

The whoosh of the elevator door declares its arrival before it even dings and slides open. Keeping my gaze trained on my hands, I do my best to ignore the thudding footsteps racing across the empty lobby and in my direction. If I look up,

Mitchell Divine will know I heard his descent from ten levels above—something supposed to be impossible for me. The last thing I need is for the founder of Donor Life Corp—also the creator/dad of my guys—to discover that I'm what Austin declared an anomaly.

"Jewel, we're sorry to have kept you waiting," Mitchell says, materializing in front of me.

I widen my eyes and cover my heart with my hand, hoping my fake surprise fools him. Composing myself, I say, "It's fine," though I really want to tell him that it's about damn time. I hadn't expected to have had to wait alone in the reception area with the armed security guard from the estate. Even Ms. Sybil, the now always super friendly receptionist, isn't here. Just me and Pedro, but I'm basically by myself.

Pedro might look intimidating as hell, but he doesn't have the same desire to keep me safe and alive as my guys do, and the last—now twenty-seven—minutes have been the first time since what we only refer to as *the incident* that I've been away from all of them at once.

Mitchell offers his hand out, and I force myself to take it. The last time I saw Mitchell Divine was when he cornered me and broke into my mind to extract information from me. Granted, it revealed the blood debt I'm to inherit from my dad, but it still pisses me off every time I think about it.

"Are you feeling okay?" he asks, immediately noticing my gross, clammy hands. "You look unwell."

Probably because I'm sweating more than even during a

strength building session with Diego. "Nervous is all."

"My sons understood the agreement. You have nothing to worry about, Jewel. You will make the perfect match to..." His voice trails off, and he looks at me expectantly.

Sneaky ass bastard. He thinks I'm going to tell him my non-existent decision early, which will mess things up if he gets even a moment to think things through before I'm presented to the board. "I hope you don't mind, but I prefer to allow my match to be the first to hear this." Shit balls, I don't like the look he gives me.

Bracing against the railing, I prepare to have Mitchell Divine corner me to try to extract the real answer from my mouth. But luckily, the elevator halts and the door slides open. Mitchell leads the way to the grand boardroom, and the same six vampires I met last time sit in leather chairs. Kingston, Austin, and Diego huddle in a small sitting area and glide across the room to me the second I enter, intercepting me from their dad.

"Took friggin' forever," I mutter as quietly as I can.

Kingston opens his arms for me, gathering me close to whisper in my ear. "Sorry, babe. We all had to propose our prepared contracts."

"And Kingston's is long as hell," Diego says, waiting for me to turn to him next.

"Seriously, Kingston?" I ask while hugging Diego, quickly brushing my lips to his.

"You can save yourself a few hours by picking me," Austin teases, though his voice isn't into it. It's all part of the act. All the vampires listen to us intently, but that's the point. I'm not to show off that Austin's been teaching me to control the volume of my voice, so that even vampires can't hear it at this closeness. The whole intense, mind-reading looking whispering my guys used to do in front of me before I knew they were actually talking is a lot more fun now that I'm included.

Turning to Austin, I slide my arms around his neck and rest my forehead to his, taking a moment to narrow down the noise to focus on our four beating hearts, mine racing in an attempt to crash out of my ribcage.

"Take a breath, Jewel," Austin whispers too quietly for the others to hear. "We're going to be fine."

Inhaling deeply, I fill my lungs with the chilly air coming in from the vent overhead. They'd never admit it, but I can tell how nervous all of them are. They're counting on me to get this right. If I don't, we're screwed. Talk about pressure.

"You got this, babe," Kingston whispers from my side.

Diego stands behind me, kneading his fingers into my shoulders, helping ease my tense muscles. "Just like we practiced, beautiful. Honest but not too honest."

I nod, straightening my back though all I want to do is to remain sandwiched between the three of them where it's safe. "Let's just get this over with, so we can go home."

The three of them move to Mitchell's side, leaving me to pad across the expansive room alone. I wish I had remembered to put my shoes back on downstairs. The stilettos, while hurting my feet to wear, were pointy enough to use as weapons in case all of this goes to shit, and I find myself in the middle of a bunch a vampires who'll try to tear me and each other apart.

"Ms. Divine," a gorgeous red-headed vampire says from her spot next to the head of the table, where a chair remains empty for me. "All we need is for you to read over the contract of the vampire you intend to Blood Match with. Once you sign, you'll be entrusted into their care, and your next of kin will be notified for you during this transitional phase while the two you decline to match will relocate from the Divinity Estate."

"What?" I ask. "They have to move?"

"You may direct your questions to your Blood Match."

I shift to look behind me at Kingston, Diego, and Austin. "Move?"

They all shrug.

What the hell? How messed up is it that I'd displace two of them from their home? And where would they go? How could we make this work?

"It's only fair to my sons. How would you feel if you were forced to remain living with the one who rejected you?" Mitchell whispers in my ear. I stiffen at his cold breath tickling my hair, his words low and sultry, only intended for me. "Especially if you were in love with them."

"In love?" I can't stop from saying the words out loud.

I shift to look at Kingston, Diego, and Austin, who remain expressionless a few feet away. My heart picks up pace as I turn back to the contracts before me. None of us has mentioned the L-word apart from loving things about each other. And the fact that Mitchell Divine points it out that all of his sons love me—*love* me—holy shit balls. Why am I freaking out?

My body betrays my mind, begging it to get itself under control, but a wave of emotions battles through me, shoving away and destroying the resolve I needed to act my way through this. For our plan to work, I need to be in control of my body. I can't even control my breathing as my breath comes in pants.

Nasty sweat from my forehead splashes across Kingston's contract, twice as long as both his brothers. And then the tears blur and escape my eyes next, smearing Austin's beautiful scripted signature of his contract. I brace my hand on the table, accidentally crumpling the top page of Diego's.

"Ms. Divine," the red-head says, drawing my attention back to her. "Your decision, please."

I swallow and shift on my bare feet, my whole body trembling. The weight of everyone's gazes burns into me the longer I stare at the contracts. I struggle to inhale air, my nose now running as everything sinks in. I'm going to screw this up. I know it. Just the thought of having to pick someone sends me spiraling down a vortex it'll take my mind, my body, and my blood to come together to help me escape.

I clear my throat. "I—um—"

"Ms. Divine," a male vampire says, sitting on the other table from the red-head. "You've had adequate time to make a decision."

"This is why I suggested she be disqualified," the only other female vampire says.

A man with long, black hair leans back in his chair, lacing his hands on his neck. "This type of decision shouldn't be in the hands of a donor. From her file, it seems she could barely manage to take care of herself."

Without thinking, I slam my hands on the contracts. "Shut up! I can't think! I'm trying to—"

The world spins as cool arms encircle me at the same time cacophonous growls rip through the air. From over Kingston's shoulder, I watch as both Diego and Austin block us while all the other vampires rise from their seats, flashing all sorts of various lengths of sharp fangs in my direction.

"Back the fuck off and let Jewel make her decision," Diego says. "None of you are helping."

"She seems rather incapable," the red-haired woman snaps, glaring at me. "And I don't have all night to wait on a donor to make what should be an easy decision. She's had plenty of time with the three of you. If she chose to use it unwisely, that's on her."

It takes Kingston pressing his lips to mine to stop me from shouting that I don't care about her damn plans.

"This is one of our futures," Austin says. "Be respectful."

Mitchell clears his throat from his place near the wall, drawing everyone's attention to him. He's only said a few words to me, and now I'm almost afraid of what more he has to say now. Because despite my panic and fury, this is the moment we've been waiting for. The moment I've spent the last three weeks preparing for with my guys. And it can only go three ways: One, Mitchell will decide on my behalf, and we'll have to burn the place down. Two, the guys will have to Rock-Paper-Scissors, and we'll have to fight our way out because they'll call a draw. Or three—

"I will ask Jewel myself who she wants to be with," Mitchell says.

"What?" I clench my jaw to keep my face straight instead of smiling like I want. The panic rolling through me melts away as our plan finally jumps into motion in the direction we need. My guys know their dad so well. As they predicted, Mitchell would insist on using mind manipulation on me to pull my decision from my subconscious to pick who I truly yearn to be with.

"I admire your compassion and desire not to hurt any of my son's feelings, but as per the contract, a decision must be made. If you do not, you breach your contract, and your beneficiaries lose—"

"Okay, do it," I snap, cutting him off. Turning to Diego, Kingston, and Austin, I hold open my arms and accept another hug from each of them. "I hope you guys understand."

"Breathe, Jewel," they all whisper too quietly for anyone to hear. "It's going to work."

It has to. Our options are shit otherwise.

Mitchell stands in front of me the moment they step back. I blink away a new stream of tears that pours from my eyes, the memory of how awful it was to be in Mitchell's control flashing back to me. But this time is different. It's not Mitchell breaking in my mind I'm worried about. He can't. Not with my guys' blood in my system. What I'm afraid of is he'll realize I'm acting like he can.

I quickly glance at the other vampires still standing around the table to bear witness to the incredibly invasive, infuriating mind manipulation some vampires are capable of. Each of their faces grins smugly, showing me exactly where they believe I belong. They obviously don't treat the Blood Match Program how the Divines intended it. I'm just another donor making Donor Life Corp a shit ton of money that I doubt will go anywhere outside this room.

"Come on, babe. Tell everyone how I'm your perfect body match," Kingston says from next to me, attempting to lighten the situation. "Tell them how you can't wait for me to rock your—"

Diego shoves Kingston into Austin. "Kingston."

I smirk at them, my heart rate managing to even out. Cool fingers cup my cheek, forcing my attention away from my three perfect vampires, and I swallow, stiffening at Mitchell's closeness. He leans into me, blurring the world around us to where I can only focus on his eyes.

"Jewel, you will not look away until I tell you," Mitchell says, attempting to capture my gaze.

Shit. Shit. Shit. I suck in a few breaths without blinking just like Kingston taught me during one of our staring contests. If I blink, Mitchell will know. And effin' A, do my eyes want to betray me by watering.

"Please relax. I will not hurt you," he says, gazing at me intently.

Drooping my shoulders, I force my muscles to react to his words.

He licks his lips, rubbing them together. If I didn't know any better, I'd say he was just as nervous as I am, but his heartbeat gives nothing away, remaining steady. "I'm going to ask you a few simple questions."

I remain frozen without responding.

"Please state your name."

"Jewel Divine."

His eyes soften. I bet he was expecting me to say Jewel Jordan. If I could see my guys, I bet they're grinning like crazy. Their sudden beating hearts summon all sorts of warm fuzzies inside me, making me relax even more.

"How have my sons been treating you the last thirty days?"

"Amazing." I keep my answers short just like Diego recommended. My mind will only give what it has to under manipulation.

"Are you in love with any of them?"

OhmyeffingG. This was not the moment I wanted to profess my feelings, feelings none of them have asked me about because the acceptance to be with all three of them was enough. My love comes in the form of actions. The words have never needed to be spoken out loud, and doing it for an audience pisses me off.

"Yes," I say, afraid my hesitation might give me away.

Mitchell only smiles.

I brace myself for his next question, knowing the time for my declaration has come.

"So, tell me Jewel, who do you want to permanently Blood Match with?" Mitchell asks, running his finger through strands of my hair to push it out of my face.

"I don't know," I say.

If my guys weren't standing close by, I'm pretty sure the gorgeous red-head would snatch me away from Mitchell from the sound of her guttural grunt that echoes through the room.

Mitchell furrows his brows. "Jewel, tell me who you desire to permanently Blood Match with."

"I don't know," I repeat.

Digging his fingers into my cheeks, Mitchell nearly makes me cry out from the sudden pain. "Why don't you know?"

"I need more time," I say, keeping my voice even despite my mind begging me to run.

"But you said you loved one of my sons."

I don't respond to his comment.

"Which one of my sons do you love?" he asks, narrowing his gaze on me.

I swallow the burning in my throat. "All of them."

Holy shit balls. The way Mitchell tenses, I know all of hell might break loose.

PERFECT VAMPIRE MATCHES

MITCHELL BREAKS HIS EYE CONTACT, releasing me from his hold. If it wasn't for Kingston catching me, I'd have landed hard on my ass. Chaos erupts around me as the board of vampires argues over my admission. Who knew a little donor like me could get under all of their skins and cause such an adverse reaction?

"That was perfect," Kingston whispers, keeping me in place even though I want to drag us to hide behind the protective shield of Austin and Diego still behind us.

Mitchell slams his hands on the table, knocking off the stacks of papers, sending them flying through the air. My chest clenches as each future my guys planned out for me drifts to the floor only to get stepped on by the flustered board.

"Just pick an heir for her, Mitchell. It is important that no one sees a flaw in our program. One perfect donor to one perfect vampire. That's how it was intended." It's like everyone has that thought memorized. Kingston wasn't joking, and I'm so thankful my guys were prepared for this reaction.

Mitchell glances from his sons to me, a strange look crossing his face. The whole room silences, half the vampires holding their breaths. I tremble in Kingston's arms and reach my hands out behind him to clasp Diego and Austin's hands.

"Jewel," Mitchell says from behind me. "You will officially match with—"

"We'd like to submit a petition for more time," Kingston, Diego, and Austin say in unison. "We'd also like to apply for a Blood Vow on Jewel's behalf."

"A what?" I ask, surprise widening my eyes. I knew they were planning to petition for more time on the basis of my supposed indecisiveness, but what the eff is a Blood Vow? It's not the first time I've heard the term either.

No one responds to my question. Instead, the board members talk among themselves for all of a minute and turn to my guys. The red-headed vampire steps forward and extends her hand out to shake each of theirs. "Due to these unforeseen circumstances *again*, we grant all of your requests for more time. Please keep the situation discreet. We will also accept Ms. Divine's Blood Vow application upon arrival. You have seven days to submit it." The woman turns to me but keeps her hands to herself. "Ms. Divine, you will have the same amount of time it takes to process your application to make your decision. If you do not, we'll consider it a breach of contract and your heirs will lose their benefits. Do you understand?"

As much as I want to ask her how much time I have or what the hell a Blood Vow is, I don't. All I do is nod my head.

The vampires leave the room so quickly that I don't have a chance to react. I spin around to face Kingston, Austin, and Diego to throw myself at them, but Mitchell Divine remains present, giving me a once over.

"A Blood Vow, my sons?" Mitchell asks without moving his mouth.

I force myself to shuffle closer, pretending like I can't hear him. "I'm sorry for all of this."

"I'm in love with her, Dad," Austin says first, keeping his gaze locked on mine, his lips unmoving in a whisper he knows I'll hear.

"As are we," both Kingston and Diego say. OhmyeffingGod. They're admitting that they love me to their dad in front of me, and I can't even react.

The three of them stay behind their dad, and Austin mouths, "Sorry."

Kingston winks, drawing my attention to him. "Never sorry, babe," he mouths slowly, his full lips begging for me to crash past his dad to kiss him.

Diego rubs his hands over his face for a moment and mouths, "I'll make it up to you." At least it's what I think he says.

Mitchell appears in front of me, his presence commanding my attention, though all I want to do is continue to look at each of my guys. "Jewel, while this is neither conventional nor easy, I cannot blame you for the desire of your heart," Mitchell says, surprising me. I thought he'd scold me for putting everyone in this position. "While the board of Donor Life Corp doesn't always see eye-to-eye with my vision, I do hope you find the new terms agreeable. Again, I'll provide your heirs with another bonus."

I open my mouth to tell him that it's not necessary, but Diego shakes his head at me, knowing what's on my mind before it even leaves my lips.

"Thank you," I respond instead.

Mitchell grasps my hand, pulling it up to kiss the back of it. "She is quite exquisite, boys. More beautiful every time I see her. I can only hope her final decision doesn't tear you apart." His mouth doesn't move as he says the words intended only for my guys, and I shiver at the vibration of his whisper against my skin. He lowers my hand and smiles. "Until we meet again, Jewel. Perhaps my sons will relent and bring you to one of Donor Life Corp's grand affairs." Obviously, he doesn't think being discreet is as necessary as the board.

I flick my gaze to Kingston's first, and he clenches his jaw at even the mention of taking me anywhere that involves mingling with a room of vampires. "That would be lovely, Mr. Divine."

"Call me Mitchell, Jewel. We will soon share blood."

He disappears a moment later, leaving me standing in front of my perfect vampire matches. They close the space to me, all of them hugging me at once, making me laugh. A million thoughts rush through my mind as tonight's events swirl through my head.

"Shit balls," I whisper. "That was intense."

"You probably have a ton of questions, beautiful," Diego says.

"You think? How much time? And a Blood Vow? What about the fact that you all admitted you lo—"

Kingston cuts off my questions with a kiss, curling his hands around my hips, taking advantage of the fact that tonight is our night, and he doesn't need my permission to kiss me anymore. Which I'm so glad about. I had no idea how much I enjoyed surprise interruptions until Kingston showered me with them.

"We'll talk in the car, babe," Kingston whispers.

"Do you have another long-ass contract for me to sign?"

He narrows his eyes at me. "I was being authentic."

Pulling away, I bend down and start collecting the scattered papers of their contracts into my arms. I can't help it. Now that I don't have a bunch of annoyed vampires snapping their fangs at me, I want to see what each of them desires of a future with me.

"Beautiful, what are you doing?" Diego asks.

"What does it look like? I want to see what you all have in store for me."

Kingston hooks his arm around my waist and hoists me against his side with my arms and legs dangling off the ground. "Oh, no you don't, babe."

"Yeah, you might reject Kingston immediately," Austin says.

"Never." I reach up to purposely squeeze Kingston's butt until he shifts me so I'm not dangling upside down. "I kind of like having him around," I tease.

Kingston chuckles. "Damn straight. Who'd break all the rules for her if not me?"

My eyes widen. "Does that mean?" I'm afraid to say the words out loud. Coming into Donor Life Corp tonight meant that Kingston could have full access to their system, which he's not allowed remotely on his on-call-only leave of absence.

He pouts, his answer obvious. "I'm sorry, babe."

"Brayla and Orlando have been removed from the system," Diego says.

I frown. "How is that possible?"

Shrugging, Kingston says, "Could mean a number of things, but nothing I want you to worry about. The Diggs remain in Haven Springs with no indication of complaints. If something happens to a match, it's usually the heirs to be the first to inform us with a complaint. The last check in from them in the system says they're more than happy with the arrangement."

Austin eases the crumpled papers I still clutch of their contracts from my hands. "But don't give up, Jewel. There are other ways of tracking people, and we'll get it taken care of now that this is over."

"But first, let's get out of here." Kingston spins me around, making me scream and laugh, and then the world blurs, only gaining clarity in the elevator. We're out of the building a minute later. Diego holds the back door to the car open for me, and Kingston slides us in together. Shifting me off his lap, he buckles me behind Austin and rests his head on my shoulder, twining our fingers together. I still have so many questions to ask, but I know I have to wait until we at least leave the city. I might not get them to open up until they're no longer on edge by the presence of too many curious vampires.

Diego starts the car and peels away from the curb, and I turn my gaze from the crowd of shadow dwellers now free to roam the streets of Dark Terrace Ranch under the darkness of night.

Kingston messes with his jacket before shrugging out of it to give to me. "I know you wanted to read the contracts, but seriously, I'd much prefer our lives to be more of a surprise," he says to fill the silence in the car.

I fake glare at him. "Sure that's it."

Diego chuckles. "Partly, beautiful. At least for myself. You shouldn't have to worry about what we came up with when the only perfect future we can create is with you and what you want from us too."

I stretch against my harness to squeeze his shoulder, loving how they bring up the conversation so easily, using it to distract me from the disappointment of another dead-end lead of Bray-la. It's easy to forget the murder on my mind elicited by Orlando with my guys promising such a future I never imagined before. "Is that why no one told me about the Blood Vow application? What does that even mean?"

All three of them glance to each other without a word. It's Austin who says, "We'll talk about that more later, Jewel."

"So, it's personal?" I ask without needing a response. It's written all over their faces that they want me to keep it between me and them individually. Which I don't mind. I love what I have with each of them separately as much as the loyalty we share together. It's what makes this work. "A vow sounds serious. How much time does it take to process the application?"

"Six months to a year," Kingston says. "At least for a Divine heir. Such an occasion must take a lot of planning."

I suck in a breath at his words. "Wait, we get six months to a year?" I can't stop the smile from crossing my face. I had expected far less and stressed we might not get any at all. "That is friggin' awesome."

"Jewel," Austin says from his spot in the front seat. "We get more than that, remember?"

"Yeah, babe. We're planning on forever."

Forever.

I frown. "But I don't have forever."

Diego reaches back and touches my knee while keeping his eyes trained on the road. "We're going to see to it that you do."

"Come here, babe," Kingston says, wiggling his fingers at me. "I want to get you out of that dress."

"You out of the suit first," I say, smirking.

Kingston's shirt falls to the floor in two ripped pieces, and I crack up, staying in place. Diego appears in the doorway to the room with a tray of dinner for me and groans the second his gaze falls on his brother. "Kingston, seriously?"

"Can't you at least wait until we leave the room?" Austin says from his spot near the bed. He messes with the blood draw equipment, getting things ready.

Kingston doesn't take his eyes off me. "You're taking forever, and our girl asked me to strip it off. I'm not denying any of her requests after that shit show tonight."

I giggle, blush crawling up my chest to bloom in my cheeks. "I'm just glad it's over. All I want to do is feed you, be fed, and change into my pajamas."

Austin motions me forward. "I'm ready when you are."

Pressing my lips together, I summon my nerve and say, "I didn't mean I wanted to do things in that order."

I turn around to face my back to them and pull the side zipper of my dress, letting it drop to the floor. The three of them each suck in a breath and hold it. I purposely ignore them and stroll into the closet, smiling to myself. Teasing them never gets old. They make me feel like the best thing they've ever seen.

Running my fingers along all of the dresses neatly hung up, I take my time and wait to see who breathes first. After we decided I didn't need my own room, the guys divided my stuff to fill their rooms. I didn't realize it at first, but they each took things they want to see me in, and Kingston's choices unsurprisingly don't exactly leave much to the imagination.

"Babe, do you need help?" Kingston asks. "Because putting your clothes on wasn't on my list of things to do with the rest of our night."

I laugh, releasing a stupid snorting sound that makes all three of them chuckle. Opening the top drawer of the built-in, I gaze at the in-his-dreams lingerie Kingston swapped my pajamas out for. I'll give him credit for his sneakiness, but just because it's there, doesn't mean I'll wear it. I haven't gone to that level with any of them yet unless you count drinking their blood, which I haven't drunk directly from them since nearly dying on the hillside at the hands and bite of Katherine Duchanne.

Running my hands through the different colored laces, silks, satins, and some soft sheer materials I can't name, I mess up the piles and glance back to the open door. Kingston releases his breath first and chuckles, knowing exactly why I'm taking so long. The cute bastard. He's not the only one who can play around. "Kingston, call security, I—"

I don't even get a chance to make a joke about a pajama thief before my guys surround me, flashing their fangs.

"Shit, you're fast," I say, frowning.

"What's wrong, babe?" Kingston pulls me against him, enveloping me in his arms.

Austin releases a sigh through his nose, composing himself.

"Are you okay, Jewel?"

I twist my lips to the side, nodding.

Diego peers from me standing in my bra and underwear to the open drawer with the lingerie. And then he laughs. "Looks like Jewel has been robbed of everything she likes to sleep in."

Both Kingston and Austin meet me with serious expressions, clearly missing the brilliance of my poorly executed joke. I didn't consider that the second I said security that they'd rush to my side. Now I'm giving them a lot longer show than I planned on. Sure, they've seen me like this before, but never all together, and I'm not sure I can handle so much intensity.

"Not funny, babe," Kingston says, kissing my bare shoulder. "But nice try."

"If you'd like, I'll bring you something from our room," Austin says, eyeing Kingston.

I smile at him while watching Kingston as well in my peripheral vision. He reacts exactly how we both expect with a low groan and a glare at the side of Austin's face.

"It's okay. I'll figure this crap out. Thanks though," I say, tightening my hand on Kingston so he doesn't punch Austin.

He behaves better than I expect, though now he's going to silently gloat about it being his night. Kingston shoos his brothers out of the closet and takes his time drinking me in. I sweep my fingers at him to get him to go back into the bedroom to wait for me. The last thing I want is to have to reject all his possible suggestions. Instead, I open up his drawer and pull out one of his cotton shirts. I unclasp my bra, grin again at the sudden intakes of breaths, and then shrug into the shirt.

"Shit, I wish it were my night," Diego muses.

A thud resonates through the air, and I step out of the closet to find Diego sitting on the ground, Austin back beside the bed with his blood draw equipment, and Kingston propped on his pillows with his hands behind his head, looking smug as hell. But I won't comment. He's already given up half his night to going to Dark Terrace Ranch.

"Hot, babe," Kingston says, patting the spot next to him.

Diego beams his irresistible smile at me. "She definitely wears it better than you."

Austin smiles without saying anything, his cheeks blooming with the blush that makes me feel better about my own inability to control the heat always threatening to set my face on fire. I smile at all three of them, bouncing on the balls of my feet as I cross the room.

"You guys look as hungry as I am," I tease. "People are going to think I never feed you."

If my sister Ramona heard me, she'd probably have a heart attack. Actually, all of Dark Terrace Ranch would probably shun me and suggest someone toss me into the shadows. But I'm beyond caring, especially with how amazing my guys treat me. I never thought I'd enjoy feeding a vampire, but here I am, willingly extending my arm to Austin for a draw.

"Probably best we keep it that way, beautiful," Diego says, getting to his feet.

Kingston groans. "Though I really fucking want to rub it

in."

Austin doesn't comment as he comes up beside me to tie a rubber band around my arm to extract my blood. Because of my blood's new ability to regenerate crazy fast, partly due to my weird transitional stage and also consuming my guys' blood, I now provide enough of it to feed all of them daily. And I'm happy to.

If it wouldn't become suspicious, they'd forgo general population blood altogether. Luckily, the Divinity Estate hosts and houses many elite vampires that none of the blood goes to waste. I crinkle my nose at the thought. If I were still a gen. pop. donor, I'd be annoyed at the thought of donating for nothing. So while I've never come within touching distance of any of the vampires and have only ever seen them moving about the terrace from one of our balconies, I'm sort of relieved they're here, and my guys aren't dumping blood down the drain.

Pulling a thermos from his bag, Austin pours dark red liquid into the only empty glass on his tray. It took a few days of figuring out the perfect amount of vampire blood to give me, but now that he has, I feel less like a donor and more like a recipient, even though the blood I drink doesn't provide the sustenance I need to survive. It does, however, prevent other vampires from manipulating my mind and suppresses the nightmares caused by the vampire I hate most in the universe. The one—

A cool finger touches my cheek. "Hey, babe?"

I blink my sudden tears away and smile at Kingston. "Sorry, I got lost in my thoughts."

Austin touches my knee while Diego holds my free hand. Kingston hugs an arm around me from behind and rests his chin on my shoulder. No one comments on the fact that I'm crying. They know why. My disappointment over the whole Brayla thing is obvious. But they do give me the support I need to ease the pain, to carry hope. Because we're in this together. Stronger together.

I slowly raise my glass up. "Here's to us."

"To us," they all repeat.

"And how much I love you. Each of you...even if I had to confess that to your dad first."

Without giving them a chance to respond, I tip back the glass and drink, the sweet mixture sending a wave of warmth through me. I turn to Kingston and kiss him first, just a light tease to show him how much I appreciate him.

"We're more than just body matches," I whisper in his ear for only him to hear. "I feel like our souls matched too."

He nuzzles his nose to mine and smiles. "I love you too, babe. And I plan to make up for the bullshit tonight."

Sliding out of his arms, I meet Austin for a hug, pulling him slightly away to kiss him, knowing how much he wants to though he won't make the first move in Kingston's room because of the unspoken rule they share.

"I know we're a perfect match for nutrients, and I love that we both provide the sustenance we both need to each other, but you're matched with my heart. And I appreciate how careful you are with me."

"You are my heart outside my body, Jewel," he whispers. "I hope you can feel how madly in love with you I am."

I smile and kiss him again. "So much so I know I can survive on it if it's the only thing I have left."

His cheeks flush, and he hides his face against my shoulder, hugging me for a moment longer. I watch him leave the room and wiggle my fingers when he gives me one last look before disappearing.

Diego closes the distance to me next, and I slide my arms around his neck and pull him down to meet me for a kiss. He smiles against my mouth, letting our breaths mingle, and waits for me to pull back first.

"I love you, beautiful," he says, beating me to professing our feelings out loud. "You have no idea how happy you make me."

I smile. "I think I do. You get me. You're more than my personality match. You match with a part of my very essence, making me feel like as long as you're with me, I can breathe."

"And you swear you hate romances," he whispers, grinning.

"They might be wearing on me."

"Good, because I've been dying to sweep you off your feet."

I cup his face and kiss him again. "You already do that."

Diego hugs me once more and disappears from the bedroom, closing the door behind him. Swiveling on the balls of my feet, I turn and face Kingston, lying shirtless on his bed. He extends his arms out to me, wiggling his fingers to invite me closer, and I rub my lips together, suddenly nervous.

Finally admitting our love out loud brings us to a new level in our relationship. His desire shines clear on his face and body as he drinks me in, inch-by-inch from my bare feet to my hair that I unraveled from my messy braid to drape around my shoulders.

I lose myself in his dark eyes, my smirk disappearing as I take a small step closer, twisting the fabric of my shirt between my fingers. My heart picks up pace, followed by the comforting sound of Kingston's thrumming as loudly as it used to with my ear pressed to his chest.

He doesn't move, letting me close the space between us at my own pace no matter how torturously slow my legs drag me forward. I slide onto the bed next to him, well aware that dawn is still a bit of time away. We've spent our last couple of nights together practicing my acting and working on my reactions to face the board, but now that we don't have to worry about them, the night finally belongs to us to do what we want.

Kingston pulls me closer, sliding his arms around me. "I thought we could just watch a movie. Dinner for you in bed. Some much needed cuddling."

I smile, shifting to drape my legs over his. "Really? That's all you had in mind?"

"Well, no," he says, kissing my neck. "But your stomach is growling like crazy, and since you're dressed for bed even before the sunrise, I figured you didn't want to do anything...except for maybe me."

"Well, when you put it like that," I tease.

"I'm just kidding, babe."

"That's too bad." I slide my hands over his taut muscles, flexing and relaxing as I explore his stomach with my fingers.

"I mean, we can do whatever you want. And I mean whatever..." He sucks in a sharp breath and releases a moan the second my fingers disappear under the comforter and graze along the clasp of his pants.

I raise my eyebrows, because he was honest about his joking. If he had really planned to explore our body match, he'd already be undressed. "But you're still wearing your dress pants," I murmur, messing unsuccessfully with the hidden hook. "What's up with that?"

He laughs so loudly at my remark that I take his moment of distraction to unclasp his pants and slide my fingers lower. His laughter fades with another deep breath, and he flips on top of me, kissing me fervently and desperately, sucking my bottom lip into his mouth to graze his teeth over it.

Whatever nerves clinging to me disappear with his roaming fingers. His hand travels down my hip and to my thigh, adjusting my body to curl around his. I gasp at feeling his body react to mine through our clothes. He steals my next breath with another kiss, drawing his mouth from mine to glide his tongue down my neck, his fingers dragging my shirt up at the same time.

"Jewel," he whispers. "Is this okay?"

I nod and lean up so he can pull my shirt off. He hovers over me, drinking me in with his eyes, and I reach up and brush my hand to his cheek, smiling at him. The way his dark eyes capture mine, warming me with their intensity, I feel incredibly loved—something I never even dreamed possible until a few weeks ago.

He brings his lips back to mine, grazing his hand to cup my breast before breaking away again to shimmy lower to kiss my clavicle, working his way down my chest. His lips map my skin, sucking and kissing and licking me in a way that has tingles exploding through me. I squirm at his slow pace, digging my nails into his back, making him moan against my skin.

"Kingston," I whisper, pressing deeper into the bed. "I—" A loud ass moan erupts from my lips, and I cover my face with the pillow to stop the noise from escaping, my whole body trembling with anticipation, wanting nothing more than to test the extent of my attraction and body match with Kingston.

But his hand drops away with the weight of his body. He pants for a moment, twining his fingers through mine, resting our hands together over his pounding heart. "I love you," he whispers. "So. Damn. Much. You have no idea what you do to me. I just—"

"It's okay if you're not ready," I whisper, smirking as he shifts on his elbow to look at me.

His brows furrow. "Wait, what?"

I untwine my fingers from his and trace his muscles to his

navel and lower, making him breathe harder. "I wasn't going to tell you to stop, if that's what you thought."

His dark brows rise, his pouty mouth slightly opening. He stares at me for another moment like he's trying to determine if he heard me correctly. I answer his silent question by biting my lip between my teeth and summoning the nerve to graze my hand over him in a way I haven't touched a guy before.

The world spins, and I land back on my pillow, laughing at how quickly his pants disappear.

"Shit," I gasp.

He grins at me. "Don't worry. I'll slow down."

Just as he bends to kiss me, the phone on his desk rings in three quick successions. He ignores it, taking extra care to slow his pace, brushing his lips gently to mine and then leaning back up to study me. "Babe, this is going to sound totally un-sexy, but if you have any questions—" The phone rings again, cutting him off.

"Oh, um. I'm good. Just don't bite me, okay?"

He kisses my nose. "Bite me all you want."

"Shit," I murmur. "I—"

The phone rings again, and we both turn our gazes to it. Kingston mutters under his breath but still doesn't move to answer it. Instead, he throws a pillow across the room, knocking the small box off his desk with perfect accuracy.

A bright light flashes from the floor before a projection lights up on the wall next to us, triggering the video sensor above it. Kingston swears, disappearing from the bed to disconnect the phone, but my sister's smiling face appears, her eyes searching through the room, trying to find me.

"Jewel?" she asks, her face morphing into a frown. "What's going on? Where are you?"

I don't move. I pray she hangs up and tries back later.

But then her gaze narrows in my direction.

She screams.

BAD TIMING

"RAMONA, DON'T HANG UP!" I shriek, scrambling to pull the comforter around me to sit up in bed.

"What the actual fuck." Her eyes dart around the room, searching to see who I'm with. Since moving into each of the guys' rooms, I've kept the camera pointed at the wall so she could only ever see the curtains or glass behind me. At least the last two times I've talked to her. She stopped answering my daily phone calls and now refuses to let my little cousins Dana and Fallon talk to me at all. She was the last person I expected to call me. She never has before.

"Please, give me a second. You caught me at a bad time." I rush from the bed, keeping the blanket around me.

"You're naked. What are they making you do? Shit, Jewel.

Is this about the sudden deposit of stipends? The council is making us move too. A bigger house."

I inhale a few deep breaths through my nose, turning my attention to Kingston leaning on the wall out of my sister's view in his boxer-briefs. He rubs his hands down his face, still trying to catch his breath. Ramona shifts on screen, trying to peer in the direction I look, but she's limited to what the camera picks up.

"What is going on?" she continues, annoyance lining her words.

I clear my throat. "Please calm down. No one is making me do anything, and my state of dress is none of your business, okay? Like I said, you caught me at a bad time. Kingston didn't mean to answer the call. We were—"

She covers her mouth, her eyes widening. Then she releases the strangest, strangled sounding noise from her throat, her face paling. "Shut up. Shut up! I don't—ew. That's so wrong. You signed up to be an exclusive blood donor, not to give into some horny vampire's desires. Please tell me he's not the one—"

"Ramona!" I yell. "That's enough. I signed up to be Blood Matched, which—"

"I know what it means." She glares at me. "I just thought you were better than—"

Kingston jets from his position to stand in front of the camera, blocking me from the screen. He flashes his fangs, worked up more than I am. Ramona's eyes widen, and she freezes, pressing her lips in a thin line. "Ms. Jordan, you will not talk to Jewel in this manner. You should thank her for all she's done for you."

"Done for me? She left me." Ramona's nostrils flare. "And you brainwashed her. My sister would've *never* been caught alive in the bed of a vampire."

Kingston tenses, curling his hands into fists. "You ungrateful—"

"Kingston," I say, my voice soft as tears threaten to choke me up. "Please, stop. She won't understand."

"Oh, I understand, Jewel," Ramona says.

I stride closer and cut in front of Kingston. His hands slide around my waist, and he hugs me from behind. My sister glowers, her aqua eyes, the same color as mine, glassing over with angry tears. She pushes her bangs off her forehead, wagging her head at me, turning into someone I no longer recognize. She's not the same girl I grew up with in The Boxes just like I'm not the same.

I release a small breath. "You don't understand anything. I love them. They treat me so incredibly well. Like an equal."

She crinkles her nose. "So you're no longer providing blood to them."

It's my turn to frown. "Well, no, I—"

"Then you're *not* their equal. You are there to serve them and feed them. And now you've lowered yourself to pleasuring—"

"Enough!" Kingston yells, startling me. "I will not stand here and listen to you degrade the love of my existence like this.

You have no idea how amazing your sister is. She's willing to give up a life beyond anything any donor could ever imagine to save you from the blood debt you are supposed to inherit from your father. Now—"

A look of utter horror crosses my sister's face at Kingston's words, and a split second later, the call disconnects. Kingston's chest heaves against my back, his anger burning through him, though it does nothing for the cold dread pouring over my head.

Tears spill on my cheeks, my heart shattering into a million pieces. Whatever threads of sisterly love I shared with Ramona were severed with Kingston's words.

"Jewel," Kingston whispers. "I'm sorry."

He attempts to spin me around, but I plant my feet to the floor. I can't believe he told my sister the one thing I wanted to protect her from. How could my life turn from incredible to devastating in a matter of seconds?

I pull away, dragging the comforter with me, and head straight to the bedroom door. I can't help it. If I stay, if I even look at Kingston, I'm going to lose it. My heart screams at me not to put it through the torture of running from a guy it wants to throw itself at, but my mind can't stop replaying what he told my sister in my head. If I stay, I might say something I'll regret.

Kingston sighs from behind me, and I hear him whisper Austin's name. I keep my gaze trained on the floor and head left down the hallway only to have Austin fall in step beside me.

Something crashes from my room with Kingston, and I hug the comforter around me tighter while I make what feels like the longest trek of my existence toward Austin's room.

Diego's shadow stretches across the hallway as he stands in his doorway. "Beautiful, I—"

I shake my head, more tears splashing down my cheeks to roll off my chin. He touches my shoulder once, leaving his room to head in the opposite direction toward Kingston. Austin closes the space between us and gingerly slides his arm around my back, rigidly and barely touching me like he expects me to yell at him to get away.

But I don't. The second his fingers rest over the blanket on my side, I sink into him, hugging him until I can't stop the sob from escaping my mouth.

"I fucked up." Kingston's voice drifts from behind me.

"It was a mistake. Jewel will forgive you," Diego responds.

"I don't deserve her."

Their conversation makes me cry harder, and Austin scoops me up and carries me the rest of the way to his room, clicking the door shut behind us. He tries to set me on his bed, but I refuse to let go of him, so he climbs in with me and rubs circles on my back until my stomach stops heaving with the torment coiling through my insides.

"She hates me," I whisper. "She's never going to forgive me."

Austin twines his fingers through mine and brings my hand to his cheek to feel the weight of our fingers together against his skin. "The transition for humans into Haven Springs is difficult, Jewel. Ramona doesn't hate you. I've told you this before, and I still believe it's true, but I think she's scared of losing you. Your family has entered a new life of privilege. As a minor, your sister, and your cousins for that matter, will never have to experience a donor life. They are far removed from society, and after a while, some humans resent it. From hearing your argument, she sounds like she has beneficiary's guilt. It also sounds like some of the more vocal people in the community might be getting into her head. It's not uncommon for heirs to cut ties with their family member who matches."

I groan and rub my hands over my cheeks. "She's definitely going to now after what Kingston s-said." My voice quivers, and I swear I hear Kingston curse from probably Diego's room. I wouldn't put it past him to listen in on our conversation, especially now. Privacy is something we only pretend to have.

"Can you blame him?" Austin asks.

I shift to meet his vibrant green eyes as glassy as mine are. "I—well, no," I admit. "She said some awful things to me."

"And Kingston's scared. We all are—"

"You think Orlando's going to come soon? Do you think this is why he disappeared?" I tense at the thought of the asshole vampire.

Austin shakes his head. "No, he's staying away for a reason we're still trying to figure out. But what we're scared of—at least I am. I can't speak for my brothers—is that you will start to believe Ramona."

I snuggle against him, shaking my head, sending strands of hair splaying across the pillow. "I'd never. You never have to worry about that, okay? I'm not going anywhere." Unless Orlando tries to collect my sister to finish paying my dad's debt. I don't say it though. I don't even want to consider it. I might be angry with Ramona, but she's my sister, and I'll still do anything for her no matter if she disagrees with my lifestyle.

"We will make sure you will never be in a position to even have to consider it," he says, reading my unsaid words in my gaze.

I nod my head without saying anything.

Rolling over, I pull Austin down to lie behind me, holding his hands against my stomach. His cool fingers stay locked around mine, his breath lightly playing with the loose strands of hair on my neck. I listen to the thrum of his heart to ease the pain in mine until I struggle to keep my eyes open.

I stand at the head of a long, wooden table in a formal dining room with glittering crystal chandeliers, silver candelabras with orange flames dancing toward the strange flags hanging from the ceiling.

Vampires sit in every seat, their blurry faces turned in my direction. Three figures stand at the other end of the table and raise goblets of red liquid into the air. But they don't drink it. At once, all the vampires dump their goblets of blood across the table, slickening the surface.

Heavy hands shove me from behind, and I crash onto the table. Cold fingers rip at my dress, shredding it as I slide on the blood toward the three figures. Blood coats my skin, clumping my dark hair as I lie exposed and placid.

"My precious Jewel," an eerily familiar voice says. "How lovely of you to offer yourself to my guests."

Orlando materializes in front of the three shadowy figures, leaning forward over me on the table. He bites his fangs into his lip, breaking his skin to bleed down his chin. His blue eyes capture mine, and I squirm, struggling to get away from him.

"Leave our girl alone," Kingston says, clamping his hand on Orlando's shoulder. "Her sister satisfies the blood debt. This donor is ours."

Orlando snaps his teeth. Diego shoves him in the back, sending him reeling forward. Before he can crash into me, Austin flips the vampire off, sending him sprawling across the table toward another figure—Ramona.

"I hate you!" she screams at me.

I don't get a chance to watch Orlando fly at her. The world spins, and I gasp, now stretched across the table, empty of vampires apart from my guys. They all stare down at me with sorrowful eyes, holding me flat with their strong hands.

I open my mouth to speak, but blood rains down from the ceiling, bathing me in crimson liquid that makes their eyes flash silver.

"You broke my heart, babe," Kingston says.

Bloody tears drip on Austin's cheeks. "Even after we promised you forever."

"All for a donor who can't stand you, beautiful." Diego

digs his fingers deeper into my leg.

"But don't worry, Jewel." Kingston leans closer, using my name. "You will make it up to us."

All three of my guys flash their fangs and lean down to bite me. I arch up, desire rushing over me, my mouth begging for them to drain me dry.

"Jewel, wake up."

"She deserves such a fate." The voice comes from everywhere and nowhere, biting into me before my three vampire matches can. "So ungrateful."

I tilt my head up, catching sight of a dark-haired figure strolling closer.

"Just forget about her," she says.

"I—"

"She never deserved your loyalty."

"Jewel."

I flip onto my side, my eyes meeting familiar aqua ones. It's me.

I scream.

My voice resonates through the air, startling me awake. I flail, thrashing at the suffocating covers. Flipping over, I roll into Austin's comforting arms, and he holds me against him, petting my hair from my face.

"Shit," I whisper.

"You're okay, Jewel," he whispers. "It was a nightmare."

"Orlando is going to get my sister," I say, panting, my heart beating wildly.

"He's not. It was a nightmare."

"I didn't even care. I said she deser—"

Austin silences my panic with a soft kiss, rubbing his hands up and down my back to smooth the trembles shaking my body. He holds me, brushing his lips to mine without deepening our kiss until I release a long breath and pull away first.

It's then that I realize I'm wearing only my underwear, pressing my boobs into Austin's bare chest. Heat floods my face a second before he blushes and licks his lips, offering me a shy smile.

A second later, he disappears and returns with a pair of my pajamas. I shrug my shirt on but forgo the pants because sweat glistens over my skin. The room is a little too warm—or maybe it's just my body.

"Thanks," I whisper, my throat hoarse, burning with tears that manage to stay in control.

Austin grabs the pitcher of water from my night table and pours me a glass. I swallow a few mouthfuls, the room temperature liquid setting off my stomach. It growls embarrassingly loud, drawing Austin's gaze to study me.

"My sister called before I could eat dinner," I say, bringing the glass back to my lips. "And I was too nervous to eat at the Blood Match Center."

"You must be starving. I can get you—"

"Mind walking me back to Kingston's room first?" I ask. "I want to talk to him."

He nods. "Yeah, sure. I need a little bit of time to get ready for our night anyway."

I smile at him. "I expect ice cream."

"You got it."

"And you to feed it to me."

He chuckles. "I can manage that."

"Shirtless."

Tipping his head back, he releases a loud laugh. "We'll see."

Summoning my courage, I grab the comforter I stole from my room with Kingston off the floor and wrap it around my shoulders. Austin guides me halfway, leaving me with Diego to walk the rest of the way with him, bringing forth memories of my dream again.

"I'm sorry I brushed you off earlier," I say.

"Hey, no worries, beautiful," he says, offering me one of his gorgeous smiles. "You don't have to explain anything."

He hugs me outside Kingston's door and leaves me the second I touch my hand to the doorknob. Slowly pushing it open, I hesitate, my nerves getting the best of me.

"Jewel," Kingston calls from inside. "Please don't leave me."

"Leave you?" I ask, my voice shaking. "I came to apologize."

"Apologize?" Kingston widens the door, standing before me, his eyes red, his black hair a tousled mess that I want to run my fingers through. "I don't deserve an apology. I owe you one and so much more."

"It's cool, dude," I say, purposely using the nickname he gets a kick out of.

His Adam's apple bounces in his throat through a whisper of a smile. I could kick myself for making him so brooding despite how cute he looks with a pout. I just—I have a hard time keeping composed. Sure I could have lived without Kingston telling Ramona about the blood debt, but she doesn't exactly make it easy on any of us, and Kingston—Austin and Diego too—don't tolerate those who intend to harm me, even if it's just hurting my feelings.

He pulls me to him, engulfing me into a hug that lifts me a few inches off my feet. "So, we're okay?"

I nod and kiss him. "Yeah, we're good. And so you know, it wasn't you who broke my heart. And you were right to call out Ramona. I just wish—"

"We'll fix this," he says, knowing I was going to mention the blood debt.

"Will you sit with me while I call her again? I think she might be cooled off enough now to see some reason. I need to explain everything I can to her."

He frowns. "I don't know. I love you, babe. But your sister is a raging—"

"Please."

He sighs. "Okay, for you. But you can't expect me to keep my mouth shut."

I sink deeper into his arms, feeling the weight of them holding me together when a part of me wants nothing more than to fall to pieces. "I don't."

"Good. Then let's get this over with. I have better plans for the rest of the day with you."

I smirk, his remarks welcomed, showing that we're going to be okay. Even if my world falls apart, I have my guys to help me piece it back together. Even better than before. Better than ever.

BLOOD DEBT

I HIT RAMONA'S NUMBER FOR the sixth time, listening to the chime ring through the air over and over again. One of the stipulations involving the Blood Match heirs is that the line of communication can't be blocked. Though it was to prevent a vampire from isolating a match or to cut them off from their family, I'm grateful that it also stops Ramona from blocking me. Because I doubt she wouldn't after our last conversation. She technically doesn't have to answer, but I'm hoping the constant ringing will annoy her enough to do so or that one of my cousins will hear and disobey Ramona by speaking to me.

"You can try again tonight with Austin," Kingston says, resting his head on my shoulder.

I open my mouth to agree, but the screen lights up. Kingston straightens his back and moves out of view from the camera. I squeeze his fingers, meeting the serious eyes of a young guy with long, blond hair waving at someone I can't see over his shoulders. The guy tilts his head the second our gazes meet, studying me.

I'm so surprised by him that all I do is gape, mouth open and all.

Shifting toward Kingston, I whisper, "I think you called the wrong number."

"No, babe. It's definitely your sister's."

"Then who the hell is this dude?" I wince at the sudden rise in my voice as I'm unable to maintain the quiet whisper that normal humans can't hear.

"I assume you're Jewel Jordan?" the guy asks, keeping his eyes narrowed on me.

"Divine," I automatically respond.

His jaw twitches. "I also assume your master stands near-by."

I scrunch my nose. "I don't have a master."

"One of your misters...or is it all of them?" he asks, shifting his jaw in an obvious look of disgust, his nostrils flared, his lips tight. It's the same expression Ramona carries, and I'm certain she picked it up from him. "Rather disturbing that Donor Life Corp allowed you to be entangled in such a situation since they push the whole donor safety bullshit we all know isn't true."

Flinging my hand out, I cover Kingston's mouth before he can breathe a word. "Where's Ramona?"

"Unavailable," the guy responds.

"Then let me talk to Dana or Fallon."

"I'm sorry. The Jordans don't want to speak to you."

"What?"

"You heard me, Ms. *Divine*."

"Then why did you answer? Who are you?" I straighten my back, meeting the guy with my own glare.

"I have a message for your masters."

Kingston nudges my rolling chair, pushing me out of the camera frame to take my place. He surprises me by keeping his anger in check, not even flashing his fangs. If I had a pair of my own sharp incisors, I'd snarl at the guy. He has no business trying to talk to me on my sister's behalf or trying to send messages to my guys.

"In private," the guy says.

"Oh, hell no," I say, climbing into Kingston's lap when I can't shove him back out of the way. He releases a quiet chuckle into my hair, sliding his arms around my stomach instead of moving me off of him. "You are not my sister's keeper nor are my guys my masters."

"*Your* guys?" His gaze flicks to the side, and I zone in and hear Ramona whisper that she told him so.

"Ramona!" I yell. "Face me! I just want to talk. What Kingston said earlier—"

"Mr. Divine," the guy says, ignoring my pleas. "This is in regards to the supposed Jordan blood debt. And let it be a warning."

The door to Kingston's room flies open, and both Diego and Austin arrive, materializing behind us. Diego touches my shoulder while Austin links his fingers through mine, squeezing the trembles from me.

The guy's face twists in obvious disgust. "Don't think for a second that I'm going to allow a vampire to take Ramona from Haven Springs. I have proof that your masters breached their contracts."

I blink a few times at his words. "They did not."

He hums under his voice. "Ramona was right about them getting into your head. You probably don't even know that they allowed another vampire to take you from them. How they managed to get you back alive is rather intriguing."

Diego releases a low growl, digging his fingers into my shoulder. I reach up and cup his hand, trying my best to keep a straight face.

"That's ridiculous," I say. "Kingston, Austin, and Diego have been perfect matches to me."

"Get it into your fucking head that these monsters are using you. They feed on you. They don't care about you. You're better off fulfilling the blood debt, because then you'll realize your place in this damned world."

"Shut up!" I scream. "You're wrong. You have no proof."

"But I do," he says. "A former employee and her family of the Divinity Estate were granted safe living here two weeks ago. A lifetime deposit from a vampire by the name of Katherine Duchanne."

"Shit," all three of my guys whisper under their breaths.

"Laurel," I murmur, too late to realize it wasn't quiet enough for the guy not to pick up.

The guy raises his eyebrows. "So, you do know her."

"Laurel Mendoza was found guilty of treachery with an immediate death sentence upon capture," Kingston says, speaking up.

"What?" I ask, turning to Kingston. He doesn't look at me, keeping his eyes trained on the guy.

"Your laws don't apply in Haven Springs. Anyone inside these gates is immune to past discrepancies."

My breathing comes quickly, my palms sweating the more the guy's words swirl through my mind. The edges of my vision darken, my eyes blurring, but I force the sob to stay locked in my throat.

Austin pulls me from Kingston's lap and hugs me, carrying me away from the camera and across the room to the door. But he's not fast enough to get me from the room.

"I'm officially notifying you on behalf of the Jordans that Ramona Jordan, head of her household and rightful heir of Jewel Divine, will file the paperwork to dispute and request your contract with Ms. Divine be annulled. Because it was your error, Jewel and her heirs will gain safe living in Haven Springs at your expense until the filing of the supposed blood debt Jewel will inherit from her father as next in line as head of household."

Kingston punches his monitor, shattering the glass with his

strength, sending it spilling across the floor. I stand in shock, my knees wobbling, and Austin being the only reason I'm still on my feet.

"Hey, beautiful," Diego says, coming up in front of me. He clasps my face in his hands, peering into my eyes. "Take a breath. He can threaten a breach in our contracts all he wants, but Donor Life Corp does not put worth on the word of a human, especially one found guilty of treachery. Filing for a breach in a vampire's side of the contract is common. Heirs attempt such things all the time. They won't take you from us. *He* won't get the chance to take you from us." Diego doesn't have to say his name for me to know he's talking about Orlando.

"I will devour all of Haven Springs if they—"

Diego jerks his head to Kingston. "That's not helping."

"She needs to know that she can count on me," Kingston snaps.

I sniffle, pulling away from both Diego and Austin. Where they're calm and collected, Kingston still flashes his fangs. I slowly close the space between us, keeping myself together not to set him off and find him abandoning me to fulfill his desire to destroy the whole community for me—something I don't want but also can't blame him for. My sister's words and that guy's attitude burn hot through me.

In this moment, I miss talking to Brayla. I try not to think about her in Orlando's arms, but just after having to deal with one shit show after another to learn that a guy clearly loves my sister enough to throw me to the shadows reminds me how different we've grown over the last few weeks.

Reaching up, I poke my finger to one of Kingston's sharp fangs, piercing my skin in the process. He retracts them, pulling himself together enough to relax his shoulders and focus on my eyes.

"Kingston," I whisper. "It's going to be okay."

He releases a long sigh, nodding his head, licking the drop of blood I spilled on his lip. "I'm supposed to be comforting you."

I motion for Diego and Austin to come closer, and the three of them surround me. I finally take a much needed breath, relaxing from their closeness. All the fear and anger that clung to me moments ago dissipates the longer I can think clearly. And with my guys, everything is perfectly clear. I've made a promise to each of them, to choose them and let them choose me.

Looking at each of their beautiful eyes—Kingston's midnight intensity, Diego's storming gray, and Austin's serene green—helps me realize that as much as they'll fight for me, I'll fight for them. I'll not stand around and hope for the best. I've proven I can survive in their dangerous world, and they don't have to rescue me. I can get us out of this. I just need to close the space between me and my sister the situation created.

I clear my throat, wetting my lips. "Before you protest what I'm about to ask, I want you all to know how important you are to me. And you should know that the asshole with my sister has a lot of nerve to try to get between us. He's going to find himself shoved in the shadows for threatening you. I'll personally introduce him to Chomper Jonas myself."

Kingston snickers, practically giggling, making me smile. "Babe, protective is hot as fuck on you."

Diego elbows him in the ribs. "What's your question, beautiful?"

"I have a feeling we're not going to like it," Austin says, keeping his face expressionless.

I bare my teeth in a frown. "You can say no."

"You think I'm going to tell you no after everything tonight?" Kingston asks.

"I was hoping you'd say that." I reach out and brush his cheek before turning to Austin and Diego. "I want you to arrange a visit for me to see my sister...tonight."

"No," Kingston says, his eyes widening at his automatic response. Then he swears. "Why that? Why now?"

"We can't even go beyond the gate with you," Diego says. "If things turn bad, we can't protect you."

Austin takes my hand in his. "I think it's a good idea."

"What?" both Kingston and Diego ask.

I can't stop the smile from lighting my face.

"Ramona is Jewel's sister. I think a visit to show Ramona that Jewel is fine while giving her a better chance to explain herself might ease any tension. I don't know about you, but I don't want to have to face constant complaints. Donor Life Corp will have no choice but to visit or require interviews if there are enough."

"So, I can go?" I ask.

"It only takes one of us to agree," Kingston mutters.

I frown. "I want you all to agree. If you don't, then...I won't ask again."

Diego's eyes soften, but Kingston groans, hooking his hands behind his head. He takes a step back, muttering under his breath a shit ton of swear words, some words that sound like profanity, but I've never heard them before.

"And you say I have a back-world mouth, dude," I say, smirking. I run my fingers around his side to hug him from behind with my chin on his shoulder.

He reaches up and hugs my arm against him. "Diego, you agree with Austin?"

"I agree with Jewel," he says. "But there's no way in hell we are sending her in alone."

"Agreed," both Kingston and Austin say.

I frown. "You can't go, though. Or can you manipulate your way in?"

"The remainder of our daytime security is loyal. Stipends go a long way," Austin answers.

As much as I want my mouth to smile, fear rushes over me at the thought of my guys actually agreeing to make this happen. I've missed my sister every day, but her lack of communication recently made me hesitate to ask. I wanted to give her more time to adjust, and now I'm afraid too much time has passed. I'm afraid we won't recognize each other anymore—or worse, I won't be able to excuse her disgust and hatred.

"So, when do we leave?" I ask, looking out the tinted glass window. "The sun will set in ten minutes."

"In seven, babe," Kingston says. "And we're not taking you there tonight."

I frown. "What if they file the paperwork in the morning?"

"They can't, beautiful," Diego says, drawing my attention to him. "It's the weekend."

"People work on weekends."

"Not vampires," Austin says.

Diego smiles. "Something we liked about the back-world."

"Fucking hell," Kingston mutters.

I swivel in his arms to meet his eyes. "What?"

"Monday's my night," he complains. "The universe is against me."

"I'll make it up to you," I muse.

Diego comes up beside his brother. "We can switch. I'd love to see how you make it up to me, beautiful."

Kingston shakes his head. "Her pity is mine."

I laugh, lean closer, and whisper ever so softly, "Good, because I was going to make sure the world wouldn't screw you again. No one will do that anymore..."

He raises an eyebrow. "Go on."

I blush, regretting my joke. "Except me."

He moans through a kiss before spinning me out of his arms. Diego catches me, and I hug him and thank him for trusting that I can handle this. Austin holds out his hand for me and laces our hands together.

Wiggling my fingers in a wave, I blow each of them a kiss. "See you at dinner."

"Bye, beautiful," Diego calls.

"Better run before I beg you to switch with me, Austin," Kingston yells.

Austin hooks his arm around me and flips me onto his shoulder, making me laugh. He skips his room altogether and puts me down on my feet at the elevator. I shiver, watching it light up as he calls for it, remembering one of the poor staff members murdered all to make a point to my guys. I can hear Laurel's voice as clear as ever.

Austin presses me into the cool wall, kissing me with the same hunger that flashes silver in his eyes. "I love you, Jewel," he whispers against my lips. It's like now that we've said the words to each other, he's trying to catch up for all the times we didn't.

"I love you, too, Austin," I say.

"I promise to take care of you, but I also promise to teach you to take care of yourself."

I grin, pulling away to smile at him. "Is everything okay?" Austin's usually more stoic, collected. He always waits for me to make the moves before initiating anything more, following my lead.

Blush tints his face, and he tucks my hair behind my ear. "It's great. I just—that was part of my plan for our future. I wanted you to know, especially after everything with Ramona.

It's part of my vow."

"You mean the Blood Vow?"

He nods. "Come on. Let's go for a swim, and I'll tell you all about it."

TRUE DIVINES

I SIT ON THE EDGE of the pool, hanging my feet in the water. Austin friggin' torpedoes around the pool faster than a fish—or probably more like a shark from one of the old shark horror movies—swimming laps a few times. He shoots up in front of me, shaking water from his hair, and smiles.

"Come on," he says, holding his arms open. "Your turn."

I groan. "I feel so...ridiculous."

"But you look cute."

He splashes closer when he realizes I'm not going to jump and presses his hard abs into my knees until I open my legs for him to stand between them. I squeeze his waist with my thighs, relenting to let him pick me up to dip me in the water.

Brushing my lips against his damp shoulder, I pepper him

with kisses, working my way up his neck to suck his earlobe between my teeth. He moans deep in his throat, moving his hands to my butt to embrace me so close that no water would dare even try to separate us.

"I know you want me to distract you, but please try for me," he whispers, his voice pleading. He'd swim with me if I asked him, but I know how much he enjoys turning things into a learning experience. I also love how proud he gets seeing me succeed at something. After the first time I swam on my own, people in hearing range probably thought I had learned to fly with how loud he boasted.

I pull away and meet his green eyes, sparkling in the soft pool lights. "Okay, just for you. But don't you even think of laughing like last time."

"Hey, I was excited for you," he says, grinning.

"You were amused."

His smile stretches more until he flashes his fangs. "Like I said, Jewel. You look cute doing so."

I glare and wiggle my nose to his. "Maybe I'm not going for cute. So no laughing."

He kisses me. "No laughing. Promise."

Peeling myself away, I let Austin set me on my feet in the shallow section of the pool nestled in a connected room. He trails his eyes from mine to my cleavage, accentuated by my one-piece, halter bathing suit.

I meet his longing gaze with a smirk. "I mean it. Not even a chuckle. And no moving. I'm coming to you."

"Despite what you think, this is more torturous for me," he muses.

"Is that so?"

"The space kills me."

"Then let this be a lesson."

He chuckles.

I hold my finger up in warning.

Clenching his jaw, he suppresses another laugh, looking super cute with how amused he is by me. I sink lower into the water, swirling my arms in front of me to warm up. Austin's brought me to the pool nearly every one of his nights this month, but I don't mind. I like it. I'm getting more comfortable swimming without his arms around me no matter how lame I feel with my ungraceful strokes. And I love how close I get to be with Austin. He's not naturally as touchy-feely as Kingston or Diego without my initiation except when we're together like this. And once I start with my affection, he continues, giving into the desire he keeps in check.

I take a breath and sink under, kicking my legs and stroking my arms. I focus on his blurry form in the water and slowly, most definitely clumsily, make my way to him. My chest tightens, needing air, but like hell am I going to pop up before I get the chance to tease him just a little. I've gotten bolder with Kingston but not with Austin, and I'd like to be. Something about Austin professing his love to me and the promise he made before we got here awakens something deep-seated and amazing inside me, letting me throw my nerves and caution away. And he's right about wanting him to distract me.

I barely get to cop a feel of him through his swim trunks before he hoists me up and kisses me without letting me take a breath. He sets me on the top step with him between my legs. I gasp into his mouth and laugh, tasting the salty water dripping from my hair.

"Jewel," he murmurs, sinking into me. He kisses me again, his voice hitching and fading.

"I'm sorry, Austin. Our contract said you were okay wit—"

He cuts off my words with another kiss, which I hungrily accept. "I'm definitely okay with anything you want to do with me. And I want to, I just...can we talk? I've been gathering my courage all night, and I'm afraid if I let myself get lost in your love that I'll lose my nerve."

His words send my heart racing.

"And now I made you nervous."

Shifting away from me, Austin sits on the step beside me. Water drips from his blond hair, running down his face. He stares at the rippling surface, his jaw moving as he lets the silence grow between us.

"You don't make me nervous," I finally manage to say. "At least not anymore. Not like I was. I'm more anxious than anything. You usually tell me what's on your mind. The last time it was hard for you to tell me something was when you asked me not to choose between you and your brothers because we make it work."

A smile crosses his lips, and he finally tilts his head to look at me. "That's what makes you incredible. You have so much love and loyalty inside you. And I'm so thankful you have it for me."

I twine my fingers with his. "Then tell me what's got you so worked up that you're extra cautious tonight. I mean—" I pause and motion to the few inches between us. "Look at all this space."

His whole face lights up, his green eyes capturing mine. Before I can lean in to kiss him, he stands up and pulls me to my feet, wrapping a fluffy towel around my shoulders. He tugs me from the steps, and we walk hand-in-hand along the perimeter out to the main pool to a lounge area near the diving board that suspends over the deepest part of the water.

My eyes widen. "Austin, what is all this?" I thought it was weird Austin brought me in through a side door but didn't think much more about it because he took me right into the dressing room...and well, my mind wasn't going to let me think about anything apart from how hot he looked changing with his back to me.

He grins, bringing my hand up to kiss. "Just something special for you. I know how much you enjoy flowers." Because I always make him stop in the garden on the way here. We never had flowers like this in Dark Terrace Ranch. At least nothing I could ever stop and appreciate.

Under a white canopy, colorful vases and pots of fragrant flowers decorate the small perimeter of the lounge area. I drag Austin with me instead of letting him lead the way. He lowers the curtains on the three sides that connect to the wall, allowing the light of the flickering candles in crystal sconces to sparkle against the blue and gold tiles. I take in the area, purposely sectioned off to give us privacy from the security cameras of the main pool.

"This is beautiful," I say, touching the soft petals of a deep red rose. "And so thoughtful."

"I'm glad you like it. I know the last few weeks have been kind of monotonous with prepping for the board and not leaving the estate—"

I plop down on one of the lounge chairs and pat the spot next to me. "Did you forget I spent every night inside an apartment nearly all my life? I hardly find spending time with you boring. I worry that you're getting bored though. I can't imagine you stayed home this often." It's only on Kingston's nights we occasionally have to go to Donor Life Corp. Austin and Diego have taken a leave of absence for the month while Kingston is always on call, but I know that might have to change.

Austin pulls a blanket-sized towel out from under the table and swaps it for my wet one to wrap around me. I invite him to share it and rest my back to his chest, snuggling close without facing each other. He hugs me from behind, resting his hands on my stomach.

"I just feel like I could do better," he finally says. "Now that we were granted the extension, I want to take you out more. Maybe to...visit my dad."

I frown. "You guys didn't look happy about it when he mentioned it."

"I know, and it's not exactly the first thing I had in mind, but with the Blood Vow application, we need to start preparing for..." He lets his voice trail off.

I swivel my body to hang my legs over the armrest to meet his gaze. "You're starting to freak me out with how you keep mentioning this Blood Vow stuff but then won't get into it. Would you be more comfortable if I asked Diego or Kingston?"

The grimace he gives me makes me feel terrible, and I regret even making the suggestion. I could kick myself for pushing the subject. Austin's always been honest with me, but he sometimes needs a moment to think. I knew this.

I close my eyes and inhale a small breath. "Austin, I'm sorry. I didn't mean to pressure you."

He brushes his lips to mine. "I know, Jewel."

"And whatever it is, I do want to hear it from you. I didn't mean anything by the suggestion."

He smiles. "I know that, too. I'm just working up my nerve."

"Nothing you say can be any more surprising than what that asshole with my sister threatened me with."

Closing his eyes, he doesn't respond to my comment. We know each other well enough to know that when he gets nervous, he gets quiet. And when I start to freak out, I can't stop talking.

Austin releases a breath and opens his eyes, meeting mine

once again. The worry lining his forehead smoothes out, and he stretches to grab something he hid under a cloth napkin on the small table he arranged a few desserts on for me.

"Jewel," he says, holding a rectangle wooden box in his hands. I know immediately that he's not going to bombard me with stall-talk and plans on getting right to the point. "When a vampire falls in love with someone outside of their coven, and they both decide they want to spend forever with each other, they often go through with something called a Blood Vow, which blends bloodlines and strengthens bonds."

And what a point that was. I mean, from confessing our love to eternity? I had planned on spending my life with Austin—and Diego and Kingston—but it's nerve-wracking to hear him talk about this seemingly out of my reach vow.

I rub my lips together, staring at the box in his hands. "So like a donor union?" I ask, trying to keep my sudden nerves in check. Because when humans fall in love, Donor Life Corp allows one human to pause their donations. It's an incentive to bring humans together in hopes that a union will increase the population. It's not really talked about, but my dad told me so.

He crinkles his nose, obviously proving that this vow is nothing like a donor union. "That's more of a contract with an incentive for humans to...procreate."

"Damn, my dad was right," I murmur.

He bows his head slightly, messing with the box. "I'm sorry, Jewel. I realize how terrible that sounds. This isn't like that, and I wish that wasn't like that either. There isn't a contract or anything with a Blood Vow past the application."

I nod. "I'm starting to hate contracts. I get why they're in place, but we're different."

"You're unlike anyone in this world—I mean, you get me and accept me. You have no idea how much I despise the damn contract right now," he says, releasing a breathless laugh. "I'm supposed to revise ours—"

"Please, don't. With all the talk of breaching contracts and shit. I just—do I still need one with you?"

He shrugs. "We'll keep the formal Blood Match one for Ramona, Dana, and Fallon. And when we find your dad. But the personal one between us? That's for your peace of mind—"

"I trust you," I say, reaching out to run my fingers across his cheek. Something about his words, about how he mentions all my family specifically and even includes my dad like he's certain we'll find him, fills me up with hope that tingles through my whole body.

His mouth pulls up in a smile, his eyes turning away from the wooden box he clutches to capture mine. He closes the small space first, kissing me feather-soft and quickly, setting off my desire like his lips detonated a bomb inside me. But Austin doesn't let me implode or explode as much as I want to, and he most definitely wants me to with one flick of my gaze down his body and hearing the thrumming of his heart, now faster than mine.

He stops me from flying at him to crash my mouth to his by popping open the box in his hands. The lid thunks to the floor, his hands shaking, making me freeze. Within the black velvet lined box rests a necklace with a blooming rose made of red stones. A matching ring, much too big for any of my fingers, sits in an inlaid compartment off to the side next to two vials—one the size of my pinky fingernail in the shape of a teardrop and the other an orb that looks like it might fit inside the ring.

I reach out and graze my fingers over each piece, entranced by how pretty the jewelry is. All three of my guys have given me jewelry to wear over the last few weeks, but something about this necklace feels different. Sentimental compared to something pretty they thought I might like.

Austin carefully balances the box on his knee to take my hands into his. "Jewel." The sound of my name on his lips draws me closer to give him my undivided attention. He smiles and drops his gaze, releasing a nervous laugh without continuing.

It's my turn to squeeze his hands to stop them from trembling. "Hey, Austin?"

He brings his eyes back to mine.

"I love you."

God, I can't get over how cute he is right now, lighting up every time I remind him how I feel. The words come so naturally like I've been saying them all my life. That I've felt the good kind of heaviness they bring to me, making me feel tethered to Austin and like no matter what, no one can get in our way. I'm invincible with him. The world is less scary and better as long as

I keep saying those three words out loud.

"And I love you, Jewel," he says. "Which is why I want to ask you to bond to me with a Blood Vow and join my coven as a true Divine by blood."

I tilt my head. "I thought I was a Divine."

He frowns. "You are, but—"

"And weren't you already going to submit the Blood Vow application? You don't think I'll be denied or something, do you?"

Austin's frown evens out, his features softening. "You won't be denied, Jewel. It's not something Donor Life Corp decides. It's just a formality."

I twist my mouth. "Oh, okay. Well, then yeah, of course I want to be a true Divine, especially if it means that I don't have to sign another contract or constantly have to worry about my family losing their benefits."

His smile falters, and I'm pretty sure he releases a tiny groan under his breath. "Jewel—"

"I'm sorry," I say, my hands now gripping his hard enough that he wiggles his fingers. "I didn't mean it to come out like that. Um, I know you said it wasn't like a donor union but it still sounds like a union of sorts, and I assumed..." I let my voice fade for a second. I don't know what I assume. Inhaling a small breath, I add, "I mean, I already plan to spend my life with you. So whatever works."

Shit balls. With the look Austin gives me, I realize I might have said something that hurt his feelings, but I don't know what. I can't get my rebel mouth to communicate with my brain for a second to process what Austin says and how I should respond besides throwing up whatever words that first come to my mind.

Silence falls between us, Austin keeping his eyes trained on our entwined hands. I shift and clear my throat, trying to think of something to say. Austin's shutting down, and whatever I said made him lose his nerve or offended him. God, I friggin' might've messed up something fierce. He's usually quick to compose himself.

Tears burn my eyes, and I can't stop from sniffling. "Austin, please—"

"I'm sorry," he blurts. A tear doesn't make it from my lashes before Austin scoops me off the lounge chair in front of him and brings me into his arms, showering me with a dozen kisses, assuring that none of my threatening tears spill. "I messed up."

"I'm pretty sure it was me who screwed whatever sweet gesture you're trying to do for me because I can't keep my stupid mouth shut for a second."

He shakes his head, kissing me until my lip stops quivering. "That mouth of yours is smart and kissable and honest, and I love it and you, and I realize that I probably make little sense to you because I'm not as brave as you are and keep sugar coating things because I can't just tell you what I want, Jewel."

I open my mouth to say something, but he kisses me, cutting me off.

"Jewel, I know we told the board that we were submitting a

Blood Vow application, but I wanted to ask you myself and not only as a way to postpone the Blood Match process. I'm asking you to bond with me to be a true Divine with an eternal vow—and I mean forever, not just your human lifetime. I'm asking you to agree to transform into a vampire to be with me always."

My eyes widen. "But Austin, what about—"

"Kingston and Diego will ask you in their own way," he says.

"I—"

"I mean, if that's what you're worried about," Austin says, filling in my words for me for the first time. "This was what we always wanted, and after everything, I don't want to wait. My life has already been long enough without you in it."

I blink a few times, trying to come up with a response. How the hell do I even respond to this? I never thought beyond my life as a donor or a Blood Match. I didn't think there was life after...but now? I'm used to living like there was an end. The idea of something different is nothing short of daunting. And then there's the whole blood thing.

"A vampire," I whisper, needing him to confirm that I heard him correctly. "But I can't provide you with sustenance as a vampire."

He snuggles against me, resting his forehead to mine. "Out of everything I've just said you're worried about not being able to feed me?"

"Well, no, but it's the only thing I can offer you."

Austin smiles against my lips. "Jewel, this isn't a business exchange. You know that, right? You could tell me you never want me to have another drop of your blood again, and I'd be okay with it. Because I have you and your love and that beautiful heart and soul of yours. And I want this forever. You're my perfect match."

A Blood Vow. Turning into a vampire. Giving up my humanity for the guys I love.

Could I?

Should I?

Ramona's words sneak into my mind, filling me with doubt. She accused me of abandoning her. She said they'd get to me. That they'd change me. It's not until this moment that I realize the significance of her fears. The truth to them. We grew up terrified of vampires. We grew up ultra aware of our place in the world. But I never imagined I'd fall in love with one, let alone three. I never thought my place in the world would change.

If I agree to Austin's proposal, it would mean that it's nearly guaranteed that Ramona would be the one to inherit our dad's blood debt. Because if I say yes, I would never devastate Austin by taking back my promise. But could I do that to Ramona? Even if she's turned against me, she's my family. My blood. I would have to sever my ties to her. The fact that she's in a human-only community assures it. She'd never forgive me.

But this shouldn't be about her. And I'm trying so hard not to let it. I just...

"Austin, I don't know," I finally manage to say, telling him the only answer I can think of.

He offers me a smile. "I know it's a lot to think about, and I want you to take all the time you need."

"You're not upset I didn't automatically say yes?" I ask.

"I wasn't expecting you to. I'm relieved you didn't automatically say no," he admits, tucking my still-damp hair behind my ear.

"Is that what you were afraid of?" I ask.

He nods. "But I don't want you to feel pressured."

I nod instead of telling him that pressure is a given. Because shit. I'd be devastated if he told me he decided to withdraw his match to me. He's agreed to a lifetime with me. He wants forever. Obviously, Kingston and Diego do from what he's said.

Forever is a long time.

I sacrificed everything I knew to save my sister and cousins. But this time I wouldn't be sacrificing anything. This decision is for me—for the four of us.

"Thank you," I whisper.

"Will you still wear my vow necklace, at least until you officially decide?" Austin asks, gently tugging the necklace from the box.

I lift my hair and let him fasten it for me. The rose rests at the top of my cleavage, cool against my skin. "What about the ring?"

"It's for me."

I carefully take it from the box and cradle it in my hand.

Austin doesn't say anything and just watches me run my finger over the heavy, shiny metal. "Will you wear it for me? Because even if I need time to think about it, I do love you and want to grow what we have into something incredible. Something more than contracts and applications."

He smiles. "And we are."

I kiss him. "Most definitely."

Austin carefully picks up the teardrop vial and uses one of his fangs to prick his index finger to squeeze a drop of blood inside it. I stare at the dark liquid settling at the bottom, my whole body tingling as he attaches it to hang below the rose to be near my heart.

I turn my gaze away from the vial only to glance at Austin's still bleeding finger. Heat crawls up my neck, my body reacting to the sight of his blood. He and his brothers have been careful with me since I was bitten, and they never let me see them bleed when we share blood, but now that I see that small drop, it's something I want—not because of what it does to my body. I'm plenty fine when it comes to the lust Austin ignites in me, but it's the act of intimacy I know he attaches to the idea that I crave. The intimacy that awakens parts of me I want to explore with him, especially in this moment.

Austin must sense my desire to bond on this level in a moment I don't need his blood to save or protect myself because he gingerly extends his finger to me without a word. I meet his green eyes, his mouth turning serious, his breathing quickening. I lick my lips and swallow. An intense hunger burns inside me, traveling from my core and up into my chest while trailing down to the rest of me, making me curl my toes.

I finally bring Austin's finger to my mouth and smear the blood across my bottom lip, gliding my tongue over it to taste it. The tangy, almost citrusy flavor dances over my taste buds. I had nearly forgotten how—and it still feels weird as hell to even think this—delicious his blood tastes to me. The mixture of all three of my guys' blood tastes good, but there is something un-explainable about each of their blood apart from each other that makes me crave them in a way I never in a million years dreamed I would.

A small moan escapes my mouth, and I suck on his finger until I can't taste anything anymore. Austin's gaze doesn't leave mine, and I'm pretty sure he didn't even blink, his whole body tense, but not in a bad way. He's tense with anticipation, his eyes only breaking away from mine to travel down my body.

He clears his throat, his eyes still roving over me, devouring me inch by inch in my bathing suit. I straighten my body and pull my long hair over my shoulder to drape down my back. He inhales a small breath, his hand trembling in mine again, his eyes so incredibly hungry like he's starving for even a drop of my affection.

"Do you need my blood now?" I ask, bringing his hand down to rest on my bare leg.

He softly runs his fingers over my skin, giving me goose-bumps. "It doesn't have to be now. I don't have any of my equip—"

Reaching my hand up, I press my index finger to his lips to silence him before I lose such an amazing moment. His bright green eyes darken, the hunger returning to them under the weight of my gaze. His fangs flash, peeking through his lips, but he doesn't move an inch, his breath turning heavy the longer I hold my hand to his mouth.

"It's just a little finger prick," I whisper, though I know how much more it means to Austin. He's never punctured me with his fangs before, even in a way that seems casual when Kingston's done it to me. But I can tell Austin feels completely different. Because allowing him to do so, even just a little finger prick, proves how much I trust him. It's easy to say the words out loud to him, but this little act shows that I know he'll be careful with me.

"Are you sure?" he asks.

"I want to do this," I say, tapping my finger to his bottom lip.

Gently wrapping his hand around my wrist, he turns my palm facing upward. I uncurl my fingers, relaxing my muscles though the same anticipation that flexes his muscles threatens to tense mine. I know if I react, he'll stop and question me, or he might change his mind altogether. And a huge part of me doesn't want to wait. This is our moment now, even if I don't have an answer to his Blood Vow proposal.

Austin flashes his fangs in a smile just for me, bringing the pad of my middle finger to his left incisor. I lock him in my gaze, my breathing quickening in a pant. The small pinch lasts a second, sending an explosion of tingles through me.

His gaze breaks away from mine to the blood drop blossoming on my fingertip. He licks his lips, and I half expect the drop never to make it into the tiny vial that inserts into his ring, but Austin carefully squeezes it off my finger, turning the clear vial vibrant red.

He reaches for the napkin on the table, but I shake my head before he can staunch the blood still pooling to run off my finger. I offer the blood to him, a part of me not wanting it to go to waste on a napkin and another much more dominant part of me wanting nothing more than to satiate the hunger burning in his eyes.

Austin sucks on my finger, his tongue flicking over the tiny puncture he made in my skin. He moans, the sound vibrating across my finger to my wrist, sending a heat wave through my core. I trail my free hand down his chest, touching his hard nipples to make my way to his pulsing stomach muscles, shifting with his swallowing.

The pressure subsides in my hand, and Austin slides my finger from his mouth, taking a moment to kiss the tender skin. He touches the napkin to it, pressing it slightly to make sure the blood stops, and then he exhales a long breath.

"That was incredible," he whispers. "You're incredible."

I grin. "It was just a drop."

He shakes his head. "To you maybe, but to me? It was everything."

Carefully pulling his ring from the box, I slide it onto his finger and hold his hand to my chest to feel the cool metal against my racing heart. He leans over to kiss me, and I devour his affection, my body and mind wanting to be close to him more than ever.

He flips me onto my back and lies beside me, his leg resting between mine. Smiling at me, he snuggles close with the towel around us, brushing his finger along my jaw to graze over my lips. I tease him by snapping my teeth, making him laugh. The softness of his voice digs into me in a good way, and I can't stop thinking about the taste of his blood or how good it felt to let him taste mine in a way he's never done before.

"Careful," I whisper, closing the space to kiss him. "I can't promise I won't try to suck more blood from your finger."

His smile fades into a look of desire, and he strokes his fingers down my side, mapping my skin without taking his eyes from mine. A dozen thoughts flicker through his gaze as he searches my face.

"I'd like that," he says, his voice deepening as he shifts his body closer. "I mean if you want to."

I inhale a small breath, knowing how serious he is. This is the first time he's ever mentioned something that he wants me to do, and I realize that I want it too. Because I like being close to Austin. He makes me feel like the best person in the world, and I hope I do the same for him.

I swallow and clear my throat. "I do."

His fangs flash with his smile. I expect him to prick his finger again, but instead, he sinks his incisors into his arm, sending a rush over my whole body. Because the side effects Austin's blood has on me are intense. We're a perfect match for nutrients, meaning that the second his blood touches my lips, I might lose myself in a rush of uncontrollable desire, basically intoxicated by him.

"I won't let you drink too much," he whispers, shifting his body closer to mine.

I lick my lips. "Okay."

He adjusts his body to completely align with mine, letting me feel the extent of his desire. Our breaths mingle, his head close, watching my lips, and then I bring his arm up and brush my lips to his blood while pressing my body into his.

I lose myself to Austin's blood and touch, to his love coursing over me, allowing it to consume me. Wanting and needing it to consume me. In a world so wrong, where everyone seems against us, wanting to destroy our Blood Match, wanting me to end up where they think I belong, Austin and I together feels so right. I can't believe that this could be forever.

I can't believe how much I want it to be forever.

But something dark inside me knows that forever for me is impossible, and I must enjoy it while it lasts.

GHOST

I FIDDLE WITH MY NECKLACE, rolling the vial of Austin's blood between my fingers. Last night replays over and over in my mind as I stare at the sun sinking into the horizon to descend on another night. It took me about an hour after returning to Austin's room before the sunrise to realize that Diego wasn't picking me up to sleep in his room for the day. All Austin said was that something came up, and he hoped it was okay if I spent the day with him.

A knock sounds on Austin's door a second before it opens. Both Kingston and Diego appear in front of me before I can even get to my feet. Austin emerges from the closet dressed in jeans and a tight-fitted T-shirt, and I blush at the sight of the trail of fading hickies running the length of his arm.

Kingston and Diego look from Austin to me, but neither of them comments, though the obvious smirks on all their faces set my face on fire. I scoop up my napkin and toss it at Diego. His smile widens, clearly remembering the first time I drank his blood. Kingston sits down next to me, bumping his knees to mine, and I reach under the table and rest my hand on his for a moment.

Silence hangs heavy in the air, but it's not awkward, just so full of anticipation. All three of them wait for me to say something, do anything, but my nerves have me shoving nearly my entire strawberry muffin in my mouth.

I chew and swallow before taking a sip of my orange juice. "You guys look hungry," I finally manage to say, keeping my voice even.

Kingston chuckles. "Starved."

"Take your time to eat, beautiful," Diego says, kicking Kingston. "You don't have to rush because Kingston forwent drinking the gen. pop blood last night."

"I'm sorry. I—" I frown, snapping my mouth shut. I turn to look at Austin. "You said they were busy. I could've fed—"

"We were busy," both Kingston and Diego say in unison, glancing at Austin.

"And don't look so worried about me skipping a meal, babe. I'm good."

"But why?" Diego made it sound like Kingston purposefully skipped drinking blood. The thought is utterly ridiculous to me. The idea of purposely not eating goes against my instincts.

Kingston curls his fingers around mine under the table. "Why what?"

"Why skip? Isn't that dangerous for you to be hungry? If I had known you didn't want to drink any gen. pop. blood at all, I would have—"

"Damn it, Kingston," Austin mutters.

Kingston raises his other hand. "What?"

The two of them vanish, the door slamming at their disappearance. Diego sits in Kingston's spot, leaning closer to me. I turn my attention away from the door to meet his smiling face, completely unfazed by whatever happened between his brothers.

"Don't worry about them," he says, running his finger along my cheek. His gaze trails down to my still swollen lips and to the rose necklace hanging on my chest. Slowly reaching up, he grazes his fingers along the chain, his eyes never revealing his thoughts of seeing it around my neck. "Or the fact that Kingston thinks that you'd get jealous if he drinks blood other than yours."

"I wouldn't if he were hungry," I say, realizing I totally admitted I would most definitely be jealous, because I now know I can provide enough blood to feed the three of them. Something about providing sustenance to them makes me feel like I'm worth their affection, though I know deep down it's not like that.

He raises his eyebrows. "Oh."

I push my plate away. "I didn't mean—Diego, please don't refrain from drinking gen. pop. blood on my account. I..." I let my thought trail off because his brows furrow, worry obviously lining his face.

I groan and rub my hands into my eyes, now realizing why Austin dragged Kingston out of here. Austin's well-aware that one of my concerns about a Blood Vow involves not being able to provide blood to them if I transform. He thinks if Kingston purposely refuses to drink anyone else's blood that it might sway my decision. And he might be right. Because it would mean that Kingston isn't fully on board with this, and I can't agree to something if we're not all in agreement.

Diego runs his fingers over my back, kneading his hands into my tense muscles. "It's okay to be jealous," he finally says. "We all get a little jealous sometimes...or a lot jealous."

"It's more than that." I rest my chin on my arms, hiding my face.

"Is this about the Blood Vow?" Diego asks. "Because you don't have to worry about it. We have plenty of time to prepare and adjust."

I turn my head to look at him. "If I agree."

He nods. "If you agree."

Diego continues to massage my muscles, letting me draw silence between us as I lose myself to my thoughts. I attempt to listen for Kingston and Austin, but they're too far away for me to hear them.

Just when I start to worry, Austin's door swings open and the two of them return to my side. Kingston surprises me by pulling me from the chair to wrap his arms around me. He buries his face in the crook of my shoulder, breathing in the scent of my hair. His lips brush against my neck a few times, and I finally react and bring my hands up to hug him back.

"I'm sorry, babe," he whispers. "I want you to know that while I find gen. pop. blood bland in comparison to your fucking deliciousness that I don't mind it. I'll drink it from now on to prove it. All I want is you and that back-world mouth of yours against mine. Possibly with that sexy ass body under, on top, or next to mine if you'd allow it."

Both Diego and Austin groan.

Kingston spins me away from them and plants his lips to mine to kiss me. Austin must've told him about my feelings toward the Blood Vow and clearly gave him permission to break one of the few rules that help my guys with their own jealousy, though they manage to conceal it so much so that I don't ever notice.

I slowly pull away from Kingston, smiling at him. "Maybe tomorrow night."

His eyes hold mine for a second, darkening with desire. "Don't think I won't figure out how to work it in even with your visit to Haven Springs."

My mouth forms an O. "You arranged it?"

He nods. "It's what Diego and I have been doing while you obviously had a great time with Austin."

I lean forward and kiss him again, sucking his bottom lip between my teeth. "Now, who's the jealous one?"

"I was being considerate," he murmurs.

I nod. "I know, and thanks, dude. I'll most definitely make some special time for you. You know, we will have all day…"

His nostrils flare, searching my face. Kingston and I have had a lot of almost-moments, but we've never actually followed through with our banter to each other. He claims to pride himself on his self-restraint, but I know he wants to make sure everything is perfect between us.

Spinning me around without commenting, he nudges me to where Austin sets out his blood draw equipment. I raise my eyebrows at Kingston, his fangs already flashing. Excitement rushes over me, and Austin smiles at me, clearly remembering our moment from last night where I allowed him to puncture my finger for a blood drop and then a taste.

Austin quickly and painlessly extracts blood for the three of them before filling up my glass with a blend of their blood from an insulated container that keeps it warm. They watch me drink, making me blush under all three of their beautiful, yet intense, gazes locked on me. Kingston downs his glass in a swallow, and if Diego didn't lace his fingers through mine, I would ask Austin if it would be safe to give each of them a little more.

"Come on, beautiful. We have a big night ahead," Diego says, pulling me to my feet.

Both Austin and Kingston follow us to the door, and I give them each a hug and a kiss before letting Diego guide me into the hallway.

"Have fun, babe!" Kingston calls through the closed door. "See you at sunrise."

"And be safe," Austin adds.

I glance at Diego. "Safe?"

Austin and Kingston chuckle, and then Kingston says, "Good luck, bro."

I frown. "What the hell?"

Diego's smile widens. "I'm in charge of making sure you're completely prepared for tomorrow."

"So, we're going to practice fighting?"

He nods. "And a little something more."

"What?"

Laughing in excitement at whatever surprise he has planned, he hooks his arm to my waist and lifts me off my feet to run with me at his speed. "You'll see," he says into my ear, squeezing me tighter as I cling onto him.

"Hopefully it'll be something slower," I murmur.

"That'll all depend on you, beautiful."

Cool air blasts my face. Diego runs me through the property, not giving me the chance to see anything or anyone. Silence hangs in the air, and I wonder if he might have either kicked out all the guests or somehow managed to get them to remain in the guest houses, at least for a moment while he takes me across the vast property.

Diego twirls me around once, making my head spin. I laugh, wobbling on my feet. He holds me in place for a moment, and I stare into his gray eyes only lit by the light of the white moon hanging overhead in the darkening sky. This is the first time in weeks that I've been able to stand outside and breathe in the crisp, citrus and ocean-scented air.

Behind Diego, the looming palace sparkles with soft lights from the windows. I catch sight of two figures standing on a balcony, and even from this distance, I recognize Austin and Kingston. Though we're within the secure walls of the Divinity Estate and there are tons of soundless, well-armed guards hiding around, my guys won't take any chances if they don't have to.

I tip my head back and stare at the sprinkling of glittering stars across the dark blue sky slowly fading to black as night shoves away twilight. Diego leans down and brushes his lips to my neck, making me dig my fingers into his sides hard enough to make him pull me completely against him.

"I've missed you," he says, begging me with his voice to turn away from the stars to give him my attention. He doesn't mean that he's missed me because we've been apart. He's missed being alone with me.

I meet him for a kiss, standing on my tiptoes until he picks me up, so I don't have to stretch so much. Our lips explore each other's, tasting the sweetness of our mouths, the softness of our tongues, just re-familiarizing our bodies with each other.

"I'm sorry you didn't get your day with me," I say, pulling away to comb my fingers through his brown hair. "I missed you, too."

He kisses me once more, just teasing his lips with mine, and I snuggle to him, letting him walk with me in his arms a few dozen feet to where I notice the car idles. I wiggle in his hold until he sets me on my feet.

"We're leaving?" I ask. "But—"

"Not exactly," he says, cutting me off before I start to spill the sudden collection of concerns I have about leaving alone. He opens the door to the driver's side and leans his hand on the frame. "But we are going for a drive...well, you're going to drive."

"Me?"

"We want to make sure that you can manage to get yourself back here if something ever happens. Getting lost on the hill is one thing, but we're going somewhere that we can't follow you. We just want to be prepared for anything."

"But you'll be outside the gate," I argue, fear sneaking up on me as I stare at the empty seat behind the wheel Diego expects me to sit in.

"I know, beautiful. And nothing will happen to any of us, but I just want you to be capable of controlling a car if you need to. We trust your safety more in your hands than we do any of the security team if we can't protect you."

I suck my bottom lip between my teeth at his admission. I know that Diego has doubts about sending me to Haven Springs. He knows he can't follow me, and if teaching me how to control the car will make him feel better about my visit tomorrow, then I'll let him even if I'm freaked the hell out to be responsible for controlling something that humans aren't supposed to be allowed ever to learn how to operate.

My sister would scream that she was right if she knew. She'd—

Diego squeezes my hand, drawing my attention away from my thoughts of Ramona and to him. He waits for me to slide behind the wheel and closes the door for me. I keep my hands locked together on my lap, afraid that even a strong exhale of breath might send the car barreling forward into Diego as he strolls around the front of it at a human speed for my benefit.

"Take a breath, beautiful," he says, plopping down next to me. His long legs nearly touch the dashboard until he adjusts the seat back to give himself more room. "It's not going to drive us off the mountain or anything."

"You sure? I know it can operate on its own," I say, taking in the glowing digital dashboard with things I don't know what they mean.

"You will definitely learn how to activate autopilot, because it takes practice to drive, especially on the winding roads outside of the cities."

"Cities? You mean I'll drive in Haven Springs?"

"No, Haven Springs doesn't have roads."

"But you said *cities*, as in more than one." It's the first time I've heard him—or anyone for that matter—mention multiple cities. It's always been Dark Terrace Ranch.

Diego presses his finger to the screen on the dashboard between us, and it lights up with a map I've never seen before— one I've never seen any of the guys turn on while I've been in the car with them. They always know where they're going like I used to know when walking the city in Dark Terrace Ranch.

Bright green lines weave around the map without a real

pattern. They interconnect together except for a long, almost spiral-like line that takes up the center of the map where a star blinks. Diego runs his fingers across the screen, and the map shrinks but adds more lines to it. Solid stars appear all over the map, and it takes everything in me not to touch the stars to see what will display. The map is similar to the one in Dark Terrace Ranch, and I know the stars mark something significant, but I highly doubt it's a Blood Match Center or more Donation Labs.

"You're familiar with maps, right?" Diego asks.

"Yeah, there is one in Dark Terrace Ranch, but I haven't messed with it since I was a kid," I say.

"Well, this one shows all the cities within a two-hundred mile radius." He taps one of the stars on the screen. "This is Dark Terrace Ranch down south of us."

I lean closer to stare at the name of my hometown glowing across the screen. "And that city?" I ask, pointing to another star.

He motions for me to tap it myself. "That's Night Vista Valley, a city twice the size of Dark Terrace Ranch with three times the population."

I blink. "Really?"

"So is Hillcrest Peak," he adds. "Except their population is only double."

"Ours—I mean, Dark Terrace Ranch's is only small because of the flu outbreak last year."

He shakes his head. "No, but it didn't help much."

"So, do all the cities have Blood Match Programs?"

Again, he shakes his head. "No, it's exclusive to Donor Life Corp's Divine Region, which is all this area here."

I stare at the circle he creates with his finger, a dozen questions swirling through my mind with new information overload. I knew that there were places beyond the walls of Dark Terrace Ranch, but I never wanted to think much about them, especially in the weeks after Dad disappeared. He was trying to get us out of the city after all and into The Orchards.

"You have a lot of questions," Diego muses, reading my expression as if I told him so with my voice. "And I promise to teach you everything, but first, it's time to drive."

I bob my head, staring at the map until Diego touches it and the screen blinks out. "Before we start, can I ask one thing?"

He smiles and nods. "Sure."

"Where are The Orchards?" It's the first time I've thought about them in a while. When Dad left, he was attempting to transfer us to The Orchards where we would have a small plot of land to grow our own food to help with the fact that he and I had to supply blood for five people in our family, and he wanted us to have something better.

Diego shifts in his seat and frowns. "The Orchards? Are you talking about Red Canyon Crest Grove?"

I shrug. "I don't know."

"Where did you hear about The Orchards?"

"My dad. That's where he was planning to take us."

"Oh, beautiful. You never mentioned this before." Diego frowns, his eyes darkening even in the soft silver glow from the dashboard. "Now I understand why your dad has a blood debt." He swears under his breath. "Red Canyon Crest Grove isn't in the Divine Region, and it takes someone of status and wealth to get into. It's known to nest Blood Rebels, which makes sense as to why your dad wanted to go with everything you've told me about him."

"You mean about his conspiracies?"

He shrugs. "Possibly. But what I don't understand is how he ended up with Orlando. The only way that could have happened is if your dad had previous ties to him. He's what we call a ghost to the system and that's why we can't find the bastard. He technically doesn't exist. While Mitchell is prominent and well known, he's also a ghost to the system, created long before the Blood Hunger Plague and The Divide. But he doesn't keep records long. We do everything for him, which is why we're the heads of the Divinity Estate."

My head spins as he muses his thoughts out loud to me without explaining them. "Diego, I don't understand what any of this means."

He groans and leans his elbows on his knees. "I'm sorry. I need to talk to Kingston and Austin before I say any more."

I attempt to open the car door, but it remains locked under my touch. "Then let's go back."

"It can wait. It won't do any good tonight."

"Diego," I snap, swiveling to face him. "You can't just drop that kind of information bomb, tell me about—"

One second I'm behind the wheel, and the next I'm straddling Diego's lap with his lips against mine.

"Diego—"

"Shhh," he whispers. "Someone's coming."

Crinkling his nose, he turns his gaze toward the windshield, his whole body suddenly tensing. Fear rises through me at the shift in his demeanor. He swears again so quietly against my mouth that without my super hearing, I'd have missed it.

"Jewel," Diego mumbles. "Don't say anything about The Orchards or your dad."

I nod my head without verbally responding to him.

A tap on the window startles me, and instead of scrambling out of Diego's lap, I sink into him, burying my face to his chest so I don't have to face whoever now has him tense and on edge. He hugs me close, whispering that I'm safe and that I don't have to be scared.

The door beeps open, and I clench my teeth at the cool air drifting in along with the deep, familiar hum I'd recognize anywhere. "This doesn't look like driving lessons," Mitchell says, his voice full of amusement.

I slowly pull myself from Diego, but he keeps his hands locked on my waist. "What a nice surprise, Mitchell," I manage to say, keeping my voice even. "I didn't know you were coming by."

"I thought it was time for a visit," he says, grinning at me, flashing his fangs in the process. "I've been dying to get to know you, Jewel. I see you officially accepted..." He leans closer to glance at my necklace, his eyebrows shooting up. "Austin's proposal."

Diego releases a low growl from his throat at his dad's amusement.

"I plan to accept all your sons' proposals," I say, straightening my back. "But Diego and Kingston haven't had the chance to formally ask me."

"Which you interrupted," Diego says quietly without looking at Mitchell. I realize he's whispering to his dad, pretending like I can't hear him.

Mitchell smiles at me without moving his mouth. "I'm sorry, son. I didn't know. Are you sure you want to even though she agreed to Austin's proposal already?"

"Yes, Dad. It's important to me that she knows my plan for our forever."

"If she chooses you."

I shift uncomfortably, knowing that all I should be hearing is silence. Turning my gaze from Diego to Mitchell, I say, "Would you mind if we got back to our date? I've been looking forward to learning to drive. If you're around for dinner, I'd love for you to join us then."

Mitchell tilts his head and smiles. "That sounds exquisite, Jewel."

Nodding once to Diego, Mitchell closes the car door and disappears into the night. Diego peers through the windows for a moment and gently sits me behind the steering wheel again.

He doesn't say anything as he adjusts the settings, helps me buckle the harness, and then straps himself in.

He doesn't move to show me anything and gazes out the dark windshield.

"Diego," I say, taking his hand in mine. "What's wrong?"

"I know I'm supposed to teach you right now, but can we switch for a bit?"

"Yeah, sure. Whatever you want."

"Thanks, beautiful. I just really need to drive."

LOVE BITES

"BRAKE, BRAKE, BRAKE!" DIEGO SHOUTS, bracing his hands against the dashboard.

I stomp on the brake pedal, sending the car skidding across the stretch of black pavement. Smoke clouds the air around us, and I release a loud laugh, accidentally easing my foot off the pedal to send us lurching forward a few more feet.

Screeching, I slam the brakes again and program the car into park like Diego showed me. He presses a button to cut the engine, leaving us sitting in darkness, both our chests heaving as the smoke clears to reveal the few inches of space between the front bumper and the massive tree.

"Shit, your reflexes need work, beautiful," he says, smiling at me. "We're going straight to the gym after—"

I climb into his lap and kiss his plans from his lips. Soaking up every drop of adrenaline coursing through me, Diego devours my mouth in a hot kiss that leaves me breathless. His hands run down my sides to squeeze my butt, making me smile into his lips.

"You said the car would stop automatically before I could hit anything," I say, working my lips from his to brush and suck along his jaw.

"I forgot to set the sensors," he murmurs. "Your excitement distracted me. You drive like Austin."

"But better, right?" I ask with a hum against his skin. I shift to press harder into him and continue to kiss and lick a trail up his neck until I nibble his earlobe, sinking my teeth deep enough that I can hear his fangs extend at the pressure.

He moans, moving his hands from my sides to flick a button that shoots the front seat back to give us more room. "Definitely, beautiful."

I straddle his lap, my dress hiking up higher on my thighs. "Is this okay?"

Murmuring his response deep in his throat, he pulls me down on top of him, roaming his fingers up my dress to explore the skin of my hips to graze cautiously over my thighs, testing me.

My body reacts to the pressure of his fingers, and I jerk forward, releasing a gasp before I kiss him harder, giving him permission to continue. Heat and pleasure blossom through my whole body as Diego helps me discover exactly what I like, creating sensations I've never felt in my life that have me grinding against him.

My breathing quickens, my toes curling. I can barely stop myself from screaming out. Diego whispers my name, moving his lips from mine to graze his fangs against my shoulder, setting my body on the verge of exploding.

And then a wave of tingles tense and relax my muscles and something indescribable crashes through me, sending me over the edge. I lose myself in a rush that has me sinking my teeth in Diego's shoulder to muffle my loud ass mouth from telling the world that Diego gave me something I had no idea I wanted or needed. Something that pulls everything good from deep inside me to spill out so I can live and breathe and love Diego as I want without worry.

Sweet, warm liquid drips onto my lips and coats my tongue, sending another wave of trembles through my body.

"Jewel," Diego gasps. "Just a little."

I pull away from his shoulder, my chest heaving, the seemingly never-ending rush intensified by the taste of Diego's blood in my mouth. He reaches up and runs his fingers across my lip, and I lean down and kiss him again.

His fingers travel back up my sides, caressing over my breasts before he pushes my hair behind my shoulders to drink me in sitting on top of him, my body begging me to let Diego continue. His eyes shift from mine to my throat, his fangs flashing again, though he tries to hide them with his hand.

I suck in my bottom lip between my teeth, locking Diego

in my stare. I know exactly what's on his mind with his heaving chest, the silver flashing in his eyes, a hunger for me that far exceeds the small moments where I give him my blood to sustain him. The hunger he carries runs deeper than nourishment, turning hot with need, and I never wanted to give him something as much as I want to let him do what he desires in this moment.

Swallowing my nerves, I pull down the collar of my dress off my shoulder, revealing my smooth skin to him. He tenses, shifting under me without a word. His gaze flicks from my shoulder and back to my eyes.

"Just a little," I say, repeating the words he told me.

He intakes a breath, his excitement pressing into me as he leans up so we're facing each other instead of me on top of him. His cool fingers glide along my jaw, his eyes searching mine and then turning to my lips. He kisses me again.

"Are you sure, Jewel?" he asks. "You said you never—"

"I love you, Diego," I say. "And yes, I'm sure. I want to do this with you. I trust you."

He brushes his hair back, capturing me in his gaze again like he's unsure if he wants to proceed. "You can tell me to stop at any time. If it hurts..."

"I'll tell you," I say. "But I'm sure you'll be gentle."

He beams me the smile I love. "Always with you, beautiful."

Diego kisses me again, taking his time to explore my neck with his lips. His fingers graze down my body, and he pulls me closer so I can curl my legs around his waist and sit in his lap. He takes his time to work me up again, knowing exactly what to do to get me to relax in his arms. I dig my fingers into his taut back muscles, my breathing quickening.

He moans deep in his throat the more I wiggle and shift, trailing my hand down to touch him in a way I've never done with him before. His fangs graze my skin, and I don't know if my body will survive another second of anticipation as my excitement and nerves beg for Diego to give me what I never thought I'd want. But I do want it. I want it so much from Diego.

"Ready, Jewel?" he whispers.

"Yeah," I barely manage to say through my gasping.

Pressure erupts in my shoulder, and I scratch my nails into Diego's back at the strange sensation that drags a loud moan from me. His warm tongue flicks across my skin, and his lips clamp down as he sucks on my shoulder, holding me tighter, moving his body in rhythm with mine until he gasps and pulls away to look at me.

He cups my face with his hands and kisses me again, slowing down until we just hug each other with only the sounds of our breathing and racing hearts to fill the silence. Diego presses his fingers to his bite mark on my shoulder to staunch the bleeding.

"You should drink a little more of my blood," he says, pulling his shirt down to reveal the still-bleeding bite I gave him.

"Shit," I whisper. "That looks painful. I'm sorry. I didn't

mean to do that."

"It's fine, beautiful," he says, grinning. "I enjoyed the hell out of it."

I blush. "It just looks...I'm a savage."

He chuckles. "Far from it. Now come on, just drink a little. I don't want you to get dizzy."

I almost ask him to bite his arm for me, but he clearly wants me to drink from the deep wound my teeth created on his shoulder. I gently press my lips against it, tasting his sweet blood coating my tongue for a second before sucking harder.

"That's probably enough, Jewel," he whispers, easing me away.

I meet his eyes, licking my lips. "Still delicious."

The smile he gives me warms me from my center, flushing my cheeks even more. Diego helps me slide back behind the wheel, and I buckle myself into the harness to prove to him that his driving lessons didn't go over my head even if I did almost ram us into a tree.

He buckles his own seatbelt. "I take it you're driving us back."

I bob my head. "Heck yeah. No wonder you like to drive. It's awesome. Brayla would be so..." I let my thought drop, shaking my head. I've done a great job at suppressing my sadness every time I think about my best friend.

"We're going to find her," Diego says. "If Orlando's who I suspect, he won't kill her."

"So he'll torture her," I murmur, the words ruining the

happy mood I was in.

"No, I don't think so. If he's like Mitchell, then I can promise you one thing. He loves humans. He wants to be worshipped by them."

"I don't understand."

"Jewel, our last name isn't human given. Mitchell picked it. There's a reason we're the Divines."

"Floor it," Diego says when the estate comes into view.

Two figures wait outside along the paved drive that wraps around the whole property. I tighten my grip on the steering wheel and stomp the throttle, jostling us both in the seats. Diego clutches the grab handle in one hand, pumping his fist in the other, and I release a small shriek, waiting for him to tell me when to jerk the wheel.

"You sure you got this, beautiful?" Diego asks, touching a few buttons on the dash for me.

I nod. "I'm blaming you if I mess up."

He laughs. "They'll get over it."

Nerves bunch my stomach, my adrenaline boiling the faster the car speeds toward Austin and Kingston. The headlights set them aglow, and they both shield their silver-flashing eyes with their hands.

"In five, four, three, two—"

I scream at the same time I spin the wheel and let off the throttle. Diego hollers his amusement, managing to hit a few buttons on the dash that lock the tires. The car screeches and spins, the whole world zooming around us.

We jerk to a stop, the hazy air blocking my view of Kingston and Austin. Diego shuts off the car and kisses me, sliding his fingers into my hair to bring me closer to him. Our tongues caress for a minute, the both of us still smiling and laughing.

"Shit," Diego says, chuckling into my lips. "That was close."

I pull away from him, my mouth automatically opening at the sight of Austin standing with his arms across his chest, a glare marring his face, directed at Diego. Beside him, Kingston flashes his fangs, his chest heaving, and I'm pretty sure the smoke still lingering in the air might be wafting from his ears.

Hitting the button to retract the window, I lean over Diego to get a better view of my guys. They stand close enough that Diego would hit them with his door if he thrusts it open, and I'm pretty sure they haven't moved an inch from their spots.

"I'm sorry," I say, trying my best to hide my smile. "It was just a joke. You know I couldn't actually hit you, right?"

Diego clears his throat. "I had to turn the sensors off for this to work."

My eyes widen. "Diego, you said—"

"Beautiful, I knew you'd do it. You didn't hit the tree."

"A tree!" Kingston's voice rips through the air.

One second I'm behind the wheel, and in the next, I'm outside the car. Austin runs his hands over me, inspecting me inch by inch. His eyes narrow in on my shoulder, and I stiffen. The seatbelt pressed my dress to Diego's bite mark, staining the fabric with a tiny bit of blood.

Austin reaches out to touch the collar of my dress, and I instinctively slap his hand away, my cheeks burning. He pulls his hand to his chest, his eyes wide for a split second before he composes himself.

"I'm okay," I whisper.

His expression remains even. "I'm sorry. I should've asked first."

I shrug, trying to smile. I shouldn't be embarrassed that I let Diego bite me. I shouldn't feel like I have to hide it. But a part of me can't help it. I open my mouth to tell him it's okay, but a loud thud sounds through the air, drawing both our attentions to the other side of the car.

"What the actual fuck were you thinking, Diego?" Kingston's voice echoes through the cool night. "She could've been hurt." He throws a punch, but Diego moves too fast, and Kingston dents the side of the car for what looks like the second time.

"I had it under control," Diego responds, pushing to his feet. "Give me credit. I won't let anything happen to our girl."

Kingston's nostrils flare, and he directs his attention to me, zoning in on the same bloody spot on my shoulder. "That better be your blood or I'm going to—"

Diego yanks Kingston back, shoving him to the ground. He throws a few punches at his brother, but Kingston gets one square into Diego's shoulder. Diego falters and drops to his knees, swearing, and Kingston freezes in surprise.

I run around the car and to Diego, kneeling next to him. I turn my gaze to Kingston. "Seriously, dude?"

"Babe, he could've got you killed," Kingston says, lacing his fingers behind his head.

"I knew what I was doing," I snap. "Now, you need to chill the hell out."

Kingston sighs without a word. I turn my attention back to Diego and touch his cheek. A small drop of blood seeps from a cut on his lip, possibly caused by his own fang. The guys move too ridiculously fast for me to follow, especially when they're heated up.

"I'm fine, beautiful," Diego says, rolling his shoulder.

I carefully pull down the collar of his shirt and wince at the purplish-black bruise forming around my bite mark. The wounds are already healed, and I'm sure the bruises will soon follow, but damn.

"Fucking A," Kingston says, surprise raising his voice. "I did *not* do that."

Diego chuckles but doesn't say anything.

"Babe, *that* was *you?*"

OhmyeffingG. Without looking at Kingston, I push to my feet and walk back to the car, slide behind the wheel, and shut and lock the doors. My face burns with fire pulled straight from the gates of hell. Unlike Austin, Kingston can't keep his damn mouth shut no matter how hard he tries. But he didn't even try, either shock or amusement ripping off his already flimsy filter.

"Babe," he says tapping on the window. "Open the door."

"Why? I can already hear you joking about wanting me to bite you too."

"Shit, not like that. I was thinking love bites not full on zombie."

Diego punches Kingston so hard that he flies a few feet in the air and lands with a thud on his back. Austin steps between his brothers, holding his hands up, though Kingston remains on the ground, peering in my direction. If it were possible to die from embarrassment, Kingston would just have to deal with getting ravaged by zombie me.

The three of them whisper too quietly for me to hear, and I turn my gaze from them to stare at the line of blood under a few of my fingernails. This wasn't exactly how I imagined my night would be, especially because I'm also supposed to meet with Mitchell before the sun rises.

"Babe, I'm sorry." Kingston's soft voice trickles to me, but when I look up, he and Austin are gone.

Diego opens my door. "Come on, beautiful. You can't sit in here all night."

"Well, if the door didn't open for you I could've," I mutter. "So much for the locks. I guess they don't work on you."

"You'd really lock me out?" he asks, amusement lightening his words. "After our amazing night? I'm not ready for it to end."

"You said you were fine," I murmur.

"I'm better than fine. I'm fantastic." Diego touches my cheek, drawing my gaze to him. "And Kingston is an asshole.

An apologetic, sometimes dramatic asshole, but still an asshole."

I groan, sinking into Diego. "I am sorry. I just—you made me—fuck. I don't want to talk about this anymore. I feel like my face is burning off."

He nods his head, twining our fingers together. "As long as you know that you can tell me anything. I love you, Jewel."

Smiling, I rest my head on his shoulder. "I love you, too."

"And speaking of love, I have something for you. I had planned to give this to you at dinner, but then you invited my dad."

"Holy shit balls. I'm messing up all over the place."

"You're not. It's fine. But there is no way I'm going another two days without asking you to accept my promise of forever. Because that's what I want with you. To be able to love you and protect you, to laugh and snuggle and...let you bite the shit out of me all you want, always, Jewel. I want you to accept my promise of a Blood Vow and to be a true Divine."

I smile at his words, my heart racing with his vows tumbling through my mind. Forever sounds amazing. It sounds so certain. It sounds like something I want. But like when Austin asked me, I can't stop the doubt from seeping into me with thoughts of my sister and our last conversation.

"Diego, I love the idea of forever with you, I do, but I need time to think about it. Everything with my sister and the blood debt..."

"We will fix it," he murmurs, leaning closer. "And when we do—"

"I'll then give you my answer."

He smiles. "I'll take it. Until then, will you add my vow to your necklace?"

Inside the small velvet box rests a rose nearly identical to Austin's apart from the shade of the red gemstones. I touch my finger to the sparkling flower and nod my head. Diego helps me add the rose to my necklace, and it locks together with Austin's.

"No blood?" I ask, touching the teardrop vile on my neck.

He carefully twists the small piece off. "Because you're our girl, we want our vows to link together."

I carefully take the box from him, running my finger across a ring identical to Austin's but in silver metal instead of the dark gray. "Will you wear my vow? Because if I agree, I do promise you forever, to love you passionately and fiercely. Most definitely protectively. Always."

Diego grins as I lift my finger, poking myself on his right fang to draw a drop of blood to fill his vile. I slide the ring on his finger and kiss him softly, keeping my desire in check instead of asking him to go on another drive so we don't have to exit the car.

"Ready to go, beautiful? We can't keep my dad waiting."

I groan. "Do we have to?"

He nods. "It'll be fine. I'm here. We're all here. We got you."

And I believe him.

BEAUTIFUL SOUL

I STAND IN MY CLOSET, staring at all the dresses. "Why do you like my shoulders so much?" I ask, peeking my head out to see Diego sitting, dressed and ready, on the edge of the bed.

He scrunches his nose. "I like them as much as the rest of you."

"But all the dresses show them off."

Chuckling, he beams a smile at me. "They also show off something else I love."

I blush as his gaze travels down to my chest, his and Austin's small pendants cool against my skin despite the steam from my shower. If Diego wasn't dressed in a suit, I'd skip the dress and put on a T-shirt to hide the still healing bite mark on my shoulder.

A light knock sounds on the door, drawing my attention away from Diego. "Jewel, can I come in?" Austin asks.

I glance at Diego, and he shrugs. "Yeah, Austin."

I half expect Kingston to follow in behind him, but he comes in alone with a garment bag in his hand. Nodding to his brother, Austin jets across the room to meet me as I stand in the doorway to the wardrobe. He keeps his eyes trained on me even though I stand in my bra and underwear with my hair cascading over my shoulders, hiding my bite mark enough not to be embarrassed.

His eyes dart to the spot anyway. "I brought you a dress I think you might like."

Unzipping the bag, he reveals a burgundy, floor-length dress with capped sleeves and a V-neckline to perfectly hide the bite mark yet still show off the curves of my body. The light fabric feels nearly weightless, and I turn my gaze to smile at Austin.

"You're the sweetest, you know," I say, leaning closer to kiss him. "Mind helping me?"

Austin pulls the dress completely from the bag. I lift my arms up and wince, my shoulder tender and aching but not unbearable. I grimace that I have to shift my hair, and Austin can't stop himself from zoning in on the two punctures.

"I'll bring you something to numb the pain," he murmurs, turning into my health keeper instead of my Blood Match. I'm thankful it's Austin and not Kingston to have brought me the dress.

I follow Austin out, and he disappears from the room. Diego gets to his feet, closing the space between us. He kisses me softly, brushing my hair behind my shoulders to drink me in. His fingers trail up my arm, gently caressing the spot that ignites hunger in his gray eyes, and then presses his fingers to my necklace.

"You look breathtaking. I wish I could be the one to escort you to dinner," he says. "And get the rest of the day with you."

I furrow my brows. "You're not taking me to dinner?"

He shakes his head. "I hope you're okay that I agreed to let Kingston. He's..."

"Moping?" I ask. "I think I can hear him pacing in his room."

Diego chuckles. "He feels awful about earlier."

I bet he does. Because even though Kingston lacks a filter sometimes, he is quite aware of my emotions by being keen to my body language, and I'm sure my intense reaction toward his zombie comment was obvious. I know he didn't intend to embarrass me. His passion gets the best of both of us sometimes.

"If you're okay with it, then I'm okay with it," I say.

"I'm fine. I have enough memories to get me through the next two days," he says, leaning down. "Though I'll miss you."

I smirk. "I'm still here, Diego."

He kisses me again. "I know. And you do an amazing job at reminding me, even when it's no longer my night."

Austin calls my name again, and Diego guides me to the door where we meet Austin in the hallway. I spot a small tube of ointment in his hands, and without saying a word, I move my hair and pull down the sleeve of my dress, allowing him to apply the cream to my skin.

I release a small breath of relief. Tingles bloom in the spot instead of the dull ache, and I roll my shoulder. Smiling, I meet Austin for a kiss and whisper my thanks. Diego wags his eyebrows at me, making sure I'm all good, and then I stroll between the both of them, taking each of their hands in mine to make sure I don't stumble on my heels.

I don't see Kingston at the elevator, and I glance at the hallway while the door slides closed. We stick to the main house, walking past the enormous foyer with the huge tinted-glass doors with ornate gold bars framing the entrance. Tapestries hang along the wall, and we cross through an empty sitting room with back-world antique furniture. A black angel spreads its wings open as it poses on a long side table, and I catch sight of the silly peeing boy fountain glowing in a spotlight outside the window.

Voices hum through the air, tightening my nerves. There are too many only to be Kingston and Mitchell. My steps falter, my heart picking up speed. My feet plant themselves into the rug outside an open door that fits right into the wall and would blend in if it were closed.

"You okay?" Diego asks.

I grip both his and Austin's hands. "There are guests. I thought we'd be alone."

I guess neither of them realized my expectations, because

they both frown. The voices start to taper off and fade, the guests obviously hearing my arrival, which makes me extra anxious. I'll now have to enter a room with all attention on me. And being the center of attention to anyone apart from my guys freaks me the hell out. It'll be like walking near the shadows in Dark Terrace Ranch. Instead of the sun keeping the shadow dwellers at bay, my guys will have to keep some of the most elite and powerful vampires in check. I know they're capable, but this makes things worse.

Kingston suddenly appears before me, making me jump. I cover my mouth with my hand to stop any more noise from escaping me. With one look into his eyes, I throw myself at him and let him pull me into his arms. Both Austin and Diego whisper that they'll assure I'm fine. They leave me to my private moment with Kingston, and he peppers me with kisses, dragging me away from the dining hall I still can't get my legs to move to enter.

He steps out the front door and into the dark morning. The sun won't rise for another few minutes, and I inhale a deep breath of the cool air. Kingston kisses me again, snuggling his face into my neck, being extra affectionate. He'd take me back to our room if people weren't waiting on us. From his rigid posture, I can tell he doesn't want me here as much as I don't want to be here.

"Babe, I'm sorry for earlier. I don't always think before I say stuff to you, and I didn't mean to tease you about...you know." He skips saying the words, obviously on the same page as me with my desire to never want to discuss what I do with Diego ever again.

"Thanks, dude," I say, offering him a smile. "I didn't mean to react like that, but—"

He silences me with a kiss. "No need to explain. I just want you to forgive me. Because I love you so fucking much that I would throw myself in the sunlight for you. I don't think anyone else in the world could handle my bullshit, and I appreciate that you're still here with me despite my flaws."

"We're soul mates, remember?" I ask him. "Body and soul."

He hugs me with a groan, kissing the crook of my neck. "I love you, babe. I want to spend forever with you, and I vow I won't go down without a fight, even if I have to wait for you to get old and gray for your response. I'd still love your sexy ass body then."

I laugh. "I promise you it won't take my lifetime to come up with an answer to our forever."

Kingston surprises me by pulling a small wooden box from his jacket pocket. I hadn't realized he was officially promising me a Blood Vow. He smirks, touching my chin to close my gaping mouth.

"You didn't think I was going to allow you to have your first official appearance as a Divine without giving you my vow, did you?" he asks. "This is just the first part. I have a bed of roses and candles, a steaming bubble bath, and a mountain of chocolate waiting for you when this is over."

I smile. "Can we skip dinner?"

He releases a deep growl from his throat, staring at the door behind me. "You know what? Yeah. Screw them."

Shaking my head, I press my hands into his shoulders. "I'm not screwing anyone."

Kingston tips his head back. "I fucking missed you and that mouth of yours all night. And there's only one person I want you to screw." I open my mouth to joke about who, but he brings his fingers to my mouth. "Don't you dare say it, no matter how much I deserve it."

"I love you, Kingston," I mumble into his fingers.

Kingston grins, nuzzling his nose to mine before helping me add his rose pendant, darker than both Austin's and Diego's, to my necklace. It connects with the other two, creating a bouquet of three, the perfect symbol of what I have with them.

"Will you wear my ring?" I ask. "Because I promise if I say yes that you'll most definitely have eternity to enjoy my backworld mouth."

"And your hot body," he murmurs through a kiss. "And your beautiful soul."

I prick my finger on Kingston's fang and let him add my blood to the vial for his ring. He sucks on my finger for a moment, keeping his dark eyes locked on mine. It takes the sun starting to rise to get us to return inside to face everyone waiting for us.

Austin and Diego hover in the doorway to the dining hall. They each hug and kiss me before patting Kingston on the back. We take a moment to let it sink in that I agreed to think about forever with them, beyond the lifetime I imagined as a Divine.

"Ready, babe?" Kingston asks, hooking his arm through mine.

I nod, inhaling a deep breath to steel myself to enter the now utterly silent room. Diego and Austin enter first, leading the way. Kingston practically carries me forward, holding me close with his arm around my shoulders, and my arm around his back, my fingers digging into his side.

"My sons." Mitchell's voice echoes through the narrow room, drawing my attention in his direction. "Their beautiful Jewel."

A wave of panic crashes over me, and I stop in my tracks, forcing Kingston with me. I can't believe what I see. It's the dining room from my dream with the long, wooden table, narrow to keep guests close. Old tapestries hang along the walls, and a series of flags suspend from both sides of the vaulted ceiling with glittering chandeliers hanging in the middle.

Five members of the staff perch in the strange built-in seats along a portion of the wooden wall, making them appear to be standing but allowing them to rest. Mitchell pushes from his chair in the middle portion of the table instead of at the head, and all of the vampires follow suit, greeting us with shallow bows and nods.

I still can't move, fear rushing over me. The golden goblets sit in front of the vampires with carafes of enough blood to satiate everyone across the center. At the head of the table, the staff arranged a buffet with everything I like. A human woman in all black keeps her gaze trained on the floor, waiting for my arrival.

"Don't be nervous," Kingston says, leaning down to kiss my cheek, hovering a moment to hear if I need to whisper something to him without drawing attention that I can do so.

I swallow, clearing my throat. "This is the room."

"The room?"

"From my nightmare."

Kingston pulls back to study my face, clearly confused. "Maybe it was just similar. A lot of vampires have similar set-ups."

I shake my head. "It was this one. Please, don't make me do this. I want to go back to the room. What if—" I pause, afraid if I don't control my emotions, someone will hear me. "What if I end up on the table?"

"I will rip apart anyone who would dare try," he says. "Including Mitchell."

The darkness clinging to his voice both scares and assures me. Because I know he's capable. So are Austin and Diego. And together they make my fierce protectors, who I know will never purposely let me down. Not with their Blood Vow proposals.

"I'll keep this short," he adds, kissing me. "And I won't let go of you."

Scooping me up, he races me to the table, making me laugh. He sits down in my seat with me on his lap. Everyone's gazes bore into me, but I only look toward Austin and Diego at my sides, acknowledging them for a moment before training my gaze to Mitchell, who flashes his fangs in a smile.

Mitchell raises his goblet. "I'd like to make a toast to the Divine heirs, my sons, their futures, and to Jewel, a match worthy of eternity among us. To my legacies."

I glance at the ruby liquid in my crystal chalice, different from the other glasses. I realize that none of my guys pick up glasses, all their cups empty. I nearly ask them if they want some of my blood, but Kingston kisses the almost-suggestion from my lips.

"Are you not allowed to drink with the others?" I ask, still swirling the ruby liquid in my glass. I know it's not blood, but I don't want to drink anything if my guys aren't. I'm not sure I want to eat either.

"If it's okay with you," Austin says.

I raise an eyebrow. This must be a vampire tradition thing. This gathering was so last minute that no one thought to prepare me or they didn't think it mattered. I'm usually pretty good at just going with the flow of things.

"I prefer you didn't," I say, trying to hold my face straight. I purposely shift on Kingston's lap to face him. "It makes me incredibly jealous."

Diego releases a howl of a laugh, and Austin touches my knee under the table.

"I deserve this," Kingston mutters to himself.

I bow close to his ear. "I can see why you like to tease me. It's fun. And don't worry, I won't let you starve."

He presses his fingers deeper into my hip. "But I would for you."

Kingston nods to the woman standing nearby, and she fills their gold goblets. They lift them to me, and I tap my crystal chalice to theirs and take a small sip of the ruby liquid. It slightly burns my throat going down, warming my stomach.

"Do you like the wine, Jewel? I've been saving it for such an occasion as this," Mitchell says.

Or he's been saving it because vampires don't drink wine. I don't say it, though. Under his scrutiny, I realize he, and everyone else for that matter, watch and listen to me like I'm here for their entertainment. And maybe I am.

"It's intoxicating," I say, using the only knowledge I have about alcohol since I can't decide if I like it or not.

"So don't drink too much, Jewel," Austin murmurs, his hand still resting on my leg.

After the novelty of my presence wears off, the vampires pick up their conversations, purposely talking in hushed tones. My guys smirk at me, clearly amused by how engrossed I become listening to the only two female vampires discussing the appeal of a greater female-to-male household staff because it increases the chances of procreation. If two staff members have children, one must donate blood to their personal stash. It's an odd way of gaining more exclusive donors without having to pay extra for blood accommodations if they find gen. pop. blood substandard.

"Or you could apply for a Blood Match," Kingston says,

speaking the words that I was clearly thinking about.

"What?" I ask, playing along like his response is the first I've heard.

He smirks at me. "I was just commenting to Brooklyn and Francisca about how applying for a Blood Match would assure they got the best of the best in blood and companionship."

The two vampires smirk at Kingston. "Kingston, my love," the woman with blond hair says, flashing her fangs. "I might consider it if you proved the truth of your words. Perhaps Ms. Divine wouldn't mind a finger prick."

Fuck. Me. Three deep growls reverberate through my bones. Kingston stands up with me while Diego and Austin step in front to block me from everyone's view like they do when we're outside the Blood Match Center.

Another pair of cacophonous growls erupts, the whole room silencing as I stand amid vampires who aren't afraid to fight. My mind screams for me to remain calm and safe in my deliciously muscular vampire sandwich, but my stupid body reacts with my anger, and I squeeze between Diego and Austin.

"How dare you suggest that," I snap.

The blonde smirks at her companion before turning to me. "You mean suggest your masters play nice and share? They already do so, and you look like you rather enjoy it, Ms. Divine. Pardon me for assuming you wouldn't mind offering a taste."

I throw my glass of wine in her face. I don't know what comes over me or where I summoned the nerve, but the vampire reminds me of Katherine, and it's easy for me to summon the fury the snobby blonde uncaged inside me. "You will respect me and my Blood Matches in our home."

The blonde hisses at me, swiping the wine from her eyes. If I didn't have three powerful vampires surrounding me, I'm sure she'd have lunged. "*Your* home? I think you've forgotten your place, Ms. Divine. Don't think because you are a donor to an heir that you are entitled the same respect. You are merely a play thing they will surely get bored with."

Mitchell slams his gold goblet down, spilling blood across the table. The memory of my dream, of sliding across the table, bathed in blood, flits through my mind. Fear threatens to rattle my bones, but all three of my guys touch me, Kingston hugging my waist and Austin and Diego take my hands, giving me enough of their strength to not cower away.

"Francisca, you will speak to the next true Divine with the respect she deserves," Mitchell says.

She growls, turning between me and the founder of Donor Life Corp, surprise turning her green eyes wild. "But Mitchell. She's not wor—"

"Jewel," Austin whispers so quietly from beside me, "Call for security."

"Me?"

He nods. "It must be you."

Clearing my throat, I draw all the vampires' gazes back to me. "Pedro."

I don't even have time to blink before the hulking vampire materializes in front of me, hoisting a massive, scary-ass gun on his shoulder. His fierce eyes flick around the room for an immediate threat and then land on mine.

"Yes, Ms. Divine," he asks.

"Will you please escort Francisca out of the building? She is no longer welcomed at the Divinity Estate," I say.

The man across from her stands up, smacking his open palm on the table. "You can't do that! It's past sunrise."

I almost lose my nerve. Almost. But then Francisca smirks at me with a raised eyebrow, the lot of vampires murmuring about the situation. "And what is your name?" I ask, turning to the man.

"Lewis," he says, glowering at me.

I turn back to Pedro. "Please escort Lewis out with Francisca."

"What?" He turns to Mitchell. "You can't possibly allo—"

"Jewel, perhaps you'll accept an apology," Mitchell says.

"An apology!" Francisca shrieks, like the thought pains her.

I shake my head. "Pedro, now please." I look at the two stunned vampires. "But do offer them an umbrella or something. That should suffice for their journey to the shadows."

Pedro looks to my guys for confirmation, and they nod, keeping their faces expressionless. Mitchell leans back in his chair, amusement crossing his face. I imagine he believes I've come a long way from the girl he first met, begging for help while being dragged away by a lunatic who thought he could match me out from under my guys.

Pedro escorts the vampires, who yell and scream the entire

way out of the dining room. The second they disappear, the whole table erupts in excited chatter, shifting back to normal like none of the spectacles I was involved in happened.

Mitchell raises his glass again, calling attention to him. "Here's to Jewel, a true Divine."

SAVAGE

I CAN'T BELIEVE I SURVIVED dinner with twenty vampires. I can't believe I might have actually fit in. Not once was my blood mentioned again nor my place within the Divinity Estate. But now? It's all starting to sink in. Something dark snapped inside me, and I'm afraid I'll never be able to fix it or if I should even try. I still can't believe my guys—or Mitchell for that matter—allowed me to order the removal of two supposedly elite vampires from the estate in the daytime.

And now I regret it.

Not because I feel bad. I'm sure neither of the vampires have clear or moral consciences. What I'm afraid of is that I've added more enemies to the seemingly long list I've inherited from my guys. I'd be totally pissed off and murdery if someone tossed me out of the safety of my apartment in The Boxes and into the shadows. But at least—or more like unfortunately—Francisca and her companion dude will only get a little burned.

Kingston comes up behind me, sliding his arms across my chest to pull me close against him. "Babe, as cute as you look lost in your thoughts, I'd rather you get lost in my eyes."

I smirk. "Am I starving you of my attention?"

"I've been standing here waiting for you to look up for at least two minutes," he says, his voice deepening as he trails his hands lower to my hips.

I stare at the sun through the tinted windows for a moment longer before spinning in his arms to meet his gaze. Inhaling a breath, I say, "Kingston."

My eyes wander from his and down his bare chest, drinking in the tight muscles of his stomach to the sharp bones of his hips and...I look back up at him with another soft breath that makes him smile. He touches my warm cheeks, releasing what sounds like a purr from his throat at my reaction.

I swallow my shyness and peek at him again. I should be used to his brazenness. He purposely walks around our room without clothes all the time, but it's usually only after his shower, and though I hear running water, he's completely dry. And now he's close. Super close. There is only one thing keeping an intimidating amount of space between us but even that doesn't stop Kingston.

"Dress. Off. Now," he whispers, touching his body to mine. Desire hums through me along with what seems like a never-ending adrenaline rush. "Ple-e-e-ase."

I giggle with my nerves, sounding more like I'm gasping for air, and touch my palms to his bare shoulders. "I guess since you asked nicely."

With a flick of his hand, he tears the side seam, sending my gown to the floor to pool around my feet. Cool air sends goosebumps over my arms and legs, and I place my hands on my hips, giving him another once-over.

"Seriously?" I ask.

"Super serious. I've been dying for a moment alone with you since my proposal."

I surprise him by hopping up into his arms, making him chuckle. He carries me to the bathroom, his lips never leaving mine, his hands remaining in place on my lower back. Steam engulfs us from the shower spraying behind opaque glass. Kingston sets me on the sink, and I draw our names on the mirror, making him smile wider as he checks the temperature of the water.

"What, no bubble bath?" I ask, peering at the empty tub.

"And lose my view of you to the mountain of bubbles? No way." He glances over his shoulder, searching my face for a reaction. The last time we were together was the most undressed I've been with him apart from a few bubble baths. I always got in first with his back turned, so this shower business really is serious. His bold confidence is both hot and nerve-wracking. It's different being caught up in a moment compared to jumping in head first.

I wring my fingers together on my lap. "I hope you don't think I'm going to have sex with you in the shower."

He flashes his fangs at me. "Always about the sex with you."

I glare. "Nu-uh. You are not going to twist this on me."

Taking a breath, he closes the space between us and cups my cheeks, peering into my eyes. "Jewel, I'm just teasing you. I'm sorry if it feels like it's always about sex with me. I sometimes can't help myself. I'm so damn attracted to you, and I love you like crazy. More than I thought possible. I want to make you happy."

"You do make me happy," I murmur. "And I do think about sex with you. I just—no shower. I saw this movie one time, and—"

He groans. "You learned about sex from a movie?"

"My high school had an old human health book, too. Dad didn't like to talk about it except for the consequences of increasing the population."

Kingston bows his head, smirking to himself. I know he didn't intend it, but now I feel silly and naïve and confused. I can't stop my cheeks from burning. I'm nearly certain I know the mechanics involved, and I am aware that sex can be more than procreation despite what my dad said, but maybe it's different with vampires.

"Why are you smirking?" I ask, knocking his shoulder with my knuckles. "How else was I supposed to learn? Donor Life Corp likes to keep humans ignorant. My dad..." I let my voice trail off.

"Babe, I'm sorry. I didn't mean for my question to make you feel ignorant. You might lack experience, but your knowledge isn't wrong. I wasn't smirking about that. I was smirking because...it's nothing. You don't like watching romance so it's not a—"

"I didn't like romance, but my mom did. She'd make us watch two for every comedy Ramona and I picked. And to be honest, you're kind of changing my mind on romance now that I know it's not out of reach."

"Damn it," he says, turning his gaze to meet mine. "I mean, hell yeah I'm going to romance you, but I have to be honest. I can't promise it'll be...as glamorous as in the movies."

I flash him a smile, loving the fact that for once he's nervous. "So, you're like a romantic comedy."

Kingston laughs so loudly that all my nerves and worry disappear. I slide off the counter and take his hand, pulling him toward the shower. I bounce on my feet, watching Kingston get in before me. His eyes stay trained on mine until I reach behind me to unclasp my bra. It never ceases to amaze me how quickly he can switch his mood, his eyes turning from playful to hungry, devouring every inch of my body like just looking at me can satisfy him for the rest of time.

Kingston wiggles his fingers at me, and I quickly, most definitely ungracefully, finish undressing to join him. The hot water streams over me, and I moan, letting it relax my tense muscles.

"You're as perfect as I imagined," Kingston whispers, grazing his fingers over my arm. "Can I help you?"

I smile and nod at him, watching him lather soap in his hands even though my bathing sponge is next to his. My whole body tingles with anticipation, the sweet scent of vanilla wafting through the air. Kingston tugs me from the water and into the warm mist raining from the ceiling.

He slowly shifts my hair over my shoulder, taking in my breasts, trailing his gaze higher until he freezes. The desire disappears from his eyes, and he drops his hand from me, adding another few inches of space between us.

"Babe," he whispers, his voice hitching as he clears his throat. "I'm sorry. I forgot about something. I'll be right back."

I stand in shock and confusion, the cloud of steam thinning as Kingston disappears, leaving me alone in the shower. The open door of the bathroom allows in cool air, and I spot my reflection in the mirror above the sink.

"Shit," I whisper to myself. I had completely forgotten about Diego's bite mark on my shoulder, and Kingston saw it when he moved my hair. Whatever cream Austin had put on me numbed it so much that it was the last thing on my mind with Kingston attempting to bond with me on a new level after I accepted the possibility of forever with him.

He's obviously upset over it, because he was the last one I had ever expected to abandon me in the shower. And I don't even know how to deal with this. We all know I love each of them and that they love me. I don't hide my affection even if we don't talk about it.

Except for this. I did hide this. I don't even know why.

Maybe because I knew Kingston would react this way. Austin reacted, but he is a master of control over his emotions. Kingston's not. Kingston wears his heart staked outside his chest for me to see. Though I know I didn't do anything wrong, and Kingston doesn't have a right to be upset, I still feel bad I caught him by surprise in an intimate moment.

Shutting off the water, I grab the towel Kingston hung over the partition and wrap it around myself. My bare feet slap against the cool tiles no matter how quietly I try to stroll to the bedroom. I half expect Kingston to be gone with Austin in his place, because Austin's the one he always calls when he doesn't know how to handle me, but Kingston sits on the edge of the bed in pajama pants with his chin resting on his hands as he digs his elbows into his knees.

Seeing him sitting there makes it obvious that it's not me who needs to be handled with care. It's him.

I cross the room and sit on the edge of the bed next to him. "Kingston, I'm sorry. I should've warned you."

He groans, rubbing his hands into his eyes. "You don't have to apologize, Jewel. What you do with my brothers is none of my business."

"But you're upset," I say, half hugging him the best I can.

"I shouldn't be, and I'm mad at myself that I am. I just thought..." His voice trails off, and he still refuses to look at me.

I open my mouth to try to guess what he chooses not to say

but decide against it. The last thing I want to do is try to put words in his mouth. I might accidentally say something even worse.

"I wanted your first non-murderous bite to be with me." It still drives my guys mad that Katherine did such a thing to me.

"Technically, it was," I muse. "And without even a first date. But you know what? I look forward to *our* real first experience together, whenever that happens."

He groans again, sagging his shoulders. I regret reminding him of our first encounter. Because the jerk I met in the lobby of the Blood Match Center who had the nerve to prick my finger isn't the same guy who sits beside me now, wearing a pout I want so badly to kiss away.

"I'm the worst," he says. "How do you even love me?"

I frown. "How could I not? You saved me, Kingston. More than once. You might make a few mistakes, but I make a ton. That's our thing, dude. No filters for us. Acting without thinking sometimes."

He shifts and smiles at me. "How do people tolerate us?"

"I know, you're so dramatic." I bump his shoulder, getting him to straighten his back so I can take his hand.

"It's called passion, babe. And you have it too. It's what makes us overreact."

I roll my eyes. "I don't overreact."

"You had Pedro escort two vampires outside in the sun. Do you realize how many more enemies we have now?" he teases, shaking his head at me. "We will surely never be invited to the

Matherson Compound ever again. And that place was awesome."

I heave a sigh. "I'm a savage."

"I know. I remember Diego's shoulder. But you're a hot, badass savage and worth every vendetta that comes our way."

"Kingston."

He leans over and kisses my cheek. "Sorry, babe. You're full of surprises."

"And so are you."

Kingston tugs me into his lap and kisses me, murmuring about wanting to go back to the shower. I answer by dropping my towel to see how he reacts. His eyes trail down my body, only looking at Diego's bite mark for a second before zoning in on my boobs. He stands up, hoisting me high enough that he can kiss the sensitive skin of my chest, gliding his tongue over my curves, making me shiver. Kingston hums deep in his throat and carries me at a human's speed, purposely taking his time to familiarize his mouth and hands with my bare skin.

"I'm not so sure I want that shower," he says against the warm skin of my throat. He shifts me lower, our bodies grazing and nearly aligned, and I hug him tighter.

"I'm not so sure I do either," I whisper, burying my face in the crook of his neck. "Can we cuddle for a bit?"

"And kiss?"

I answer him by meeting my lips to his.

"And touch?"

"I should probably familiarize myself with you."

He chuckles.

I don't.

Inhaling a small breath, I reach down and stroke my fingers across his body, making him practically fly me back to the bed. Kingston pulls the blankets up and kisses me so passionately that my whole body buzzes as my anticipation builds.

His lips leave mine to burn a hot, tingling trail lower and lower down my stomach, making me excited and nervous with trembles that he smoothes away with his fingers.

But then he suddenly stops, his eyes opening to peer up at me. He props himself on his hand to prevent his torso from pressing between my legs. His eyes turn silver, and he flashes his fangs, glancing toward our door and back to me. I tense. His desire turns dark, dangerous even, and fear collides over me in a cold wave to snuff out all the good heat emanating from my skin to warm Kingston.

He shakes his head, smoothing out his fierce expression, noticing my reaction. "I'm sorry, babe," he whispers so quietly that I know no one except me can hear the words. "We have to hurry and get dressed."

One second I'm lying under Kingston on our bed and in the next he's pulling one of his shirts over my head in our wardrobe. He bends down, pulling me close. His lips graze my earlobe. "Mitchell's coming," he whispers. "Remember what we worked on."

I grimace. "What we worked on?"

"How to trick him."

"But why—"

Someone knocks on the door, and Kingston lets go of me and disappears back into the bedroom. I clench my jaw, trying my best to compose myself. I mean, what the hell? Why is Mitchell coming here in the middle of the day? Something about his visit has Kingston on edge, and I can't stop the panic tightening my chest.

Music filters in from the hallway as Kingston answers the door.

"Was I interrupting something?" I hear Mitchell ask Kingston, his voice low enough that if I didn't have super hearing, I wouldn't be able to make out what he was saying.

"Actually, yeah. Can you come back later?"

"I'm leaving at sundown, so no. I'd like a word with Jewel. It has come to my attention that she asked to visit her heirs in Haven Springs."

"Yes, we arranged an outing come nightfall," Kingston says.

"Are you sure that's a good idea, son? If she accepted your Blood Vow, she must—"

Kingston sighs. "You don't have to remind me, but this is important. We've encountered some...problems."

"Elaborate."

"You know how the blood exempt act."

"Kingston, that is not an answer."

I can't stand pretending like I'm not listening to their conversation, so I rattle a couple of hangers, grab one of my robes, and exit the wardrobe to confront Mitchell. Both he and Kingston turn in my direction, Mitchell grinning while Kingston glowers. I tighten the belt on my robe and cross the room, forcing my mouth to return Mitchell's friendliness.

"Is something wrong?" I ask, sliding under Kingston's arm to snuggle against him in the safest place I could be with Mitchell intruding on our privacy.

"Not at all, Jewel," Mitchell says for Kingston. "I only wanted to stop by to make sure I caught you before I leave at sunset."

"Is this about dinner? I'm sorry if my actions were out of line—"

Mitchell barks a laugh, the sheer sound of it startling me. "You are head of the daylight household, Jewel. If someone has overstayed their welcome, you have every right to ask them to vacate the premises. The Divinity Estate isn't a hotel. It's your home."

And I'm pretty sure the remaining twenty vampires from dinner will remember that. I hadn't thought of myself as the head of the daylight household since I never leave one of my guys' sides, but Mitchell is technically right. It was in my Blood Match contract to oversee...I didn't read most of that part. Oops.

No wonder Austin told me that I was the one who had to call for security. And it makes sense that I was at the head of the table. I did sort of invite Mitchell to join us for dinner, and Diego told me after that it's customary that all guests join the founder of Donor Life Corp for such an affair.

"Then what honor do I have for your visit, Mitchell?" My question comes way too late, and I can't control the sarcasm in my tone.

He smiles, either completely oblivious to my annoyance or amused that he stirred it from me, yet he doesn't give much away. "I wanted to discuss a few matters that have come to my attention. Kingston was telling me that he arranged a visit for you to Haven Springs."

I purse my lips. "That's right."

"Why?"

"Because it's been a month since I've seen my sister."

"I saw to it myself that your heirs are well taken care of, Jewel."

Like I could ever forget. Mitchell somehow managed to get to my sister and cousins against my guys' wishes and mind manipulate them in an attempt to extract information about Orlando after it was discovered I would inherit a blood debt. I still haven't forgiven him for that. Or for manipulating my mind without my permission for that matter. He—

"So I would like you to reconsider your trip. It's best you stay away from the exempt of Haven Springs. That is no place for my soon-to-be heiress," Mitchell says.

My face betrays me with a grimace, and I tilt my head to glance at Kingston, who hasn't said a single word since I stepped from the wardrobe to confront Mitchell. "It's one visit. I want to share the news with her." It's a flat out lie, but I don't know what else to say. I don't exactly trust the guy who got into my head the first opportunity he had.

"Kingston said there were other problems."

"It's not a big deal."

"Then not going shouldn't be either. I'm sorry, Jewel. I'm overruling my sons' decision. Your heirs will be alerted of your Blood Vow upon approval of your application and after you make your final decision," Mitchell says.

"But—"

"Dad," Kingston says, finally speaking up. "This is important to Jewel, which makes it important to me."

"The answer is no." He leans closer to Kingston. "I don't care what kind of problems you think you have. You will deal with them appropriately and without Jewel." Mitchell whispers the words, oblivious to the fact that I can hear him.

"Da—"

Kingston flies across the room and crashes into the wall mirror above his display case of weapons. Glass shatters, sparkling across the floor. Kingston launches to his feet, and Mitchell disappears from my side. I try to follow their blurring forms, but they move too quickly for me. It takes Kingston smashing into our headboard, splintering the wood and then landing face down on the bed for me to realize that he's no match for Mitchell's strength.

I try to run to Kingston, but Mitchell cuts me off. My back thuds into the bedroom door, and I release a cry I'm sure Diego and Austin could hear. Mitchell flashes his fangs, his eyes turning silver. His handsome face morphs into one like the murderous vampires that plague my nightmares. I whimper, my chest heaving, tears burning my eyes.

"Jewel, do not look away until I tell you to," Mitchell says, capturing my stare.

Panic kicks me into action, and I force my body to slacken, knowing all too well that he's attempting to manipulate my mind. Everything my guys have taught me over the last few weeks comes rushing back, my body finally listening to what my mind commands.

Mitchell narrows his eyes on mine, pushing loose strands of hair from my face. "You will not make a sound. If one of my sons calls to you, you will tell them everything is fine and to go back to bed."

I remain still and placid in his arms, only staying on my feet because he's holding me in place.

"Now, Jewel. Tell me, why is it important that you go to Haven Springs?"

My eyes burn with tears. "I miss my family."

Leaning closer, he breathes an annoyed breath in my face. "Kingston mentioned an issue with your heirs. Tell me what it is."

A dozen thoughts swirl through my mind, but I don't have time to think about it, so I stick to the truth. "My sister has become aware of our family's blood debt. She's angry. I want to make sure she's okay."

His fangs flash in a smile. "Tell her that she may apply for a Blood Match upon her eighteenth birthday. You are a Divine. She is no longer your responsibility. Your heirs have been immensely rewarded."

I don't respond. It takes everything in me not to cry and give myself away.

"You will sever your ties to your human family. You will no longer have the desire to see them," he whispers, keeping his voice low.

It's now that I realize he doesn't have to say the words at a volume normal humans can hear. I don't think any of my guys could hear him speaking to me. And I'm furious. He not only tries to get into my mind like before, but he also attempts to manipulate my emotions, something far more invasive.

If I were closer to the balcony door, I'd attempt to fling it open to throw Mitchell to the sun to show him what the pain he's attempting to inflict on me feels like. But I can't move. I can't speak. I can't do anything except play along and make him believe that he's the puppet master, and I'm his little doll.

A knock sounds on the door, drawing his attention, though his eyes remain on mine. "Hey, Kingston? I heard a crash. Is everything okay?"

"Tell him Kingston is in the shower," Mitchell whispers.

"Kingston is in the shower," I say, keeping my voice even.

The doorknob jiggles, but Mitchell locked it, and Diego would have to break it down to get to me. "You okay, beautiful?"

Without waiting for Mitchell's command, I say, "Everything is fine. Go back to bed."

Mitchell nods his approval like I'm even supposed to have a choice. "Tell him it's your time with Kingston and not to bother you again."

"It's my time with Kingston. Don't bother me again." My heartbeat starts to speed up, but Mitchell doesn't react. He's too busy listening to Diego on the other side of the door. And what Mitchell doesn't know is that I'd have never told Diego something like that. I see all my guys every night no matter what, and I'd never tell them to leave me alone.

"Okay, Jewel," Diego says through the door, his use of my name a clear indication he knows something is up. "I'll see you later."

Mitchell listens to Diego's shuffling footsteps fade and draws his full attention back to me. Leaning forward, he inhales a breath near my neck and pulls back to give me a once over before searching my eyes again.

"You will not speak of this to anyone. When Kingston comes to, you will assure him that you are fine and that I left immediately." Mitchell raises his arm to his mouth and bites into his own flesh. Blood seeps from the wounds, and he holds his wrist to my lips. "Now drink."

Holy shit balls. My stomach rolls at the thought, but I do what Mitchell says and press my lips to his skin. His blood coats my tongue, tasting odd and strangely spicy that I nearly cough.

"If my sons try to open your mind, you will go along with it. You will tell them that I did not get into your head. You will tell them that I made a good point about cutting your ties to your human heirs. Now sleep."

I automatically close my eyes, and Mitchell removes his arm from my mouth. He wipes something across my lips, the world jostling with his quick movements. I have never been so grateful that my body does not react with unbidden desire to his vampire blood. Austin had told me that side effects of drinking vampire blood vary, and effin' A. If I found myself with even an ounce of desire toward Mitchell, I'm nearly certain a part of my soul would die.

The door quietly clicks closed, and I remain unmoving in my spot, counting my quick heartbeats as my heart rams against my ribcage, trying to escape my body. After I finally manage to push out all the chaotic noises of my insides threatening to make me sick, I focus on the other heartbeat in the room.

I shift onto my side, slowly opening my eyes to peek through my eyelashes. I half expect Mitchell to rush back into the room to realize that his mind manipulation didn't work, but he doesn't, and I don't think he will. He seems confident enough in his ability that I'm pretty sure he'll be far away from us and will disappear come sundown.

I press my hands into the floor and push to my feet, catching sight of Kingston still face down on the bed where Mitchell threw him. "Kingston," I whisper, just in case. I'm only slightly sure that Mitchell left out of hearing range. "Kingston, can you hear me?"

Kingston doesn't respond to my voice. If I couldn't hear

his heart, I'd be freaking the eff out, but I know Mitchell wouldn't have killed his son—I think. At least, I'd hope he wouldn't. I honestly can't put anything past a vampire who would betray and purposely make his sons breach our contracts like this. Because if the rules still applied to me and my guys, Mitchell's act of betrayal would fall under the whole keeping me safe from other vampires clause. But Mitchell's above the law—he *is* the law. I don't care if he has a board of vampires at his side. If it came down to it, I'm sure he could rewrite the rules to fit his needs. He already did it by going to Haven Springs to see my sister.

I carefully knock off the broken pieces of wood from our headboard and climb next to Kingston, digging my hand under him to give me leverage to flip him over. Tears bursts from my eyes the second I see his beaten face, both his eyes purpling with bruises, one swollen. Blood stains his lips and chin where his fangs must have punctured through. More blood trickles from his now crooked nose.

Bringing my hand up to his cheek, I gently brush my knuckles over his skin. "Kingston," I whisper. "Please, wake up."

I summon the nerve to shake him, but he doesn't respond. Mitchell knocked him out cold. I'm too scared to call for Diego and Austin, because if Mitchell is still on the premises, it's possible he could hear me, and then he'd know that he wasn't able to mind manipulate me. Things will grow complicated if he did. My guys keep my drinking their blood a secret for a reason, the same way Mitchell tried to.

"Please, Kingston," I beg, touching my fingers to his lips. I should be careful about waking him because he could accidentally attack me, but my anxiety grows with every passing second. It's worth the danger to me to wake him up.

His fangs extend to show from his parted lips, reacting to my touch. I suck in a small breath at the sight of them, because I know exactly what I have to do. When I got hurt, the guys gave me their blood to help me heal. My blood should at least give Kingston enough energy to open his eyes. He didn't touch any of the offered gen. pop. blood at dinner because of his weird logic of making sure he never makes me jealous, and Austin wasn't going to come by until breakfast to assure we were set for our journey to Haven Springs. I had drunken enough of Diego's blood before dinner that I didn't need more of theirs.

Bringing my arm to Kingston's mouth, I use my free hand to stretch his lips to give me a better view of his fangs. His slackened jaw makes it easy enough to open his mouth, and I press my arm hard to his fangs to break my skin.

My arm stings with pain, and I blink the tears from my eyes. This definitely doesn't feel like my moment with Diego. There's nothing fun or intimate about purposely shoving my arm into a sleeping vampire's mouth. I just hope Kingston doesn't chomp down.

"Kingston," I whisper again, my warm blood dripping from the two puncture holes and into his mouth to coat his tongue. "Don't bite down. Please, I'm begging you. Don't bite."

A soft moan escapes from Kingston's lips, his breath tickling my skin. The stinging sensation worsens the longer I hold my arm to his mouth until I have to pull it away because the pain suddenly turns into agony, my skin feeling like it's been set on fire.

Kingston jerks his hands up, latching his fingers to my arm, startling me. His eyes snap open, the midnight color flashing silver, and he flails back, shoving me away. I fall back at the force and tumble off the side of the bed, releasing a shriek.

I don't hit the floor.

Cool arms envelop me, lifting me up. "Jewel, fuck. Did I—did I bite you?" He spins me and lays me on the bed, stretching out my throbbing arm. "Shit. Austin!"

Haze shadows the edges of my vision. "Kingston, you're okay," I say, trying to touch him.

He links his hands on the back of his head and stands. "Austin!"

The door bangs open, but I can't take my eyes away from Kingston and how sad and distraught he looks, his wide eyes turning wild with every glance at me. Austin and Diego materialize next to him, and I stretch my arms out to them. None of them move to touch me as they stare at me and my bleeding arm.

"Jewel," Austin says, "What happened? You were bit. Was that Kingston?"

I shake my head. "No one bit me."

Kingston swears. "It was fucking Mitchell. I'm going to ki—"

Diego slaps his hand over Kingston's mouth, cutting off his words. "Shut up. You can't threaten shit like that."

"It wasn't Mitchell," I say, trying to sit up. My head throbs at the sudden spinning room. "It was me. I did this."

"You?" all three of my vampires ask.

I blink a few times. "Kingston wasn't waking up. He needed blood, so I gave him mine."

"Babe, with a knife, right?" Kingston asks, sitting next to me to pull me into his lap. He releases a groan, staring at my obviously not inflicted by a knife puncture holes.

My tongue numbs, my face feeling weird. The room won't stop spinning, either. "I feel strange. I felt like this when Katherine..."

"Fucking hell," Diego says. "You did bite her."

"Don't get mad, Diego," I murmur. "You bit me too."

"But I didn't bite her! I was unconscious," Kingston snaps at his brother, ignoring me. "There's no way that was me."

A cool hand touches my forehead, and Austin leans closer to make me focus on his face. "Hey, Jewel. Tell me what happened, so I can help you."

"Mitchell beat up Kingston," I manage to say.

"And then what?"

The world turns dark for a second or a minute. I can't be certain. Something's wrong. Maybe Mitchell did manage to get into my head somehow even if I remember.

"Jewel," Austin asks again. "It's just me and you now. Will you tell me who bit you? It's important we know how it happened. If Kingston bit you while he was unconscious, we need to discuss—"

I squeeze my eyes shut. "I told you no one bit me. It was me. Kingston needed my blood. I told you."

"He needed your blood?" he repeats.

I nod. "He wouldn't wake up."

"And you used his fangs?"

Darkness pulls me away from Austin again before blinding light shines in my eyes.

"Jewel, please try to stay with me. I need you to confirm it was Kingston's fangs."

I blink some more. "Yeah. I'm sorry. Am I in trouble?"

He swears under his breath without answering me and flashes a light in my eyes again. Sitting me up, he brings a cool glass to my lips and helps me drink the familiar, sweet blood of my guys. I hum my pleasure, licking my lips, but still, the shadows crowd my vision.

"So much better than Mitchell's blood," I murmur.

"What?" Austin asks, raising his voice.

I nod, managing to focus on the cup in front of me. "He thought he was manipulating my mind and gave it to me to stop you from getting in my head."

Austin growls.

Reaching out, I touch my finger to his lip. "I'm so sorry. I didn't know what to do."

"It's not your fault," he whispers. "Now, please. Drink a little more for me. If you don't feel better in a second, I'll—"

I throw up all over Austin, my insides twisting and turning the more I remember my encounter with Mitchell. My stomach heaves so hard, wanting to expel every ounce of blood from me regardless of who it came from. I gasp, trying to catch my breath. My head hurts even worse. Muscular arms encircle me, the world shifting again. Whispers prod at my ears, but it's too hard to focus.

"Jewel," Austin says. "Don't fall asleep. Keep talking to me."

I open my mouth to respond, but nothing comes out. My tongue weighs a million pounds and refuses to partake in any of this speaking business he asks of me.

"Babe, listen to Austin," Kingston says. I didn't even hear him come in the room. Cool fingers entwine with mine. "Keep your eyes open. It's going to be okay no matter what."

I groan and shake my head, trying to do as he asks.

"It's important, beautiful," Diego says. I tilt my head in the direction of his voice, but I can't seem to do anything else. "You accidentally triggered Kingston's venom, but you're going to be fine. We're here."

I what? I don't get the chance to ask. My body betrays my mind's commands, and I black out.

ADVERSE REACTIONS

MACHINES BEEP OVER AND OVER, yanking me from my sleep. I gasp and sit up. Wires stick to my skin, and I instinctively rip at them, trying to get them off me, including the painful needle stuck into the top of my hand.

Strong arms push me down, holding me in place. "Jewel, hey. Hey, it's okay. Take a breath. I'll get everything off you. Just calm down."

I thrash again, my body rebelling against Austin's calm words. I accidentally punch him in the stomach, and he jumps back, his eyes widening.

"Did she get stronger?" Diego asks.

I blink the haze from my eyes, my vision clearing. Austin straightens his shoulders and returns to my side. I focus on him carefully untangling the wires from me that I messed up. He offers me a closed-lip smile, never taking his eyes off mine as he finally removes all the medical equipment, taking it completely out of the room to leave in the hallway.

My stomach growls immediately before I can even open my mouth to ask Austin what the hell happened. It's pitch-black outside his window, so several hours must've gone by since...ohmyeffingG.

The memory of mine and Kingston's confrontation with Mitchell explodes through my mind, leaving me scared and confused. "Am I a vampire?" I blurt. "Did I transform? You said I triggered Kingston's venom." Holy shit balls.

"Jewel—"

"Ah, hell. I'm so hungry." I rub my hands together, my stomach burning, begging me to put something in it. "Is this what it's—"

Austin cups my face and cuts off my words with a kiss, combing his fingers through my hair and down my shoulders. His lips don't leave mine until I relax in his arms and kiss him back, scooting my body to close the space between us.

Slowly, he eases away. "You're not a vampire."

"I'm not?"

He shakes his head. "False alarm. We thought he did because he was unconscious when you gave him your blood, but you got sick because of Mitchell. Like with anything, too much of something, such as blood, can have adverse reactions."

I frown, my bottom lip puckering out. Am I pouting? I am

friggin' full-on pouting, and I don't even know why. I mean, come on? I can't be sad that Austin informed me that what I did to help Kingston didn't trigger his venom or my transformation. I should be cheering that I get to experience another human day. That I can still step out onto the balcony in sunlight if I want to. That I can still manage to feed...

"Are you sure?" I ask.

He nods, remaining serious. "There's a reason I try to keep things precise. I leave some room for variances in case you want to enjoy a private moment with one of us," he says, keeping his voice even and professional like any other time he manages my health. "But I never imagined—" Austin spins and slams his fist into the wall, creating a crater with his strength.

I startle, my eyes widening. It's rare for me to see Austin lose his cool, and it makes me get to my feet to shuffle to him. He only lets me get a foot on my shaking legs, lacing his hands around me to hug me to him. Hiding his face in the crook of my shoulder, he breathes against my skin until his body stops trembling.

"I want to kill him," he whispers so quietly. "How could he do this to you? To us?"

I squeeze him tighter. "I'm okay, really. It was nasty, sure, but he didn't hurt me or anything. I was scared. You shouldn't threaten to kill everyone who scares me."

"He betrayed us, Jewel."

"I know." I don't know how else to respond. Seeing Austin shook up somehow manages to keep me calm for the both of us.

While I'm not excusing Mitchell's gross and horrifying behavior, I do know that he had specific reasons. He wants to sever my ties to my family and Haven Springs, and I think there's more to it than what he told me. All I know in this second is that I can't have my guys threatening to kill their dad, and I'll say what I can to cool the tension until we can figure out how to approach—or even if we should approach—the situation with Mitchell. Look how he handled Kingston? I've never seen anything like it. I'm also not so sure Mitchell's blood is the complete reason for my getting sick. Something still feels off about it.

"But I am okay now...I think. Are you sure about the venom? I mean, the punctures felt more like Katherine's than Diego's." I need to get his attention on something else besides his dad.

He pulls back to meet my eyes. "It healed quickly. Your blood work looks normal."

I frown. "Maybe it just didn't work. I mean, I know now vampirism wasn't caused by a real plague, but my dad once told me that there was a vaccine against it. It was part of his conspiracy theories."

He grimaces at my words. "The only vaccines given prevent human illnesses to keep the human population healthy. I should know. What your dad told you was a rumor from long ago to stop the chaos and fear. Humans killed each other if they thought one was turning. Donor Life Corp kept things simple and easy to understand."

I only bob my head.

"I really don't believe that Kingston's venom got in your system. And as for Katherine's, whatever amount she released obviously wasn't enough. I am still looking into the side effects. I just don't have an accurate way to test my theories, but I think our blood negated the process. I will continue to monitor you for signs of progression."

"And I guess we'll know for certain if I do decide to officially accept your Blood Vow," I muse.

He smiles at my words and kisses me. "So Mitchell didn't ruin this for you?"

"I was a little bummed," I admit. "I thought I'd be more scared, but I'm not. I just worry about my sister."

"And we'll figure this out," he says.

"Where are Kingston and Diego, anyway?" I ask, suddenly in desperate need to make sure everyone's okay. "You guys are probably starving. What time is it?"

"We're right here, babe," Kingston says, drawing my attention away from Austin to see both Kingston and Diego sitting in Austin's library.

I smirk, surprised by their distance. "What, no smothering me?"

"As soon as the doc gives me permission," Kingston quips, glancing at Austin. "Apparently he thinks it would be a little crowded if we all cuddled you in his bed. I, on the other hand, think a little love from me is what you need."

I snort, covering my mouth with my hand. "You bet. Get

over here."

Kingston picks me up off the bed and buries his face in my hair, squeezing me hard enough that I laugh. Cupping his face in my hand, I make him look at me. All signs of bruising are long gone, his nose straight again, his lips full and pouty and begging for me to kiss them.

So I do. I brush my lips to his, kissing him long enough to make him groan softly as he keeps himself in control.

"I was so scared for you, Kingston," I whisper to his mouth.

Kingston nuzzles his nose to mine. "You saved my life, babe."

"Oh, shut up, Kingston," Diego says, coming up beside us. His eyes beg me for attention too. "You were nowhere near death."

I laugh, pushing my hands into Kingston's chest. "Even so, I'd risk losing my arm all over again." I turn to Diego and Austin. "I would've done the same for you both. I might have contemplated throwing your dad out in the sun."

"That's my badass babe," Kingston says, setting me back on my feet.

Diego immediately sneaks into my open arms for a hug. "But thanks for not following through, beautiful. Mitchell was out of line and what he did was unforgivable, but—"

Austin punches him in the shoulder, sending him a foot away from me. "Don't excuse him."

I slide between them, opening my arms to Diego again to

draw his attention away from Austin. Diego relents, choosing to hug me over trying to finish a fight with Austin. I've witnessed enough vampire brawls to last me the rest of my life. Diego relaxes under my touch, his expression softening as he looks into my eyes. "We'll get this figured out," he murmurs, bending down to kiss me longer and deeper than Kingston, sending my body tingling.

Easing back first, I say, "I know we will."

I stare at my three guys, turning to each of them. They all look like they could use another hug, so I attempt to wrap my arms around all of them at once, making them laugh. It takes everything in me to pull away, because I feel the safest surrounded by their muscular bodies, feeling their love for me radiating from them without them even having to say the words.

I turn to Kingston. "I know it's your night, but if you're okay with it, I'd like us to stay together."

He shifts his gaze to Austin's. "It's not my night."

I frown. "What do you mean it's not your night?"

"It's Austin's," he answers.

"I've been out for over a day? What the hell?" I can't believe so much time has passed.

"You missed my night too," Diego says.

"And another one of my days," Kingston says. "Two nights I could've been filling you with all the bliss your sexy ass body could ever want...gone."

"Maybe it's a sign from the universe," Diego says, nudging Kingston.

I roll my eyes and bat his shoulder. "Knock it off, Diego. Kingston's been through enough."

Diego raises an eyebrow without responding, and Kingston looks smug as hell, smirking at me. It takes Austin wrapping his arms around me to pull me from his brothers to get them to quit trying to speak to me with their eyes, though I love the way they look at me with amusement. It makes me feel like maybe things aren't as bad as my nerves tell me, even with my lost time.

"I'm sorry about all this, Jewel. I wanted to make sure you were comfortable," Austin says.

I hug him. "You don't have to apologize. I trust that you do what you think is best for me."

His whole face lights up, sending my heart racing in the best possible way. Austin's always hyper-aware of my feelings despite my needs, and I can tell he worries a lot about always making sure everything is good for me. "And as for hanging out all together, that was mostly the plan, except for the trip to Haven Springs."

My eyes widen. "Wait, what? We're going? I thought Mitchell forbade it? He even tried to manipulate my mind. If he finds out—"

"This is his doing," Austin says, keeping his face even.

I grimace, unsure what to make of this. Why go through all the trouble to fight with Kingston and then threaten my very matching with his sons to get me to comply with his desire to isolate me from my family only to permit me to go? "His doing?

Why?"

"Things have changed."

Shit balls. His tone ignites all sorts of unwanted panic inside me. Changed? I mean, what the hell does that mean for me? "I don't like the sound of that. If Mitchell said it was okay for me to go, he must have a reason." I look at Kingston, his frown giving him away. "He *does* have a reason. Why didn't you all start with this?"

"Because you're more important than a trip to Haven Springs," Diego says from his spot beside Kingston.

"We wanted to make sure you were okay," Kingston adds. "We know you well enough to know that you would have pretended to be okay even if you weren't."

I place my hands on my hips. "Well, yeah. Because I want to go. Especially if...oh, shit! It's been too long. Did Ramona file—" Now everything makes sense. I fist my hands and release a pathetic sounding growl. But I can't help it. "This is why Mitchell had a change of heart, isn't it?" Because we were supposed to get to my sister to try to fix things before it came to this. But now the whole board, including Mitchell, would have seen my sister's claims of a breach in my contract.

"Yes," Kingston says curtly, his dissatisfaction obvious in his tone. "But don't worry. She has no concrete evidence to prove we breached our contract. Laurel won't come forward as a witness. If she did, she would incriminate herself. The exempt think our laws don't apply to them, but they're sorely mistaken."

"So, if everyone knows and her claims are unproven, why am I allowed to go?" I ask, suddenly nervous. Mitchell beat Kingston up to get to me. He attempted to manipulate my mind. He forced his blood into my mouth so that no one could supposedly manipulate me to see if I was telling the truth about not wanting to go. Something feels utterly wrong.

"You're not only allowed to go, but you have to go."

"I *have* to go?"

"Okay, so don't freak out—"

"Now, I *am* freaking out," I say, cutting him off.

"Damn it, Kingston, you don't tell someone not to freak out," Diego says, pulling me to him in an attempt to smother my raging anxiety with a hug. "Now she's going to think the worst."

"It is pretty bad," Austin says with a sigh.

They both growl at him.

"Just tell me!" My voice screeches through the air, making all three of my guys shut their mouths and pout at me. "I mean, please? Tell me why you're taking me to Haven Springs if it's not about a breach in contract."

Kingston sighs and brings his gaze up to mine. "You're the only Divine technically allowed within the gates, and the one who can request a meeting on behalf of Donor Life Corp with the Haven Springs council. We usually send the head of our human security as a human liaison if there is a serious issue a remote meeting can't take care of but not this time. The board and Mitchell agree you need to make it clear that we're doing the community a favor and unfounded threats against contracts—especially your contract—will not be taken lightly anymore."

I shake my head. "No friggin' way. That's like asking for the exempt to murder me to make their point that they won't stand for this."

"We thought about the danger and have put a lot of consideration into this, beautiful," Diego says. "Most of the exempt are pretty peaceful, and no one wants to start a fight with us, especially one they can't win. But there are always troublemakers."

"Like the asshole with my sister?" I ask.

He nods. "Yes, like him. So, while we're technically not supposed to enter the gates, and the Haven Springs guards have every right to attack us upon sight, we're still going in with you."

My eyes widen. "What?"

Kingston shrugs. "It's not the first time a vampire has gone in. We have plenty of exempt allies that don't want to risk their comfortable living and who rather enjoy bonuses. It's how Mitchell got to your heirs before."

"I don't like this," I mutter. I never in a million years thought I'd say this, but here I am now ready to cut my ties to my family. "I've changed my mind about wanting to go. I don't care if someone says I have to. I'm not willing to put you guys at risk."

Austin takes my hand. "It's not that simple. We don't have

a choice. While the board denied your sister's request to release you from your contract, they want us to assure such accusations stay under wraps to prevent backlash on the program. You need to distract the council so we can do a sweep."

"A sweep?"

"We have to get Laurel."

I swallow, fear threatening to send me to my knees. Deep down, I knew it could come to this. I knew that Laurel wouldn't stand a chance if my guys found her—and she doesn't deserve my mercy for what I went through—but a part of me clings to the girl who was raised in The Boxes. Jewel Jordan would've never been okay with turning against another human, but of course, she'd have never fallen for a vampire. For three. Jewel Jordan vanished the second she Blood Matched. I'm not Jewel Jordan. I'm Jewel Divine, and this is the life I've chosen...but it doesn't mean I have to agree.

"No." My words surprise even me, and all three of my guys look at me like I've lost my head. "I can't do this. I can't go along with something that could put not only us at risk but also lead to harming someone no different than me."

"She is nothing, and I mean nothing, like you!" Kingston shouts, throwing his hands up. His voice surprises the hell out of me, and if both Austin and Diego weren't crowding me in the way I like, I might've flown back.

I blink, trying not to react to the fact that he yelled at me. It's not like I haven't yelled at him before, but hell.

Diego glowers at Kingston, but his tense, rippling muscles

display that part of his reaction is toward my words as well. He's just better at aiming his frustration toward someone else that isn't me. "She committed treason after all we have done for her. She is the reason we were forced to breach our contract. She took you knowing you could die—she was counting on it."

"She did what she thought she had to. Look at me. As much as it hurts me to think about it, I'd have never applied for a Blood Match if my dad hadn't gone missing," I whisper. "People do whatever it takes to survive."

"That's bullshit, Jewel, and you know it," Kingston says. "Every staff member and their families are well taken care of here. Your situation was extremely different than hers."

Diego reaches for me, noticing the burning tears threatening to spill on my face. I cross my arms in an attempt to stand my ground no matter how much I see it bugs my guys. I don't want to lose myself in Diego's love. Not when I have to stand strong. He sighs and folds his arms, my own annoyance mirrored on his face.

Austin puts his arm around my shoulders though I've closed myself off. He's not forcing his affection on me, just showing that he's here no matter what.

But as much as anyone wants to deny it, Austin sees humans differently than his brothers, and he was like this even before me. "You know I don't like admitting this, but Kingston is right. Laurel had a good life here. She did what she did because she was selfish. She was jealous that the Blood Match Program failed her."

"Because she didn't match with the vampire she wanted?" I ask, remembering what Kingston had done, applying to match with her because he knew she would've matched with a known body drainer.

Kingston rubs his neck. "Exactly."

"I don't see why they couldn't be together if they were in love," I say.

"It's complicated." Kingston twists his lips. "If a vampire and human could just be together, you bet your sexy ass we'd cancel all our contracts. Hell, I'd quit Donor Life Corp, and we could run away together."

"All of us," I say.

Kingston sighs. "If you insist."

"Duh, dude."

Both Austin and Diego grin at me.

If only it were that easy.

I can imagine the four of us getting rid of our contracts, and the three of them could all officially be with me how we want. Exemption can be bought, but Mitchell Divine would never pay for my family from the goodness of his heart. The contract guarantees loyalty, something he obviously worries that my family might ruin between us. And my guys' wealth is Divine wealth. We don't run for a reason.

I push the thought away, knowing that I'll damn well do anything for my guys if I have to. And I might have to after our extension is up. Bringing my thought back to Laurel, I say, "But our situation is different. Couldn't he have done something?"

Austin brushes his blond hair back. "Yeah, Giorgio techni-cally could have if he bought her work contract from us and she agreed to let him. Instead, he talked Laurel into applying for the Blood Match under the notion that he wanted to make things official while providing for her heirs. But the thing is, Laurel's mom was only a year away from exemption. All Divine staff gets it if they make it to retirement, but it doesn't include heirs."

"I don't understand. Why couldn't Giorgio do it for her mom early? Or use the money he put toward the fees to buy Laurel's contract?" Because I know there are a lot of costs for a vampire to apply for a Blood Match. They cover all the fees and inheritance for their match's heirs. Forever. There's no expira-tion. Katherine paid Laurel well to give her exemption to the one place vampires can't go. Laurel's vampire love could have easily done that for her mom.

"Because he never planned to follow through with Laurel and make it official. Giorgio's feelings weren't mutual. He was a long-term guest here and would've worn out his welcome rather quickly if we found out he was stringing Laurel along, especially because she'd been personally feeding him. We have a policy against that with guests for the staffs' protection. Gen. pop. blood or nothing. Having her match with someone else would've gotten her away from here and solved his problem of Laurel's attachment to him. I only found out why Laurel ap-plied because Martina asked if I could influence the outcome, which I couldn't because Giorgio chose and matched to someone else days before Laurel's appointment," Kingston says. "That's why I applied and got us disqualified. I was looking out for her."

"And look how she repaid you," I say, a mixture of emotions swelling through me that Kingston went through so much trouble to help Laurel. I knew part of the story, but this is the first time Kingston's decided to tell me all of it. And I can see how hard it is for him. He might joke and tease me, make comments to his brothers, but when it comes down to it, he's hard on himself. He worries if he's good enough for me. He even stresses about things like my jealousy over whose blood he drinks.

"So do you understand why this must be done?" Diego asks me, though I don't take my gaze off Kingston, who now stares at the floor. "We cannot take the chance. The risk isn't worth it. We're not losing you."

I sigh. "I'm sorry. I just—you can't hurt her. Figure something else out. Manipulate her mind. Bring her back here. Send her to The Boxes. I don't care."

"But—"

I hold up my hand to cut Austin and Diego off. Kingston still keeps his eyes trained on the floor. "My life isn't worth more than hers. Kingston went through great lengths to assure she lived, so..." I shrug, letting my voice trail off.

I want to throw out that Laurel was in her position because of Giorgio, but they might misinterpret me to mean vampires. It wouldn't be the first time I blamed something on vampires or

Donor Life Corp. But my guys aren't their dad or Donor Life Corp. I want to assure they'll never be.

"Babe," Kingston finally says, keeping his voice low. "You're right. We'll figure something else out, but this isn't for Laurel. I still don't agree she deserves your mercy after her betrayal. This is for you."

"And you," I say. Turning to Diego, I add. "Also for you." I reach out and touch Austin's hand. "You too, Austin. You once told me you never killed a human. You chose your interest in human health because you like us and were once human."

Austin presses his lips into a line, hiding them. "You're not just my perfect match, Jewel. You're the best part of me. You help me remember the best parts of me."

"And me," Diego says, touching my cheek. "Thanks for not letting me forget that."

"Never," I say, kissing him.

Kingston closes the space to me and engulfs me in a hug, lifting me a few inches off my feet. "Fuck, I missed you. Four nights of not hearing your voice nearly destroyed me. I just want to cuddle and kiss and—"

"And touch?" I ask, smirking.

"All the touching. But no biting," he says.

I giggle and snap my teeth at him. "And to think I was starting to like it."

He releases a throaty groan and turns to his brothers. "Can I please sit in back with Jewel?"

Austin shrugs his shoulders. "If Jewel's okay with it, I'm

okay with it. Just this once, though."

I raise my eyebrows. "The back? Really?"

"Um, yeah. What's wrong with that?" Kingston asks.

Diego chuckles. "I think Jewel wants to drive."

CHANGED

KINGSTON TAPS A FEW BUTTONS on the navigation screen, turning the car from manual mode to autopilot. I take my hands off the wheel and swivel in my seat to face my guys. Kingston sits in the front seat next to me with Diego and Austin in back. The bright moon hangs in the sky through the side window, lighting a path on the ocean stretching into the beyond to places I'll never go.

Headlights flash behind us, and I peer at the security detail following us. Pedro drives with three human passengers from the daytime security, all given bonuses to take care of me on my journey into Haven Springs.

"Come here, babe. Time to switch with Diego," Kingston says, not giving me a chance to argue by unbuckling me and pulling me into his lap. He secures the harness around both of us, keeping his arms on my stomach. "We're going to pass through Midnight Valley, and it's better if Diego's in control."

Diego taps a button on the driver's seat, and it reclines, giving him room to climb into it. "I think Jewel would be fine to get us through. She's a natural."

I smile. "I'd just run everyone over who got in our way."

All three of them chuckle.

Stomping the throttle, Diego speeds forward, sending me back into Kingston. The headlights cut across an old road in need of repair that leads to a looming wall tall enough to hide the city within it. Guards aim weapons at us from their posts, their silver eyes flashing in the night. A few of them jump down from the wall and land right in our path.

Fear tenses my muscles, but none of my guys react, which lessens my uneasiness a tiny bit. It helps that Kingston's hands wander from my stomach to my legs, rubbing from my knees to the hem of my dress that miraculously remains in place to hide my thighs.

"It's just a checkpoint, babe," Kingston whispers, kissing my temple.

Austin reaches forward and squeezes my shoulder. "If asked, Kingston is your Blood Match. Our triple match is not publicized around the general vampire populace. All guests at the Divinity Estate sign non-disclosure agreements with absurd fines that would send any of them to the shadows."

"Oh, but it's your night," I say.

"Too late to switch laps," Kingston says, kissing me again. "You're mine now, babe."

Diego punches Kingston in the side of the leg, making him jump with me. "Knock it off. Possessiveness only looks good on Jewel."

I smirk at Diego and sneak my hand to touch his thigh. He covers my hand for a second before returning his to the wheel. Slowing down the car, Diego keeps the vehicle steady, heading right toward the vampires. I bring my hand back to my lap where Kingston locks his fingers with mine.

Diego stops inches from the vampires but doesn't cut off the engine. The burly vampire on the outside of the line jets to the driver's side window and stares through the glass. Unlike at the Divinity Estate, Diego doesn't retract the window. He casually grabs a card from a compartment on the dashboard and holds it up.

"Nice to see you, Mr. Divines," the vampire says.

He bends down for a better look, focusing directly on me. His dark gaze bores into mine, making me extra uncomfortable. I squirm in Kingston's lap, trying to figure out how to hide from him while I'm strapped in.

The vampire speeds around the hood to stop at my window. I swivel to look at him, taking in his strong jawline and sharp nose. He flashes his fangs in a smile, tilting his head lower to nearly press his face to the glass.

"What's his friggin' problem?" I ask, turning away. If the harness would allow it, I'd shift and hide my face in Kingston's jacket.

The vampire taps on the glass. "I'm sorry, Mr. Divines. I can't get visual confirmation of your passenger. Please roll down your window."

I tense, licking my lips to prepare to yell at the guy that he's gotten a great enough view of me and if he can't see me then maybe he needs his eyes checked, though I know vampires have perfect vision.

"Jewel, stay calm," Kingston whispers. "Don't say anything. You're not supposed to hear him through the soundproof glass."

"This is normal," Austin adds. "He's just curious."

Kingston taps a button, retracting the window into the door. A cool breeze wafts in, making me shiver, and I wiggle even more, pressing harder into Kingston. He releases a soft moan into my hair, too soft for anyone but me to hear, and digs his fingers into my legs to keep me in place.

"Welcome to Midnight Valley," the vampire says. "Can you please look at me, miss, and state your name?"

I flick my gaze to his for a split second and turn back to the line of vampires inching closer on the road. "Jewel Divine of the Divinity Estate."

"Sorry, Ms. Divine. I need you to look at me a moment longer."

Austin releases a low growl from the backseat.

"That was good enough," Kingston says, keeping his voice even. "Must I remind you who you're speaking to?"

"My apologies, Mr. Divine. I just need to confirm Ms. Divine's eye color."

Kingston mutters under his breath. "Go ahead and look at him, babe."

I turn my head toward the vampire without meeting his gaze dead on. A bright light blinks on, blinding me. A cool finger touches my chin, making all three of my guys roar in a way I've never heard them. Things happen so fast that my mind has trouble wrapping around them. Kingston locks his hand around the vampire's and twists, snapping his wrist. A scream rips through the air, and I spot Austin outside the car and behind the man. His fangs flash from his scowl, and he looks ready to rip the vampire's head off.

He never gets the chance. The vampires blocking the car break formation. I gasp, air seemingly impossible to breathe in as the group surrounds Austin and the vampire. Diego exits the car next, standing taller than everyone. Kingston closes the window and unfastens our harness. I twist in his arms to face him, meeting his calm dark eyes.

He smiles and kisses me. "Relax, babe."

"They're going to hurt them," I say.

"The only vampire more powerful than us is Mitchell. These guards enjoy living too much to test us."

"You broke that asshole's arm."

Kingston brushes his lips to mine. "He's lucky I didn't break every one of his bones. He shouldn't have touched you."

I shift again to look out the window, and Kingston touches

my cheek, bringing my attention back to him. He attempts to kiss me again, sliding his hands down my back. I don't let him. I bring my hand up to his lips, making him kiss my palm.

"This isn't the time to make out," I murmur.

"It's always the time to make out, especially with how much you're squirming. It's driving me crazy, babe," he says against my fingers, flicking his tongue across my hand until I move it.

Narrowing my eyes, I slowly, purposely, slide my ass around. He inhales a breath, leaning forward to attempt to kiss me again. "Still, not the time to make out."

The car doors slam, startling me. I automatically swing out my arm with a screech. Diego grabs my hand mid-air, rubbing it to his stubbly cheek. I release a huge breath and sink against Kingston as my nerves relax. Austin touches my shoulder from the back, and I climb between the seats and throw my arms around him.

"You scared me, leaving like that," I say, hugging him. I turn to Diego. "Both of you."

"Sorry, beautiful," Diego says.

Austin squeezes my hand. "It's not uncommon for those beneath us to test our authority. I'm sorry if you were scared, but to not act would only garner more unwanted attention, especially toward you."

"Oh." I turn to look out the window, spotting the group of guards helping the asshole who harassed me to his feet.

Diego puts the car in drive, vaulting us forward. I glimpse a few figures blur past as we enter the now open gate that leads into a city in much worse shape than Dark Terrace Ranch. I couldn't see the buildings from over the wall because any that would have been tall enough have been half demolished and remain unlit.

Austin adjusts the middle harness around me, locking me in place. I'm slightly annoyed that the position obstructs my view. Kingston lasts all of a minute in the front and somehow manages to slide next to me without lowering his seat. Diego glances at me in the rearview mirror and then looks behind me. I turn to spot the headlights of our security team still following us, keeping Diego's speed.

I scoot as far over as I can to peer out Kingston's window. Lights drag across my vision, Diego racing us over a smooth road along the perimeter. Sighing, I fiddle with the restraints, drawing Austin's hands back to me. We play fight for a minute, both laughing, and then he gives up and secures his arms tighter than Kingston ever does, locking my legs in place after I climb onto Kingston to get a better view of the city.

"You guys should look into cleaning this place up," I say, taking in the trash blowing from the street from our tires. "It's kind of gross. I thought Dark Terrace Ranch was bad, but I feel awful for the humans here."

"Not our zone, beautiful," Diego says. "Midnight Valley belongs to the Vaduva Coven. You've met Viorica Vaduva. She's the redhead on the board. Feisty. Short-tempered. Head of her all-female coven."

"I don't think she liked me," I say.

"Not true, Jewel," Austin says. "She's the one who personally denied your sister's request."

"Oh."

"I think it's because she's enamored that all three of us want forever with you," Kingston says. "And she hopes we'll murder each other so she can swoop in and invite you to be a Vaduva—or what we call the Widows."

"She's a little annoyed that four of her daughters didn't make it past the questionnaire portion of your Blood Match test," Austin adds.

"Four?"

Diego peers at me in the rearview mirror. "We're sort of rivals. She was one of the reasons Roger nearly matched you out from under us. She approved to disqualify us."

A scowl twists my face at his revelation. "Are you friggin' kidding me?"

Austin rubs his hands up and down my legs. "Diego, really? You're upsetting her."

Kingston leans closer to me. "Female applicants are rare, babe. Why do you think I intercepted Ms. Sybil after she denied you? She's good at her job but does not stray from the rules."

Diego clears his throat. "And Dark Terrace Ranch has a rather appealing populace."

I frown. "Why's that?"

All three of them shrug without answering.

"Tell me."

Kingston groans, hugging me tighter. "Some other time."

I slide from his lap and back into the middle seat to turn to Austin. Reaching up, I touch his cheek. "Please, tell me."

Kingston pulls me back. "I don't think so, babe. Not cool to try to use your affection to get Austin to talk."

I glare at him and lean forward to wrap my arms around Diego. "Diego."

He chuckles. "Damn it, beautiful. You know I want to, but you need a clear head tonight."

Huffing, I plop back into my seat and cross my arms.

Kingston groans and takes my hand. "Fine, but you can't get mad at us."

"Kingston," Diego warns. "Later."

"Please, Kingston. I won't get mad," I say, inching closer. He's usually least likely to talk, but something has him breaking even his own rules tonight. I'm not even sorry about taking advantage of his mood. He tries to do the same to me.

Kingston nods, glancing at me for only a second. I realize it's because he doesn't want to see my reaction toward what he's going to say. I brace myself, straightening my shoulders to put a real effort in mastering a serious face to hide any reaction I might give.

"And you complain about my inability to tell Jewel no," Austin mutters under his breath.

Kingston ignores both his brothers and says, "The flu outbreak last year might have devastated the human population, but those who survived are considered desirable because of it. It basically means you're the strongest, most resilient donors."

I clench my jaw to stop myself from reacting and let silence drag between us. Bringing my gaze from my lap, I stare out the windshield, realizing we've already left the city. Both Austin and Kingston inch closer to me so I'm sandwiched between them. Diego reaches his hand behind him and rests it on my leg. I automatically take it, squeezing his fingers.

"I guess I get it," I finally say. "And I'm not mad at any of you, so you know. I just—when I hear stuff like this, it reminds me of where I come from and how much I've changed. How much I'll continue to change. And I'm scared."

"You might change, Jewel, but you won't ever turn your back or excuse poor behavior. I know this," Diego says. "And you won't let us either."

"You can't be sure," I whisper.

"Hell yeah, we can be," Kingston says. "You've changed us as much as we've changed you."

"And we want to continue to change," Austin says.

"Except the world is against us. If it wasn't, we wouldn't be here. My sister wouldn't hate me. Brayla wouldn't be with Orlando. You wouldn't be infiltrating a human safe zone. Or breaking wrists of people who touch me."

"Um, babe. I would still be breaking all the wrists," Kingston says. "I mean, I even have the urge to break my brothers' wrists, and I like them."

His certainty makes me laugh. "You better get that urge in

check, but you know what I mean. If the world wasn't against us, I could tell Donor Life Corp I choose all of you without having to worry about forfeiting my contract or putting our way of life in jeopardy. Or about the fight you'd surely have with the board."

"And Mitchell," they all say.

I sigh with a groan. "Or him."

Austin wraps his arms around me while Kingston takes my free hand. I squeeze Diego's fingers again, wishing he wasn't driving so I could ask them to sandwich me with all their love and hugs.

Diego must read my mind, because he hits the dash screen and puts the car in autopilot and squeezes his torso between the seats, opening his arms for me. I exhale a soft breath, knowing that even if the world is against us, we can still beat it.

"We're going to get everything settled," Diego says, pulling back only enough to see if I'll kiss him, which I do.

Austin leans into me next, his vibrant green eyes lighting up with his smile. "He's right. I promise you."

"And if we don't, we'll still manage," Kingston adds. "Because you're my badass babe. I mean, people should beware. You bite harder than any of us."

Diego punches him in the arm. "Kingston."

I giggle. The more he teases me, the less I care. Kingston snuggles into me, begging for a kiss of his own, so I snap my teeth at him.

He laughs. "I deserved that."

I finally kiss him. "And maybe this too." I pull away and look at each of my guys. "As much as I want everything to be okay, I have a promise to make you. If it's not, I'm going to fight for you all no matter what. Starting tonight. I won't let you down."

"We know, babe. It's never you we worry about."

I smile. "I know you won't let me down either."

HAVEN SPRINGS

I STARE AT THE HIGH wall of Haven Springs looming in the distance. Nestled on a hillside, the community has only one way up and down, and from their position, they have a total view of the valley below. Bright lights blink on as we go, announcing our arrival like a beacon.

"You'll have two hours, okay?" Austin says, pulling out a box from under the seat. He pops it open, and I spot the familiar thermos with a concoction of my guys' blood. "And I want you to drink a little extra blood tonight. It gives us time to get to you if something doesn't go as planned."

"It's going to be fine," I say, clutching the thermos. The words are mostly for myself, but I do hope they believe them as well.

"I know, beautiful," Diego says. "The guards will protect you."

Kingston slides a bag from under the driver's seat. "And I'm going to arm you like a fucking vampire assassin." He unbuckles my harness and nudges me to lean forward to drape a jacket over my dress. "Leather and all."

"Doesn't this give the wrong impression?" I ask.

"The only impression I want you to give is that you can't be messed with," Kingston says. "Because they'll try."

"I hope not," I murmur.

Austin motions for me to start drinking the blood as we speed up the road. "You'll be fine, Jewel. You have an hour with the human council, open to all of Haven Springs, which will assure no one tries anything. There will be children there. Humans always care for their young first. It's your hour with Ramona I'm a little worried about, but it's supposed to be family-only. The exempt still have their own laws, so I hope the asshole respects them more than us. Do try to find out his name, so we can look into his family history and see what coven he's attached to."

"I have a feeling he's a descendant from the failed matches," Kingston says.

"They tend to be more hostile," Diego adds.

I pout. "What if Ramona decides she doesn't want to see me? Then what?"

Diego offers me a small smile from the driver's seat. "She will. The request was accepted."

I bob my head and quickly finish the thermos of blood. Diego turns his attention back to the road, taking the car off autopilot to navigate us the rest of the way up the hillside. I slide my arms behind both Austin and Kingston, sinking lower in my seat. Austin draws soothing circles on my knee, calming my heart, and Kingston has a little too much fun strapping on different kinds of holsters, claiming his favorite being the one he hikes up my dress to fasten to my thigh.

"Don't you think this is a little excessive, dude?" I ask. "How am I going to move properly?"

"Jewel's experience lies in pocket knives," Diego says. "And gun safety. I never got around to anything else."

"Are you fucking kidding me, Diego?" Kingston says. "What the hell have you been doing the last few weeks?"

"Don't give me that shit. I was easing her into more intense fighting. She is terrified of the idea of using a weapon, especially after the traitors of our staff left her no choice but to defend herself against them. Look at Jewel's expression right now and imagine it ten times worse. Now tell me you don't want to do everything you can to get her to smile."

All three of them direct their eyes on me. Kingston reaches up and touches my bottom lip, puckering out his own lip. I lean closer and kiss him, just grazing my lips feather soft to his. His hands start roaming over me, and I realize he's removing half of the weapons he strapped to me.

Kingston rests his head on my shoulder. "You're right, babe. I'm being excessive. And I'm sorry if it scared you. I just—I hate this. I don't want to send you in at all."

"None of us do, Kingston," Austin says, speaking up. "But Jewel can handle herself."

"She handles you exceptionally well," Diego adds.

Austin and Diego bump knuckles and laugh. "Don't forget she can hear things normal humans can't, so she can hear possible threats coming and call for us immediately. She's resilient and smart and capable of dealing with anything that comes her way."

"Then why do you all always treat me like a fragile doll?" I ask. I can't help it.

Austin takes my hand in his. "I can't speak for Diego and Kingston, but I like to handle you with care because you deserve it, not because you can't handle anything more."

I smile at him, letting his words sink in. It helps build my confidence enough that I don't feel like my knees will give out on me the second I try to stand from the car. They make me feel worthy of carrying the Divine name.

"Yeah, babe. I don't call you a badass for nothing," Kingston muses, kissing my cheek. "And to be fair, Diego does *not* treat you like a doll, so don't get all swoony on him."

Diego growls at Kingston. "Shut up, asshat. You have no room to talk."

"You nearly let her hit a tree...and me for that matter."

I swivel and put a hand on each of them. "I love the way all of you are with me, so please quit it. I don't want to deal with fighting tonight, but especially between you. Diego is careful with my emotions, Kingston. You're careful with me physically, and Austin is sensitive with me when I need both. I don't want any of you to change that, all right? I'm cool."

They all smile at me.

"Good, because we're here, beautiful. Hold onto your cool for us," Diego says, putting the car in park.

I peer out the windshield, spotting at least two dozen figures on risers monitoring the road. "Holy shit balls. I don't know if I want to get out." They obviously have been waiting for us. And with the look of their friggin' big-ass weapons they aim at the car, they won't hesitate to attack my guys.

Kingston sets a packet of papers on my lap. "This is everything you need for your meeting with the council. Give it to Niall Maher."

"Niall Maher," I repeat. "Got it."

Diego hands me a small bag from a compartment in the dash. "This is full of stipend chips, a com, and a tracker. I hope you don't mind, beautiful. We know our way around Haven Springs only by the maps from the last blueprints submitted. Things could have changed in a few months, and there's no way we're not going to know where you are."

I nod, letting him strap on the bracelet, decorated with glittering sapphires that match the color of my dress.

Kingston groans. "Fuck. You guys find Laurel. I can't leave Jewel. I don't care if they'll try to shoot me on sight. It's not like they'll kill me."

"Yeah, just kill Jewel in the process when she gets trapped

in the crossfire," Austin says.

I take Kingston's hand. "You know what? Just load me up with all your weapons if it'll make you feel better. I'll manage."

He pouts. "I swear, babe. If anyone even touches you, I'll destroy this place."

It's my turn to sulk. "Kingston."

Groaning, he kisses me, squeezing me to him. I pull away because I know if I don't, he'll never let me go. Austin helps me from the car and hugs me next, reminding me that I'll be fine for the hundredth time. He leaves me with a kiss that makes me crave a thousand more. Diego guides me toward the wall and quietly gives instructions to the three human guards from the daylight household.

"We have to park down the hill," Diego says. "Be safe, beautiful."

I kiss Diego and squeeze his hand, staying in my spot with the silent human guards from the Divinity Estate until the guys follow Pedro's vehicle down the hill to disappear from sight. Nerves cling to me, making my hands shake, but I know they won't be far. Part of me hates it because of the danger they'll be in. Another part of me is thankful. I just hope things go as planned. I hope I can handle Ramona. She's what scares me the most about tonight. I'm afraid this might have to be my final goodbye.

Haven Springs looks exactly like one of the small towns I've seen a dozen times in the classics. Quaint shops with smooth exteriors line the main street that leads to a huge fountain in front of a white building with pillars, a triangular roof, and a dozen steps leading to a set of double doors.

Rows of identical houses with grass yards and white-picket fences glow with soft lights for what seems like as far as I can see. If the huge wall protecting the community to the right wasn't a glaring reminder of the fact that there is a world outside, I'd think I'd traveled back in time to an era long before the Blood Hunger Plague.

"How many people live here?" I ask the armed guard striding ahead of us. I was nearly certain he was going to demand that I remove all the weapons, but all he did was do a visual assessment.

"That's classified information, Ms. Jordan. I hope you don't take offense, but I'll not be answering any of your questions. Please understand."

I grimace. "It's Ms. Divine."

"Not in here," he says. "Here, you're not an asset or piece of property to any vampire."

"I'm neither of those things outside these walls, either," I say, straightening my shoulders. "So, please. Call me either Jewel or Ms. Divine."

Holy shit balls. If looks could slap, the guard looks like his would most definitely smack the sense he obviously thinks I'm missing back into me. But I can't let him belittle a life with my guys that I love. One I chose to remain in even though I had the chance to come here. My guys were willing to forfeit their contracts after Katherine to see to it that I got a life with my family in Haven Springs, but something stopped me, and it wasn't just the blood debt. I love Ramona. I love my cousins Dana and Fallon. But I can't imagine a life here, on a hillside, far from the ones who match with my mind, body, and blood. I don't care what anyone thinks.

"I think I'd rather not call you anything then," he mutters under his breath. "Fucking brainwashed."

I stiffen at the rush of annoyance toward words he doesn't know I can hear. He glances at me over his shoulder and offers me the fakest smile in the entire world.

"Okay, Jewel," he says, finally responding to me. "Any more questions or concerns can be directed to Hayden Andrei."

"I was told I'd be speaking with Niall Maher."

"Niall's been removed from his position but don't worry. Hayden is well aware of your situation, and he's rather excited to meet you."

Something feels incredibly wrong. I nearly call out for my guys to save me, but I know if they do, we'll all be at risk. They won't accomplish what the board tasked them to do. The last thing I want is to find myself in a battle between humans and vampires, especially when I don't want either side to lose.

I tighten my jaw, glancing at my quiet guards, who keep their attention directed to the area around us. "Does Donor Life Corp know of these changes?" I ask.

The man turns to look at me, obviously annoyed that I continue to ask more questions when he told me he wouldn't answer them. "It's none of their concern. This is Haven Springs. Vampire laws don't apply."

Friggin' hell. He sounds like—

"You!" I shout, spotting the familiar jerk that had threatened me step out from the double doors.

My guards step in closer, blocking my way but not to protect me. I'm pretty sure they're trying to stop me from running from them to attempt to pummel the asshole. He jumps from the top step like an obnoxious showoff, grinning at me as he closes the distance.

"You look surprised to see me, Jewel," he says from the other side of my wall of guards.

I stand on my tiptoes and glare at him. "Where's my sister?"

He crosses his arms. "I was informed you're here on business not on a familial visit."

Shoving myself between my silent, yet incredibly sturdy for being human guards, I manage to free myself to face the jerk straight on. He gives me a once over, practically sneering at me as I step closer.

"That's a lot of unnecessary weapons you're wearing. Why? Your vampires aren't here to hurt you anymore," he says, his jaw twitching.

Something dark inside me snaps. Without thinking, I swing my arm back and sucker punch him in the nose. I don't know how on earth I managed to knock him off his feet, but he lands on the ground, groaning and cupping his bloody nose.

A scream rips through the air, piercing my ears. I jerk sideways a moment too late. Someone crashes into me, ramming me into the ground. Gasping, I blink through my blurry vision, trying to make sense of what's happening. Then I see her. Ramona climbs on top of me, her chest heaving, her face twisted into a scowl she's never given me.

She raises her hand, aiming at my face. A soft, nearly inaudible growl sounds from my right. It's Austin. I'd know the sound of his protectiveness anywhere, and I also know that even though he's a master of keeping his emotions in check, when he can't, he's capable of ripping a vampire to pieces.

Reaching up, I lock my hand to Ramona's wrist to stop her from trying to slap me. "I'm okay," I whisper to Austin, praying he hears me.

But then I hear the subtle sounds of everyone in the vicinity drawing their weapons.

My guards prepare to shoot.

Taking a breath, I scream, "Don't! Please! She's my sister."

Ramona looks me square in the eyes as she yanks back, her anger burning away the softness of her features, making her look older under her short hair and bangs. I barely recognize her.

She spits in my face. "I have no sister."

Like that, she severs her connection to me. Four words to shatter me. Four words that cut me so deeply, I'm sure I'll feel the pain for the rest of my life. Possibly forever.

I thought I had experienced the worst agony in my life already, but I was wrong. Nothing compares to this. My heart hurts so badly that I'm not sure I can survive.

"Ramona," I whisper.

"Shut up! Don't talk to me! You're a fucking monster," she screams. "Just leave. I never wanted you here. I don't need this bullshit."

"Ramona," I repeat.

She shakes her head. "Just. Go. Away."

BLOOD REBEL

"BABE, WE DON'T HAVE TO do this," Kingston whispers from the direction I heard Austin's growl. I peer past my sister, catching sight of all three of my guys lurking within the trees that make up a grove toward the outskirts.

It takes everything in me not to run to them. Not to start bawling my eyes out in front of the sudden audience that inches closer by the second, all here for the spectacle my life has become.

"Turn around, and we'll meet you outside the gate," Austin says.

"We'll figure out a different way to handle this," Diego adds.

I straighten my shoulders, summoning the strength my

guys' nearby presences give me to keep my shit together even though I want to fall apart. Because we've come all this way for a reason. As much as I want to say it was for my sister, it wasn't. It's more than her. I'm here on behalf of Donor Life Corp, and the last thing I want to do is mess up no matter how much it pisses me off that they've made me come here.

"Ramona, this isn't about us, and I'm not leaving. I have a meeting with the council of Haven Springs to discuss some serious matters. I was told I'd be seeing Niall Maher, but apparently your community neglected to inform Donor Life Corp of these changes."

"The paperwork was going out in the morning. The vote just happened hours ago," Hayden says, meeting my glare with his own.

"Sounds awfully convenient to have such a vote just before my arrival," I say.

Hayden doesn't react. "It's been a long time coming."

I roll my eyes. "Doesn't matter." I motion toward the white building, noticing the placard declares it to be City Hall. I didn't even know that sort of government was still around. "Shall we go inside? As head of the daylight household of the Divinity Estate and future true heir to the Divines and Donor Life Corp, I have a message to deliver."

"What?" Hayden and Ramona both say in unison.

I guess my guys failed to mention my visit's intentions to them. Or maybe Niall didn't.

Holding out the envelope with the stack of papers, I hand

it over. "All the details are in here. Now, please. I don't have much time, and I plan to use most of it to visit with my family." Because I'm not leaving before I see my cousins even if Ramona doesn't want me here.

Ramona glares. "I told you—"

Hayden pulls out the top sheet and hands it to Ramona, cutting her off. "It seems Dana and Fallon approved her visit on your behalf, Mona."

Mona? A new name to go with her new look. Her new life.

"Can't I overrule it?" she asks.

Hayden tightens his jaw, continuing to flip through the rest of the paperwork. "No. It's their right."

"I'm their guardian."

He shakes his head. "They're over thirteen. No one their age requires a guardian here. If they did, things would be complicated. The majority of new arrivals are considered minors."

"Hayden, I don't like this. They shouldn't see her so brainwashed."

I intake a sharp breath, drawing her attention to me, and I regret it.

Hayden wraps his arm around Ramona's waist, pulling her farther away from me, clearly not going to continue his discussion in front of me. I wish he'd say more about how the community is run. I mean, I couldn't imagine if Dark Terrace Ranch considered thirteen and up to be an adult. And it bothers me that they are here. I was lucky enough to get to live my childhood in naivety no matter how quickly it ended with my first blood draw. They should still get that.

"Don't worry. They're smart. They'll see things our way, and if they don't, I'll take care of it. I promise," he whispers, not realizing I can hear him. "I have other ways. I know people. You have enough stipends that we can make it happen."

Ramona glances at me from over her shoulder. "And the blood debt?"

"I'm still working on it. Jewel's arrival—these documents she brought—complicate things, but you have to trust me. I'm not letting anyone take you."

As much as it pisses me off that he threatened my Blood Matching as a means to see to it that she wouldn't face a blood debt, his words get to me. I nearly believe him. And I want to agree with him and tell Ramona that I'm on her side. But I doubt she'd believe me. She's beyond reason. I can see it in her eyes. She blames me. She blames my guys. When in actuality, she should blame our dad. He might have left to try to help us as a family, but he's why we're in this position. If he wasn't so against Donor Life Corp and the Blood Match Program, I could have applied, sacrificed the freedom I got from donating, and my family would have been together and fine. Now? We're ripped apart even more.

Clearing my throat, I say, "I'm sorry to interrupt whatever plotting you're doing against me, but I don't have all night. Can we please get this over with so I can see my family and leave?"

Ramona flares her nostrils. "Call me when it's over, Hayden. I'm going to talk to my cousins."

"Ramona," I say, fear sneaking up on me. What if she convinces them not to see me?

My sister ignores me, not even glancing in my direction. She kisses Hayden and strolls away in the direction Kingston, Diego, and Austin lurk. Ramona disappears around the building, and it feels like a piece of my heart goes with her. I just don't understand what has gotten into her or why she's acting like I'm a monster for making this happen for her. For being better than ever because of it.

Hayden motions me toward the building, drawing my attention. My guys disappear, and I straighten my back, standing tall to meet Hayden's muscular, well-built frame. "Okay, *Ms. Divine*. Let's get this bullshit over with. Your guards can wait outside."

"Yeah, right. So you can murder me when I'm alone?" I snap, motioning the guards to follow us to the building.

"Despite the lies your masters have told you, I would much prefer it if you were alive," he mutters as he walks ahead of me. "Though I can't say the same for Mona's feelings. She thinks you're better off dead."

I press my lips together, steeling myself to all the hurtful stuff he can throw at me. He's purposefully doing it to get me to react. I can see it in his dumb smirk that makes me want to sucker punch him harder next time.

Hayden leads the way into the building. Another armed guard waits inside, giving me and my protection detail a once over, allowing us to pass. I don't know what they're expecting, that maybe one of them is a vampire, but they don't even question the purpose of all my weapons. Maybe like Hayden, they assume it's to be used against vampires.

As we walk down a long corridor, I try to push away the mundane sounds that everyone makes. From the thuds and squeaks of shoes on the tiles to the collections of out of sync beating hearts, and even the annoying tick of an antique clock on the wall. If I can push away the sounds, I could hear—

A guttural moan trickles through the air, coming from one of the closed doors on the right. The sound is too soft for a normal person to hear, but I hear it. And whoever it came from sounds hurt. If Hayden didn't walk so fast, I'd slow down and try to investigate. The sound is too strange to ignore, but I can't react.

"In here, Ms. Divine," Hayden says.

I stop in my tracks outside a small, windowless room with a single empty table and two chairs. "This doesn't look like a meeting room."

"I've been selected solely to represent the Haven Springs' council tonight. We're more morning people, but it seems you can't get yourself away at a decent hour."

I raise an eyebrow. "I'm not going in there. I demand to meet with the entire council."

Hayden smacks his hand on the doorframe. "You can't demand anything! This is our town. Our rules. If the council elected me to represent them, then that's what I'll do. This is more personal business anyway, is it not?"

"No, it applies to everyone here," I say. "You cannot continue to threaten recipients about breaches in contracts."

"It's our right."

"Not if you're making up bullshit stories," I say, crossing my arms. "You had Ramona file a complaint against my matches. You're jeopardizing my life."

He glances at the guards surrounding us, quietly taking in our conversation. "I'm not trying to, but you're so brainwashed. I want to help you. I want to help Ramona. You did not deserve to be put in this situation."

"I *chose* this situation. For Ramona. You can't honestly think I'm sitting around, celebrating that my dad made a deal with a—with a friggin' gho—"

Hayden slaps his hand over my mouth, startling me. All three of my guards raise their weapons, clicking off the safeties. My heart pounds in my ears, and I consider attempting to bite him, but his wide eyes hold mine for a moment, and I realize he was only trying to get me to stop talking.

"Please, Jewel. Let's discuss this in private," he asks, motioning toward the room.

His pleading eyes get to me, and I can't stop myself from nodding.

I motion to my guards to remain in the hallway. Hayden hands over his weapons without me having to ask, but he allows me to keep mine. I cross the room, but I don't sit down at the table. He does, though. Opening the envelope, he stacks the papers in front of him, combing his fingers into his hair, holding it off his forehead.

"You know, after everything Mona told me about your parents, this was the last thing I had expected," Hayden says after a moment.

I shift on my feet. "I'm not sure what you mean."

"Your dad is a Blood Rebel. If his debt is to a ghost of the system, then he'd have rather died than see you in the house of the Divines." His words swirl through my mind. Diego said something similar, but I haven't had a chance to discuss it. "And here you are, wearing their vows, turning your back on humanity, especially because humanity needs someone like you, Jewel. Fearless. Strong. Loyal. If only it were to the right people."

I purse my lips, refraining from snapping that my guys are the right people, but Hayden has his mind made up about me. "I love them," I say. "You think I'm brainwashed, but I have never seen things more clearly than with them. They're not like other vampires."

"They're worse."

I sigh. "They're not. They've given me a life. A home. A promise. They're helping me take care of the blood debt of my dad. If anything, you should be mad at him. Not me. And so you know, I will not let Ramona inherit the debt. You never gave me the chance to even talk about it. We have a year to figure this out, and I will figure it out."

"You're in over your head, Jewel," he says. "You think the Divine heirs will release you from your contract if you don't? If that's what you think, you're more ignorant than I thought."

"Funny, because I think the same of you. Threatening the Divines was a huge mistake."

He groans, sifting through the papers. "Obviously. I knew Donor Life Corp was full of shit when it came to Blood Matches, but their new terms and conditions are ludicrous."

"They only want you to stop filing false claims," I say. "Especially with unreliable sources with vendettas. Laurel is a liar." And so am I. "She accused such a thing because she's jealous I matched with Kingston. She likes him. She was angry they didn't get matched, and she was disqualified from the program."

He frowns. "What? No. She told me what happened. The proof is in her exemption fees."

"You mean from Katherine Duchanne? The vampire pissed she didn't match with me? Yeah, they sound like honest people. There is no way that their stories are true. Look at me. I'm alive. I'm in good health. I'm well taken care of."

"But what about those who aren't?" he asks.

Brayla automatically comes to my mind. "You can still file claims for them."

He barks a laugh, startling me. "This says we can't. Not without solid proof. They won't investigate or anything now."

I frown. "Huh?"

"You didn't read it?"

Eff me and my inability to pay close attention to contracts. "I read some."

"The new policy says there are now fees and penalties for denied claims."

"Fees?"

He swears, smacking his hand on top of the contract. "Donations. Of-fucking-course. Penalties are worse. Losing benefits. Denying future heirs."

"What?"

"Jewel, Donor Life Corp is guaranteeing you'll have no rights. That you'll have no future. This is about Haven Springs, but look at this. This affects more than the exempt. It affects you."

I plop in the seat next to him and peer over the documents, reading over every terrible point that Donor Life Corp came up with. My stomach twists, anger burning through my core. I can't even believe what I'm reading. Or that I was the one to deliver this sort of message.

"I'll fix this," I whisper, a tear spilling to smear the ink on a page. "I mean, requiring non-immediate heirs to donate? Everyone's supposed to be exempt. Dana and Fallon—"

"They'll be required to donate—but not to the gen. pop. This says to the match's household."

I nearly puke at the thought. Kingston, Diego, and Austin would never agree to drink the blood of my family. That would mean...Mitchell. OhmyeffinG. What's the point of the Blood Match Program? One exclusive donor to one elite vampire in exchange for a family's exemption.

"Shit balls," I say. "I'll never let that happen. My guys

won't agree to such a thing."

"Don't you get it? They're not *your* guys. You are theirs. They knew about this, Jewel. They probably helped write it. You think they love you, but the only thing they care about is your blood and what you can do for them."

"But they want me to accept their Blood Vows," I say it more to myself, trying not to let Hayden get into my head. There's no way that Kingston, Diego, or Austin knew about this. They'd have told me. They'd have fought against it. Right?

He tilts his head back to look at the ceiling. "And that guarantees your family will forever be donating to the Divines. To you."

"I'll fix this," I repeat. "My guys won't let it come to this."

"You're going to put the fate of Haven Springs in the hands of the Divines? Jewel, there's only one way to fix this," he says, swiveling to meet my gaze. He captures me in his stare, worry lining his eyes, a thousand unsaid emotions crossing his face. "You have to tell them that Ramona's petition wasn't unfounded. You have to tell them the truth."

I frown. "I told you the truth." At least, what I want the truth to be.

"I'm not stupid, Jewel. I know more about the world than you think. Haven Springs is my home, but I'm not removed from society. I'm not a happy little compliant heir. I'm like your dad. I'm like you. Like Ramona. We're Blood Rebels. We're the future of humankind."

I blink a few times at his words. "I don't even know what

that is."

"I can explain everything, but you have to do the right thing," he says.

The right thing? The right thing for whom? Obviously not me.

Sighing, I shake my head. "I—I can't. I won't. There is always another way."

He opens his mouth to say something, but the sound of gunshots startles me, and I jump and nearly fall out of the chair. Fear rushes through me, and I scramble toward the door. Hayden calls my name. I don't stop. He doesn't hear what I hear.

Running as fast as I can, I head toward the exit. A scream rips through the air, speeding up my heart, and I realize a little too late that my guards aren't behind me. They weren't even in the hallway.

"Jewel, stay inside," Kingston says, his voice reaching me even from his spot somewhere outside the door. "Everything is going to be fine."

"What's wrong?" I ask.

A strong hand grabs my shoulder, spinning me around. Hayden glowers at me, his wild eyes searching my face. "You knew they were here."

My quivering lip gives me away. "Please, don't hurt them."

"Jewel, we're fine," Diego says.

But Austin yells out.

I swing my arm and clock Hayden in the jaw, getting him to release me. I shove my hands against the double doors, thrusting them open. My heels skid across the steps, and I screech, nearly slipping on the pool of blood seeping down the step. Not just anyone's blood. My human protection detail lies dead on the bottom steps.

I suck in a sharp breath. "Shit."

"Jewel, please step back inside," Hayden says.

"No."

"Jewel."

"I said no!"

Hayden spins me around, stealing a knife right off my side. He shoves me back, aiming it at my chest, his whole face morphing with his anger and disgust. With a bunch of horrifying emotions that steal my breath away.

He doesn't see the blurry figure flying toward us at an inhumanely fast speed.

But I do.

And so does everyone else.

Gunfire rings through the air, piercing my ears. A boom shakes the ground beneath my feet and knocks me back.

The community breaks out in complete chaos as the humans attack. Another boom rocks the world, and Hayden throws himself at me and presses me into the wall, protecting me with his body.

Blood rains from the air, cascading around us to soak my skin in hot, dark liquid.

"Jewel, don't look," Kingston whispers.

But it's too late.

I can't stop myself.

All that remains on the steps is pieces of someone, shredded clothing, and blood. Vampire blood.

I scream.

TRUE MONSTERS

MUSCULAR ARMS ENVELOP ME, RIPPING me away from Hayden. The noise from the humans mutes the sound of my racing heart. Tears burn my eyes, trickling hot streaks down my face. Bright lights flash on, blinding me. I can't see anything but hazy figures. Dozens of them—probably more.

"Hold your fire!" Hayden calls. "These are the Divine heirs!"

I tremble, trying to press myself into Kingston. "What happened?"

"Fuck!" someone says. "Bobby, you killed a Divine. We're screwed!"

"They have no right being here!" another man yells.

Ice travels through my veins, stealing every bit of warmth

from me. "Kingston," I whisper.

"Everyone, calm down. Bobby is right. They're trespassing, but it has come to my attention that Donor Life Corp put our contract up for negotiation. We need the last two alive along with Jewel to settle things. Jewel can't file a contract breach if they're dead. She will still be property of the Divinity Estate. Her promised vow will pass on to their coven leader."

His words spin through my mind. Last two. Last two. Last two. Last *two*! I can't stop thinking the words over and over. Nothing else matters.

"I will never file a breach of contract!" I scream, fury being the only thing that keeps me upright.

"Babe," Kingston whispers into my ear.

I can't stay calm. I push against him until he lets me go. "Austin? Diego?" My voice comes out hoarse. I'm so scared for the response—for the lack of response. This can't be happening. They are the most powerful vampires. Humans shouldn't be able to hurt them. *Kill* them. But the weapons—my ears still ring. The whole ground shook.

"Jewel, stay calm. It's—"

A strangled sob rips from my mouth, agony and relief battling through me at the sound of Austin's voice. But Diego. Oh, God. No. No.

"Jewel," Hayden says, bringing my attention to him. "I know you're upset, but—"

"Don't!" I scream, yanking a knife from a sheath under my jacket. "Don't fucking talk to me. Your guard killed my—"

"Beautiful, it wasn't me. You have to stay calm. Humans have terrible reflexes in tense situations."

Another sob escapes my mouth, my whole body shuddering at the sound of Diego's voice. "Diego," I whisper too quietly for any humans to hear.

"I'm fine. Take a breath. I can hear your heart from here. Stay calm and listen to Kingston and Austin. We're getting you out of here. I got Laurel."

"The blood and...body parts," I whisper, wiping the tears from my eyes again. "Whose blood is all over me?"

"Pedro's," Kingston says.

"It was an accident," Hayden says, raising his hands up, interrupting my whispered conversation.

I realize I'm aiming my knife at him, my hand even and ready to thrust it right through his expanding chest. "It wasn't."

"They broke the rules—"

"I don't care!" My voice rises, my whole body running on fury and adrenaline. Fear. I wasn't close to Pedro, but he was nice enough to me. He didn't deserve this. "I can't believe I felt pity for you. Or that I wanted to try to help you. You think my matches are monsters, but the only monster I see is you."

The crowd mumbles, the low hum of voices growing louder and louder.

"Everyone, stay calm," Hayden says. "She's distressed and not thinking clearly. She thinks she's in love with them."

Dozens of whispered words of disgust trickle through the air—some words of pity, but only for me. I'm the poor girl brainwashed by vampires.

I jerk my head up, swiping my eyes, peering around. Only Kingston and Austin stand with me, and we're surrounded. I was utterly wrong about it being a dozen humans. It's far more. Maybe a hundred. Men, women, even children. They stand ready and armed.

"I don't *think*. I *know*. I accepted their promises of forever, and I intend to follow through. Because look at you. All of you. You stand here ready to attack, shunning me, whispering words about my life like I'm beneath you when it's people like me, people who understand what true sacrifice is, who have made this possible for you. Or did you forget?" I point at Hayden. "Who in your family entered the Blood Match Program?"

He doesn't respond.

"Have you forgotten?" I ask, sneering. "Have all of you forgotten?"

Silence falls around us, a hush stopping the crowd from speaking as they think over my words.

Kingston and Austin step closer to me, surrounding me with their strength. I never in a million years thought it would come down to this, but I realize that I have to make a choice. One that will change my entire existence. One I was on the fence about before coming here.

"That's what I thought," I say, keeping my voice even. "You've forgotten the people who made this possible for you. You turned my own sister against me. You can't expect me to help you, Hayden. You deserve what happens to you. Maybe it's time for a change."

"What is she talking about, Hayden?" a woman asks. I can't tell where her voice comes from, maybe somewhere behind me.

He sighs. "It's nothing to worry about. The renegotiations won't go through. Jewel will come to her senses. She'll file the breach in contract."

"I won't!" I scream.

He narrows his eyes at me. "You will. We're not letting you leave otherwise."

Both Kingston and Austin growl, tensing and preparing to fight even though we're scarily outnumbered. Hayden slowly reaches into his jacket, pulling out a gun. But he doesn't aim it at me. He trains it on Austin. Another guard steps forward and aims hers at Kingston.

"Be smart, Jewel. We've been preparing for this all our lives. If you don't do it, you'll all die here," Hayden says. "And you know what'll happen if you do. Do you want to be responsible for caging all these people? For killing them? Think about Mona. Think about Dana and Fallon. Look around you. Could you live with yourself? You entered the Blood Match Program to see to it that they'd be exempt from donations, and Donor Life Corp wants to take it away."

I blink hot tears from my eyes. "Just let us leave. I told you I'd figure out another way."

"You know there is only one way. You sacrificed your freedom once before. This is your chance to take it back. Because even if you think you love these monsters, you need to see that they don't love you. They're using you. You're their opportunity to change the foundation of our community. Think about what this means for your cousins."

"Babe," Kingston whispers. "Don't let him get into your head. We love you."

"I just want to leave," I plead. "Please."

"Jewel," a soft voice says from behind me. "You're leaving? Ramona just told us you were going to stay."

I slowly swivel to face the crowd behind me, catching sight of Fallon and Dana standing amid the crowd with Ramona holding onto each of their shoulders. Next to them, I spot Mrs. Diggs, Brayla's mom, hugging onto Dougie. She frowns at me, a dozen unsaid words bouncing between us.

"I—" I snap my mouth closed, my legs moving before I have time to process. I run to my cousins, wrapping my arms around each of them. Ramona steps back out of the way like being within a foot of me disgusts her.

Dana bawls her eyes out, squeezing me so tightly that I can barely breathe. "We've missed you so much. Ramona said the Divines weren't going to let you see us, but then we saw the request and—"

"She's not here because she misses you," Ramona snaps.

Fallon gapes at her and then turns her eyes to me. "What?"

I stand in shock. "Of course I missed you. I think about you every day. Whatever Ramona has been telling you has been a lie. She doesn't want you to see me."

"Ramona? Is that true?" Mrs. Diggs says, surprising me.

My sister sneers at Brayla's mom. "It's none of your business. Stay out of Jordan matters."

"Does that mean you haven't been passing on Brayla's letters to Jewel?" she asks, ignoring my sister's comment.

"What?" I ask.

"Enough!" Hayden yells. "This is your last chance, Jewel. If you want to leave with these monsters, you have to file the breach in contract."

"Jewel," Dana says. "They breached your contract?"

I don't answer her. Instead, I shake my head. "Let us go. I know you don't want to see your community perish. If you loved my sister, you wouldn't do this."

Hayden scowls, and I know I'm right about him. He's bluffing. He's trying to scare me into complying, but I've faced worse. He won't do anything to jeopardize the community. When it comes down to it, he's the one who's scared. If he wasn't, he wouldn't threaten me. "If you loved your family, you'd do as I ask. Can you look your cousins in the eyes and tell them that you've decided to put vampires before them? That you're willing to seal their fate under a vampire's fangs?"

"What?" Dana and Fallon ask.

"Shut up," I warn.

"No, they need to know. The community needs to know what kind of person you are." He straightens his shoulders and looks over the crowd. "If Jewel leaves here tonight without submitting a personal breach of contract, we lose everything that our heirs sacrificed their freedoms and lives for. New restrictions will come into place. People will be excluded from exemption."

I swallow, sweat beading on my forehead.

"Jewel, please come back here," Austin whispers to me.

"I don't trust them," Kingston adds. "I can't promise I won't fight for you if they try anything."

"I don't understand," Fallon says.

"Explain what you're talking about, Hayden," another man says.

"Fallon, Dana," Hayden says, turning to my cousins. "Jewel doesn't care about humanity like we do. If she leaves here tonight without doing what I'm begging her to do, you'll be allowed to stay here, but at a cost. You'll be required to donate. Only immediate heirs will receive benefits."

Commotion breaks out, people yelling, some shoving each other to get closer to me. I stumble away, turning my gaze from my family the second I see Hayden's words sink in. There's nothing I can say to take back his words. The unrest of the community makes it hard even to hear myself think. No one will let me explain. I'm nearly certain no one will let me leave.

Strong hands grip my waist. Kingston risks the yelling crowd to drag me from my family and into the spot between him and Austin. I turn to look at him. His dark eyebrows furrow over his midnight eyes, and he searches my face for a moment. Austin takes my hand, squeezing it in his, ready to yank me with him if he needs to.

"Do you see now? Look how she looks at them," Hayden says. "She doesn't care about you girls. Not like me and Mona. But don't worry. We won't let it happen."

The crowd inches closer, coming together to make it impossible to leave without having to fight. And I don't doubt people would get hurt if we tried. A man reaches for me, and I scream out and smack him away, stopping my guys from moving.

"Stay back! I need a moment to think," I say. "Please. Just give me a moment."

Hayden fires a gun into the air, stopping the crowd. "Decide now."

"Babe, get ready," Kingston says.

But I don't get the chance. Someone fires their weapon from behind. Kingston spins me out of the way, grabbing onto the closest guy to shield us. People scream, more shots ring through the air. Austin grunts next to me, and I gasp at the sight of blood seeping into the front of his white dress shirt. Kingston jerks in front of me next.

"Get ready, Diego," Kingston says.

"Ready. Throw her now."

I don't have a chance to process what's happening when Kingston hooks his arms around my waist, spinning me so fast that I can no longer see the world. My body twists, my heart colliding into my stomach. More weapons fire. People scream.

I fly helplessly through the air, wind whipping through my hair, the motion stealing my breath, stopping me from making a sound. I land with an oomph, gasping in Diego's arms. He hugs me for a moment and sets me on my feet. I startle at the sight of Laurel just standing with her eyes closed beside me.

"Protect Jewel with your life," Diego says to Laurel.

She snaps her eyes open to look at me.

I reach out and grab Diego. "Don't leave me with her."

"I'll be back. I promise."

"Diego."

He turns to me and brings his lips to mine. "Please, stay here."

Diego disappears, leaving me alone with Laurel, who quietly stands next to me. I can't summon the nerve to look at the one responsible for starting this mess. Instead, I shuffle away from her to get a better view of the angry crowd. Laurel creeps behind me, following my every move. I slowly make my way closer, ignoring Diego's instructions.

Voices cut through the air, and I freeze, realizing that the crowd isn't going after Kingston and Austin. They're turning on each other. My guys had mentioned that there were allies within Haven Springs. They said there were people who wouldn't want their comfortable living messed with. And they're speaking out now.

I spot Diego on the outskirts of the crowd, quickly locking humans in his gaze. They stop fighting and walk away from the chaos in an eerie, trance-like state, sending goosebumps over my skin.

My gaze travels over the crowd, fear tightening my muscles.

I spot Dana and Fallon leaving with Mrs. Diggs, surrounding her to protect Dougie. Kingston and Austin shove people away, disarming them in the process. They do the same as Diego, manipulating the minds of those they can as they break through the crowd. My knees tremble, and I clutch onto the nearest tree trunk. Blood coats both their clothes, but they manage to withstand every weapon the humans attempt to harm them with.

My heart hammers in my chest, threatening to crash through my ribcage. It takes everything in me to remain in my spot. All I want to do is run back to the crowd. I just want everyone to stop fighting.

A flash of light draws my attention to the double doors of City Hall, and I frown as a man stumbles his way out of the building. I can't stop my feet from moving, and I continue to head down the hillside. Laurel remains close enough that she'll ram into me if I stop too quickly.

"Beautiful, stop. We're almost done. Don't come any closer. It's dangerous," Diego says, catching sight of me.

I take another step forward, and he breaks away, rushing toward me. My lip trembles at the sight of his tattered shirt, torn and bleeding in what I realize is a mixture of human blood and his own. He frowns as he looks me over, worry stealing away the softness he normally carries for me in his eyes.

He touches my cheek. "You guys got it?" he asks, talking to Kingston and Austin without turning his gaze from me.

"Just get her out of here. We'll meet you at the ca—"

A holler rips through the air, cutting off Kingston's words.

Diego attempts to block my view with his sheer size, but I peek around him as the stumbling man rushes toward Hayden still holding his ground.

"That's Niall," Diego says to me.

"Hayden said that they removed him from the council hours ago," I murmur.

He reaches for my hand. "Only Donor Life Corp can do that."

"But he—holy shit balls!" I scream, my eyes widening.

Hayden turns his weapon on the man and pulls the trigger, sending him sprawling to the ground. The man squirms in his own blood, opening and closing his mouth. I take an automatic few steps forward. Diego stays by my side letting me instead of getting me away like Kingston asked.

Another gunshot rings through the air, piercing my ears.

"Fuck!" Kingston yells. "Blood Rebels. Austin, watch out!"

I jerk my gaze from the old council head on the step to Austin, clutching his stomach. A man stands in front of him and pulls the trigger again. Kingston stumbles toward his brother, his unsteady movements freaking me the hell out. The last time I saw him move like that was with Mitchell.

"Five of them," Austin says. "All unbreakable."

"I'm coming," Diego says. "Don't let them corner you."

Diego abandons my side to meet his brothers. The remaining people continue to fight, not giving my guys a chance to get close. They're firing too much to let them get far either. Fury jumps me into action, and I rush forward. I know my guys are strong, and I know they regenerate quickly, but they're not in-vincible. No vampire is. I've seen it. I've helped kill one myself.

Austin roars, his voice cutting through the air. He flashes his fangs, biting the throat of the closest man. Kingston lifts another off his feet and tosses him into the building. Diego knocks the remaining two off their feet, and I close my eyes, unable to watch what happens next.

A high-pitched scream sounds through the air, stealing my breath away. I snap my eyes open and find Ramona jerking the aim of a gun between all three of my guys. They stand utterly still, watching her lose her shit as her fury consumes her.

"Put the gun down, Ramona," Austin says calmly.

She pulls the trigger, sending him sprawling back to the concrete.

"No!" I scream, racing forward.

Kingston and Diego rush my sister. Kingston disarms her while Diego lifts her off her feet. Hayden steps closer, aiming his weapon at Kingston. Austin struggles to get to his feet, slip-ping on his own blood. The fact that he falls scares the shit out of me. My guys swore that human weapons hurt like hell if they're used but they wouldn't kill them, but then I remember Pedro.

"Everyone stop! I can't take this!" I yell. "Put Ramona down. Don't shoot anymore, Hayden."

Diego sets my sister on her feet, and she yells again, turning her wild eyes in my direction. She charges toward me, baring her teeth, clenching her fists. I've never in my life seen her look like this, and it freaks me the eff out. Ramona was worried my guys would change me, but it's she who has changed.

"I'm going to kill you!" she screams.

I hold my hands up, bracing myself. "Kill me? What the actual fuck is wrong with you? I'd do anything for you."

"Liar. If that were true, you'd have filed the breach in contract yourself already. So, it's not me or what's wrong with me. You are what's wrong. You and your gross infatuation with vampires. Your desire to care for them."

"Shut up!" I yell.

"You disgust me, Jewel. Your masters are the ones responsible for turning people into nothing more than a food supply—and it's even worse for you. You're better off dead."

Austin growls, and all weapons turn on him. My whole body tenses.

"Ramona, make them stop," I plead. "I'll sign the damn petition if you just stop. I don't know what you expect out of all this. You should know and trust that I love you. All I ever wanted was to protect you. It's why I entered the program."

She doesn't stop. "Liar! You did it to try to save yourself from the blood debt!" Reaching under her jacket, she yanks free a strange weapon I've never seen before—like a...shit balls. A stake. A sharp as all get out silver stake. I scramble back, attempting to run. Because I'm not going to fight her, and I'm damn well not going to let her try to stake me.

"Jewel!" Kingston yells. "Duck."

I drop to the ground on his command, covering my head

with my hands. Something—no someone—flies over me, crashing into Ramona, knocking her to the ground. I push up on my hands, my eyes wide. Laurel straddles my sister, wrapping her fingers around her neck.

Diego's command spins through my mind. He manipulated Laurel to protect me with her life. But now she's doing so against my sister.

"Laurel, stop!" I yell.

But she doesn't. I can't command her.

"Laurel, stop!" Diego shouts, flying toward us.

Laurel freezes.

Ramona doesn't.

I watch in horror as my sister rams a stake through Laurel's chest, sending her sprawling back into the dirt.

Laurel gasps, blinking her eyes. There's nothing I can do, because Ramona turns on me next.

All I can do now is scream.

RUINED BY LOVE

"MONA, NO!" HAYDEN YELLS. "STOP! She said she'll sign the petition. Don't hurt her. We need her alive."

Ramona jabs the stake into the ground, piercing it through strands of my hair. I shake under my sister, my whole body trembling so hard that my teeth chatter. Tears leak from my eyes, dripping down my temples. I'm afraid to move or speak or even breathe.

Hayden scoops my sister off me, pulling her back. Silence falls around us apart from the collection of heartbeats and breaths of a dozen men and women who close in on us again. It's like every time someone leaves, more people come. Diego kneels at my side, studying my face, touching my wet cheeks with his fingers, slowly looking over me for signs of injuries.

"You okay, beautiful?" he asks, yanking the silver stake from my hair. Strands fall to the ground, a small section of my hair cut off from the sharpness of the strange weapon.

I lick my lips, swallowing the burning in my throat. "Y-yeah. A-Austin? King-Kingston?"

"We're here, Jewel," Austin says, slumping beside me. "We're okay."

I turn on my side, facing Austin. His skin loses more color by the second, and his fangs peek out from under his lips. I'm not so sure he could retract them if he wanted to. He looks the worst out of my guys with his white shirt now blood-stained and torn. I shift closer, snuggling into his side for a moment before Kingston helps him to his feet while Diego helps me to mine.

"Jewel, they have to leave right now," Hayden says. "I will assist you with the petition. You're welcome to stay or leave after. I don't give a shit as long as you sign."

I sneer at him. "They're not leaving me."

"And you're delusional if you think she's signing anything," Kingston says.

I hold out my hand to him. "Kingston, I'm sorry. I have to do this. I have to. The changes with..." I let my words trail off at the look of pure sorrow crossing his face. I'm too scared to even look at Diego and Austin. "I have to do this. For Ramona."

Kingston pouts at me. "She doesn't deserve you, babe. I know all you've wanted is to protect her, but you're the one who needs the protection. *From* her."

"I agree with Kingston. You don't have to do this. You shouldn't do this," Diego says. "We can leave."

"You're not going anywhere until she signs," Hayden says. "If she doesn't, this place is over, so might as well take care o—"

"Shut up!" I yell. "I said I'd sign the petition. But they aren't leaving. Now get your people to back the eff off."

Hayden motions them back. "Fine, but if they try—"

"They won't," I snap, scowling at him. "You pushed them into this. None of this would have happened if you'd have just let us leave."

He doesn't respond. No one does. All he does is motion for Ramona to go to his side. He wraps his arm around her waist and tugs her along with him up the steps of City Hall. Hayden might seem older with how hard his eyes are toward me, but he looks young when he gazes at my sister. There's no denying he cares, but his love ruined her. It ruined everything.

An armed guard motions for us to follow him, pushing me to stop thinking of what life was supposed to be like and to deal with what it actually is like. As much as I can see it killing my guys to follow the orders of a human, they do it anyway. They're only doing it for me, though.

"We'll just give them what they want and get out of here," I whisper. "I don't want there to be any more fighting. You guys look terrible. How are you even still moving?"

"A couple bullets and stab wounds are merely uncomfortable annoyances. We're tough, beautiful," Diego says. "Nothing would have touched me if I wasn't manipulating those riled up by the Blood Rebels to back off. The whole place is lucky we were respecting your desire not to kill them all."

I pout. "I'm sorry. You're so much better than all of them, and thank you for that. I'm afraid they'll push you into it if I don't do this. But it's going to be okay...I hope."

"I hate to say this, babe, but it might not be. What you agreed to do is some serious shit," Kingston says. "It's not so easy to cancel or have the board reject such an allegation coming personally from you. It's easy to deny heirs, but if you do this, they might investigate and figure out how to place blame on two of us. It would be convenient for them to get you to make your final decision, especially if these Blood Rebels start spreading the word about the flaw in the Blood Match Program."

I think about his words for a moment. "Even so, we know the truth. We can figure it out. I just—my priority is to get you guys out of here alive and safe."

Kingston pulls me closer to him, hugging me. "I fucking love you, but worry less about us and more about you and what this could mean for this community as well. This is an act against us. Against Donor Life Corp. Not only might it mess shit up for us, but it will have the opposite effect of what they're attempting to do. They killed the head of our security. They killed the head councilman, basically overthrowing the government we put in place for a reason."

I frown. "Then we tell Hayden what could happen if he

makes me."

Austin hobbles on my other side. "No, it's not safe. I'm not in the best fighting condition, Jewel. I'm afraid if you scare them, they'll react by trying to kill us all, and then we won't have a choice but to eliminate those uprising, including Ramona. And no matter how strong and capable you are, you have limits. I'm not putting you in danger."

"He's right. They're not your normal Haven Springs residents, beautiful," Diego whispers into my hair. "They're Blood Rebels. I couldn't manipulate their minds. They've been consuming vampire blood."

I suck in a deep breath. "You think Ramona too?"

He hugs me from behind, walking with me. "Yeah, but I don't think she realizes it."

The strange moan I heard earlier trickles in from a closed door. Kingston, Diego, and Austin glance at each other, and I know they heard it too.

"Speaking of vampire blood," Kingston whispers. "I hear their source."

Goosebumps prickle over my skin, and I look at each of them. They keep their expressions serious, not giving anything away, but I can't stop the grimace crossing my face. This friggin' night sucks on every level I don't enjoy, and I want so badly to speak up, to sucker punch Hayden again, to scream at Ramona, but I don't get the chance. Hayden opens a door on the left and motions us to go inside.

"We're not all going in there," Diego says to Hayden.

He straightens his shoulders. "If you even try—"

I jerk my arm and backhand him across the shoulder. "Shut. The. Hell. Up." I enunciate each word, glaring death daggers at him, wishing my eyes could wipe the smirk off his jerk face.

Ramona hisses at me, sounding like a few annoying vampires I've encountered. I nearly tell her so.

"I'll go in with her," Austin says, offering his hand out to me. "We'll be fast."

Hayden looks at his guards. "Keep an eye on them. They move, you shoot. I'll be back. Jewel, take a seat. I have to grab a camera and com."

"A camera?"

"This time, I'm getting everything right."

I pace around the room without sitting in the chair, the events of tonight replaying over and over in my mind. Thirty minutes have passed, and Hayden and my sister still haven't returned. If I couldn't hear Diego and Kingston whispering on the other side of the door, I'd start freaking the hell out more so than I already am. Kingston's words dig into my mind about what can happen to Haven Springs and our Blood Match if I go through with this, but I can't see a way out of it. I don't want anything to happen to Ramona or to have my guys resort to killing people. I know they're capable of it. I've seen them kill vampires. But there is something about knowing all these people could die because of me that haunts me even to think of the possibility.

Doing this buys time. The outcome could be devastating but not going through with it guarantees it.

Hayden won't let us go without a fight. He's far beyond reason and caring. He's most dangerous because he feels he has nothing to lose. He thinks we've taken everything already. It doesn't help that if I don't do this, my legacy might forever be the girl responsible for destroying the one safe place for humanity.

I didn't mean to let Hayden's words from earlier about me being a traitor to humankind get to me, but they do. He managed to get into my head without being here, but it's because he's right about one thing. I don't know how I'll live with myself if something happens to Haven Springs and the people here despite how they made me feel or what they've done. People do what they have to do to survive. It's obviously true with me or I wouldn't be sitting in this room.

"Babe, you're driving me crazy. What's going through your head? I can practically hear your thoughts racing through the door," Kingston says, keeping his voice at a pitch only me and my guys can hear.

"Everything. The petition. The contract...Donor Life Corp making policy changes on exemptions. Why didn't you tell me about any of this before we got here?" I whisper, thinking about the stupid threat from Donor Life Corp that put us all in this position.

"Because it was only a threat. Something to get the council worked up enough to give us time to find Laurel, but we did not expect Hayden to have overthrown the community's infra-structure."

"It didn't look like only a threat."

He sighs softly. "Even so, it would've been temporary. Your family doesn't meet the donation requirements yet. They'd have been okay."

My chest heaves, and it takes everything in me not to start crying. "Kingston, it's more than about my family."

Austin hangs his head, staring at the table. "Jewel, we're going to work this all out. I know Kingston is worried about our Blood Matches and the board taking advantage of the situation, but I don't think they will. Things will go back to normal."

"Can you promise me that?" I ask.

"We'll do the best we can. We won't let you down," Diego whispers, answering for Austin. "We promised you forever, remember? Pretty sure that means making it a good one."

"Forever," I whisper. "Together forever. No matter what."

"I mean, if it's what you want, babe," Kingston says.

Austin shifts in the chair, propping his head on his hands, but he keeps his eyes trained on mine. I wish I could see Kingston and Diego, too. I inch closer to Austin and touch my hand to his shoulder blades, and he slumps even more. "We know you have your doubts—"

I shake my head at Austin, rubbing my hands over his shoulders, trying to get him to sit up. "I don't. Not anymore." Because thinking something happened to my guys brought me unbearable pain. It makes me realize I can't live without them.

Ever. "This place—it's made me realize a few things. I can't stand the thought of not having you. You guys are mine and I'm yours, and I won't let anyone ruin that for us. I accept your Blood Vows no matter what. I want eternity with you."

Austin straightens his back and perks up, a smile crossing his glum face. "You do?"

"You sure, babe? Ramona—"

I nod even though he can't see me. "I know you'll take care of the blood debt, and it won't come down to it. I trust you."

"Damn it, why didn't I volunteer to go inside with you?" Kingston complains.

"Because Austin needs to—shit. Austin, you okay?" Diego asks.

Austin wobbles and falls onto the table, smacking his cheek to the smooth surface. Fear clenches my chest, sending my heart racing. I bend down and touch his cheek, getting him to lean back up again.

I brush his sweaty hair from his forehead. "He doesn't look good."

Austin bobs his head. "I'll be fine. I'm fine."

Both Kingston and Diego groan softly outside the door but neither attempts to come in.

Touching Austin's cheek, I get him to look at me. He offers me a small smile, showing off his fangs. His pale complexion worries me as much as the constant silver flashing in his eyes. His hands tremble on the table, and it takes me clutching them to get them to stop rattling against the wood.

"You're lying," I whisper.

He frowns. "Jewel, I..."

He doesn't even have to finish his words for me to know what's wrong and what he needs. The fighting took a huge toll on him. Everything has been so scary and confusing that I nearly forgot the one thing that'll help Austin feel better.

Sucking in a small breath, I raise my arm up to his face. He startles, his nostrils flaring and his wide eyes meeting mine, dark hunger igniting his expression. "You need blood," I whisper.

His jaw tightens, and he shakes his head. "I can't, Jewel. Not like this. I might—"

"I'll be fine," I whisper. "I trust you."

"I don't trust me."

I bring my arm back up again. "Please, Austin. If something happens to you, I—I can't deal with that. You look like you're about to pass out. I'm tough, remember? I can handle it."

"Listen to her, bro," Kingston says. "But don't enjoy it too much."

I fake glare at the door. "Come on. Drink."

Closing his eyes, Austin laces his fingers around my arm and holds it an inch from his lips. His eyes meet mine again, and I nod, pressing my arm to his mouth for him. I remain utterly still as his fangs pierce my skin, the small pinch only hurting for a second. Unlike with Kingston, my arm doesn't burn or anything. It actually makes me squirm a little, wishing we were somewhere else as desire sneaks up on me in the worst possible moment.

Austin's tongue glides over my pooling blood, sending tingles down to my wrist and into my fingers. He drinks slowly at first, lapping my blood with his tongue, and then he starts sucking, sending my heart racing but not in a bad way.

Austin straightens upright as color returns to his face. He draws me closer to him, pulling me to sit on his lap. I press my lips together, stopping myself from moaning, and hug my free arm around his shoulders to dig my fingers into his arm. He releases a soft hum under his breath, sliding his arm around my waist to hold me even closer. Bowing my head, I rest it on his shoulder, feeling his teeth graze my skin. I brace myself for him to bite me again. I'd be okay with it if he wanted to. But his sucking turns into feather light kisses that make me shudder a breath before he puts pressure on the wounds still dripping blood.

"Was that okay?" he whispers, holding my gaze.

"Wish we weren't here," I murmur, leaning in for a kiss.

"Everyone agrees with that, babe," Kingston says, stopping me from saying more. "But now's not the time to make me jealous."

"They're coming," Diego adds through the door.

Austin tenses, and I rush to pull down the sleeve of my jacket. Muffled voices murmur through the door, and I expect Austin to plop me back on my feet, but he holds me tighter, hugging me against him. And I let him. I don't want to be anywhere else but in the safety of his arms where I know he'll protect me.

I slide my fingers through his and straighten my back at the sound of the doorknob twisting open. Hayden and Ramona stand in the doorway, their expressions turning from serious to outright disgust as their gazes lock onto me sitting on Austin's lap, our hands together, his chin on my shoulder with no space between us.

"Get off of him, Jewel," Ramona says, baring her teeth at me. "That's disgusting."

"Like she never plays lapsies with that fucker," Kingston mutters under his breath.

I grimace at him, most definitely not needing the reminder that my little sister has been obviously exploring her own desire with an asshole who brainwashed her into a loose cannon. Anything will set her off, and she'll attack without warning. She killed someone without a thought. It's the first time I've thought about it, and it terrifies me. Ramona used not to even kill the bugs that snuck into our apartment in The Boxes. She doesn't even show remorse. Her face is far less expressive than the asshole responsible for changing her, who keeps looking at me with weird expressions as he tries to figure me out.

"Whatever, Ramona," I say, commenting a little too late.

Austin doesn't give me the chance to get into it with my sister and stands us both up, but he doesn't let go of my hand, squeezing it tight enough that I have to wiggle my fingers before I lose the feeling in them.

I regret the action immediately.

Warmth blossoms over our fingers, and I tense as a few blood drops seep from the wounds on my arm to splash onto the white tiled floor. Both Kingston and Diego take an audible breath, drawing Hayden and Ramona's attention in their direction. I quickly step on the blood to hide it.

"What the hell?" Ramona asks. "Are you bleeding, Jewel?"

Holy effing shit balls. Glancing down, I stare at the stray ribbon of blood rolling down the side of my leg. I shift on my feet, smearing the blood I stepped on around. Austin lets go of me, and I curl my hand around my sleeve to hide my now bloody fingers. Austin does the same by shoving his hands in his pockets, but he doesn't step back. I doubt they'd realize the blood on him is mine considering how much of his own stains his clothes.

Ramona and Hayden look from him to me and back to him like he's going to suddenly fly at me and bite my head off.

"Ah, babe. Your shitty day got shittier. I think you started menstruating," Kingston says from the door. "That sucks. I can grab you something to clean it up."

OhmyeffinG. Craning my neck, I burn him a look, flaring my nostrils and all. If I had something to throw, I'd chuck it at him. All he does is press his mouth into a thin line, suppressing what I know would be the biggest teasing smile.

"Ugh, ew," Ramona says. "Fucking nasty vampires. Of course he wants to clean it up."

Swallowing my embarrassment, I say, "I guess my stomach ache wasn't because everyone was trying to murder us."

All three of my guys laugh, taking great amusement in Kingston's mortifying fake explanation as to why I'm standing in blood to hide the fact that we all know I let Austin drink from me. But I'm sure that revelation would be much, much worse in my sister's eyes. Ramona pushes past me to exit the room, and Hayden continues to stare at the blood with fascination, making my stomach churn. Even my guys don't give it such an intense look.

"Can we proceed with the petition or will you spend the rest of the night trying to wrap your head around the magnificence of a human female body?" Kingston asks. "Some of us don't have all night, and you're creeping Jewel out with your weirdness toward something so natural."

Hayden scowls and takes a few steps in Kingston's direction before stopping short. Swiveling on his feet, he turns back to the table and the stack of documents he piled up. On the top is a handwritten letter in Ramona's sloppy scrawl. I blink a few times, staring at the words she wants to put in my mouth.

I jerk my head up to look at Hayden. "Are you kidding me? No one will—" I snap my mouth shut. "This is ridiculous."

"You have five minutes to rehearse, and you better make it believable, Jewel." He turns to Austin. "I considered recording it to send, but I think I want you to connect me to the head of Donor Life Corp personally."

I can't stop the groan from escaping my mouth. It's going to go from bad to effin' awful. The last person I want to contact is Mitchell. What if he sends people here immediately? My guys said that this was just going to make things worse for Haven Springs, and it's the last thing I want despite every horrifying thing that has happened tonight. My family's here. So is Brayla's. There are more allies and heirs who want nothing but to be left alone. Innocent people will get caught up in this battle brought on by these Blood Rebels.

"That's a mistake," I murmur. "Please, just let me fill out the paperwork."

"You think he'll retaliate?" Hayden asks. "Because I'm not stupid. I know exactly who and what I'm dealing with, Jewel. Haven Springs is ready for all threats that head our way."

I cross my arms over my chest. "And what about the innocent people who don't want to get involved?"

"Maybe it's time to make them."

I open my mouth to argue, but Ramona enters the room and shoves a towel at me. I drop it to the floor without doing anything with it and meet her gaze. "Ramona, please reconsider this. It can't end well."

"Give me your necklace," she says, holding out her hand without responding to my plea.

All three of my guys growl, making me tense. Hayden reaches for his weapon, but he doesn't do anything except hover his hand near it. It helps that no one moves.

"Why?" I ask, touching the teardrop with all three of my guys' blood in it with my fingers.

She furrows her brows with annoyance. "I know what it means, and since you're filing a petition to cancel your Blood

Match, the vow must be withdrawn too. I want it off your neck. Just the sight of it makes me what to puke."

I don't attempt to unfasten it. If she wants it off my neck, she'll have to remove it herself, and I'm pretty damn certain my guys won't let her even try, especially now after I've officially accepted their vow despite what it means to Ramona.

Tears burn my eyes. "No, I'm not taking it off."

"Jewel," she snaps. "Just do it. Don't make this any harder."

"I accepted a promise. I made my own vow," I say. *My own vow.*

I suck in a breath at my words, realizing exactly how I'm going to get us out of this situation, but I need to buy a minute to prepare my guys. Because once I follow through with my sudden idea, I need them ready. All it'll take is a moment of surprise. Hayden and his guards might have a bunch of weapons, but they don't have the amazing reflexes of my guys.

"Jewel." Ramona repeats my name like I'll suddenly start listening to her. She should know better than that. I was always the one put in charge when Dad was gone. I was in charge after he went missing. She's my little sister. I still won't let her be in charge of me now.

"Just give me a damn minute," I snap, leaning over the stack of papers. "I'm reading and signing these first. Where's my pen?"

Hayden smirks at Ramona and tosses me a pen he pulls from his pocket. "You're doing the right thing, Jewel."

I roll my eyes. "You don't even know what that is."

Taking the pen, I scribble across the paper Ramona had handwritten about farcical events from what she imagined my life on the Divinity Estate to be like, which includes details that feel like an eerie remake of what used to be a frequent nightmare of me on a table for a room of vampires. The imagery she creates makes me gape and grimace, pushing me to the verge of uncontrollable laughter because it's absurd, but I push past it. My guys would never fantasize about doing the appalling things she thinks they'd enjoy to put me through.

Austin points out a few things. "Cross all those out."

"She signs it as is," Hayden says.

I shake my head. "No. You're stupidly excessive in trying to incriminate my guys."

Ramona groans at the term.

"Mark this out too," Austin says. "It's beyond disgusting."

I'm pretty glad Austin's reading the contract for me because my eyes want me to gouge them out if I consider even attempting to go on. This was definitely not Ramona's imagination. We grew up the same, and were taught the same things from the same people.

"That bad, Austin?" Kingston whispers.

"Be glad it's not you reading it. This is sick," Austin murmurs back too quietly for Ramona and Hayden to hear.

"Please stop reading, beautiful," Diego says. "It might trigger your nightmares."

I draw a line across another paragraph. "I stopped after...ugh I can't even repeat it."

Austin continues to point out things, and I blindly follow his finger, doing as he says. Hayden and Ramona grow more agitated by our edits that Hayden attempts to snatch the pen from my hand. If Ramona didn't yank him back, I'm sure Austin would have ripped off his arm. It's when I get to the last page that I slow down to pretend to read the fine print.

"Do you guys trust me?" I whisper, drawing my finger across the paper like I'm using it to help me read.

"Yeah, what's up, beautiful?" Diego asks lowly enough that no one hears him.

"I have an idea to get us out of here without going through with all this," I say. "At least I hope."

"What is it?" Austin asks from beside me.

"The Blood Vow," I say. "They won't know any better."

Kingston releases a small chuckle under his breath. "Fuck, babe. You're going to give your sister a coronary."

"You okay to fight if you have to, Austin?" Diego asks.

"I'll take Jewel," he says, hooking his arm around my waist.

"Ready when you are, babe," Kingston says.

Releasing my sleeve from my fingers, I slide my hand out of my jacket and press my palm flat on the paper. It sticks to my hand, and I shake it off, letting it fly to the floor. Ramona gasps at the sight of the bloody handprint on the paper.

Hayden swears. "What the hell?"

I tighten my jaw. "I told you I made a vow. Thanks for leaving us alone long enough by the way. It was quite helpful."

Ramona brings her hand to her chest. "Oh, God. Jewel, no. You didn't. You didn't do this to me. You're my sister."

I shake my head. "You told me otherwise. And yes, I did this. I'm not signing your petition. There's no point now." Shrugging out of the jacket, I let it fall to my feet. "All it takes is one bite. And a Blood Vow."

Ramona screams. "How could you!"

I hook my arms around Austin. Commotion breaks out in the hallway, but no weapons get fired. Even the guards are in shock.

Taking a deep breath, I look at my sister one last time. "How could I not?"

CONSEQUENCES

HAYDEN AIMS, FIRING HIS WEAPON. He misses us by a foot. Austin spins me in his arms so fast that my legs fly out, and I knock both Ramona and Hayden off their feet and into the wall. Ramona cries out before screaming. And she keeps wailing. I nearly beg Austin to stop so I can check on her, but he's quick to carry me into the hallway.

Kingston and Diego pile up the bodies of the guards that were supposedly keeping us in control, and Austin whispers that they've only been knocked out before I can panic. Diego takes a moment to dismantle all long-distance range weapons while Kingston shoves all the blades into the wall too deeply to easily be yanked out.

"Ready?" Austin asks them, adjusting me onto his back.

"Hold on tight, Jewel. I need my arms free in case."

I do as he says and wrap my legs around his waist with my arms locked across his chest. I rest my chin on the crook of his shoulder, brushing my lips across his skin, getting him to relax just a bit so I don't feel like I'm holding onto a concrete statue.

"Diego, lead. I'll watch Austin's back," Kingston says.

The hum of voices sounds from down the hall. I spot a security camera blinking in the corner and motion to it. "Hurry."

The world blurs around me for a second, but Austin stops in his tracks behind Diego. A few guards stand ready to fire outside the glass double doors. They've probably been waiting the whole time and whoever monitors security alerted them.

"Let's find another way out," Diego says. "It's too dangerous for Jewel."

Soft footsteps sound from behind us. Austin spins at the same time Kingston muffles someone's scream. My mouth drops open in surprise at the sight of Mrs. Diggs standing with Kingston behind her, covering her mouth.

"Let her go," I say, wiggling to jump from Austin's back, but he doesn't let me.

Kingston hesitates only long enough for me to glare at him and drops his hand. "If you're here to hurt Jewel—"

"No, I've been waiting for her," Mrs. Diggs says. "Come on. I know another way out of here."

"If this is a trick—"

"Kingston, this is Brayla's mom," I say, cutting him off.

"She could be—"

Mrs. Diggs whacks Kingston in the arm with the back of her hand, surprising him. "I love Jewel like my own daughter. I've been trying to reach her for weeks. I had no idea Ramona had gotten herself involved with vigilantes. I'd have talked some sense into her had I known. But she's never home."

"What?" I ask.

She shakes her head. "No time. Come on. Follow me."

More voices sound from the hallway we came from, and I listen to Hayden call out a command for the guards to storm the building and kill on sight. Diego growls from his place near the door and breaks off the handle and shoves it into the bottom of the door to act as a stopper.

"Go on," he motions to us. "I'll catch up."

I grimace. "Stay with us."

"I promise I'll be back, beautiful. I just—I need to take care of something."

Mrs. Diggs breaks out into a sprint, not giving us a choice to wait for Diego. A few gunshots ring out, sending my heart sliding to my stomach. Austin brings his hand up to hold my arms around his chest, softly stroking my skin in an attempt to keep me calm.

"This way," Mrs. Diggs says, pushing open a door.

Behind it, soft light illuminates a concrete stairwell that forks in two different directions, one going up and the other going down. I expect her to rush down, but instead, she heads up the flight of stairs.

"There is only one security guard on the roof," she says,

keeping a brisk pace. She's no stranger to stairs since The Boxes never had elevators. She's incredibly agile for her age compared to some of the older ladies I grew up around.

"I'll handle him," Kingston says.

Mrs. Diggs smacks his arm again. "The only one handling my life partner is me."

Kingston rubs his arm, giving me a face that clearly shows how impressed he is with Brayla's mom's fearlessness toward him. No one usually dares touch a vampire, but Mrs. Diggs has always been tough. She taught Brayla the trick to surviving the shadows by carrying blood, and she hasn't survived all this time because she's defenseless.

More gunfire sounds out from the main level, drifting up the stairwell as someone opens the door below. Austin twists to look down the stairs, and I startle when Diego materializes in front of me, leaning close enough to block my view of the world.

He kisses me from over Austin's shoulder. All boundaries blur tonight under these terrifying conditions. "Told you I'd be back," he says, straightening himself up.

"All good?" Kingston asks.

He nods. "No one will follow us."

I frown. "What did you do?"

He tightens his jaw. "I'm sorry, beautiful. I had to."

"Huh?"

Kingston sighs. "Diego released the vampire the rebels were using as their blood source. They now have a bigger problem on their hands."

I inhale a deep breath. "You're putting everyone in danger."

"We couldn't leave him. It was too risky," Diego says. "But he was in bad shape. They'll have no choice but to end him."

Mrs. Diggs pushes open the door at the top of the stairs, drawing my attention away from my thoughts. Kingston secures it to make sure no one, including the angry loose vampire, follows. I suppress my worry for Ramona and hide my face in the crook of Austin's neck to catch my breath and calm my racing heart. I understand why Diego did it. The Blood Rebels were drinking vampire blood, caging the vampire exactly how they see themselves being caged. And with drinking vampire blood, the rebels have a more level playing field. They can't have their minds manipulated. It's exactly what my guys do for me for my safety. I can't help wondering if Hayden knew, and that's why he called me a Blood Rebel too.

"Jewel!" My cousins' voices screech through the air, and I spot them standing next to Mr. Diggs, who holds a weapon, ready to fire.

Fallon rushes forward, throwing her arms around me despite the fact that Austin tenses between us. I've never seen her so brave to risk getting so close to a vampire, but she obviously can see how he's not a threat to her. He chuckles and groans, taking an elbow to the face as she snakes her arm between our heads to hug and kiss my cheek. Austin relents and sets me on my feet to hug my cousin properly.

I thought I lost them forever. I thought Hayden's words got to them, and that they'd never want to see or hear from me again.

But now I'm being smothered by two girls who are quickly maturing into women. I can't even believe how much they've changed or how they recognize how much I still love and care for them despite choosing to stay in the vampire world with the guys I love.

"We were so scared," Dana says, cradling sleeping Dougie in her arms.

I gently run my fingers over Dougie's plump cheek, so relieved to see how much he's grown over the last few weeks. Dana hands Dougie over to Mrs. Diggs and wraps her arms around me. She sniffles into my hair, squeezing me so tightly that my ribs ache.

"I knew Ramona was lying," she says. "I told Fallon a million times that you were fine and she was overreacting. Did you know that she invited Hayden to live with us? He's so weird. Always lurking around and watching."

"We've been staying with Mrs. Diggs and helping her with Dougie," Fallon adds. "We almost missed accepting your request to visit because of it. We were starting to get worried, but Brayla said that you were probably just busy with...your three boy toys."

I laugh. I can't help it. Hearing her repeat something very Brayla-like helps ease the fear I've been carrying for my best friend. "So you talked to her too? How is she?"

"Annoyed as all get out at you for not making time to contact her...or any of us," she says.

Kingston releases a long sigh, peering over the side of the building at the chaos below. "All that work and rule breaking and Brayla's been reaching out all along. Your fucking sister," he mutters. "She's going to be responsible for a complete re-evaluation of heir benefits, you know."

I frown. "Don't blame her. It's Hayden."

Mrs. Diggs closes the distance and touches my shoulder. "When it comes down to it, Jewel, we must all be held accountable for our own actions. Hayden might be a grave influence on Ramona, but she has always had a good head on her shoulders. She is well aware of the consequences."

She's right. I can place the blame on Hayden, but Ramona follows his lead. That's how vastly different me and her are—now glaringly more obvious as I stand here, thinking about how to leave without hurting anyone while she's probably thinking about how to blow the place up despite the innocents who'll get hurt in the destruction of her hate.

I swipe a tear from my eye. "I hate this."

"I know, babe," Kingston says, coming up to my side. "And we'll figure it out. But we have to go. There's going to be a lot of damage control to take care of."

Screams sound out from below, and I tense. I glance from my cousins to the Diggs. "We can't leave them," I say.

"They can't come. It might not feel like it, but it's safer here. I'll assure their safety. We'll petition to get their trusts separated from Ramona's. We'll revoke hers if we have to. It seems Hayden might be using it to his advantage anyway."

Could I do that? Should I? I don't think I'll have a choice.

"Jewel, we'll be fine," Dana says.

"I'll keep them safe," Mr. Diggs says, speaking up. "I know your parents would have done the same for our children."

Diego closes the space to my cousins and holds out his palm-sized tablet to them. "Take this. If anything happens, call us. I've programmed our personal extensions into it for you. You can reach Jewel at any one of them. Do take care to hide it, though."

Fallon reaches for it first and cups the device in her hand like it might explode at any second. "Thank you."

"Come on, Jewel," Austin says, motioning for me to return to him.

I hug my arms around both my cousins. "I don't know when I'll get to see you again, but don't forget about me, okay? I love you. I'm going to fix the world for you."

They both nod, blinking through their tears. Dana turns to my guys. "Do you all really love Jewel?"

The three of them nod, but it's Austin who says, "We promised her a Blood Vow. We want her..."

I consider not telling them what it means, but they should know. Ramona already thinks I'm going to change into a vampire, so it's better to prepare them in case. "I agreed to transition into a vampire and become a true Divine."

Everyone stares at me in shock apart from my guys, who

practically puff with pride that I've made it official and cemented my decision by telling the ones I love as much as them.

"I don't understand," Mrs. Diggs says. "You've been inoculated, Jewel. You can't transform."

"It was a lie Donor Life Corp told. I can't get into it bu—"

"Your inoculation had nothing to do with Donor Life Corp. Noah went through great lengths to assure all you girls were vaccinated. Your grandparents helped arrange it and ultimately gave their final donation to guarantee it."

Her words spin through my mind. "I—"

Kingston touches Mrs. Diggs shoulder. "We'll talk more later, but we have to get Jewel out of here. You'll receive a reward for your generosity in helping us tonight."

She hugs me. "I almost forgot." Reaching into the zipper pocket of her jacket, she hands me an envelope. "This is from Brayla. It has everything you need to contact her. Orlando said it was okay to pass it on."

I hand the envelope to Austin to hold onto and hug my cousins once more. "I love you all. Be safe, okay? I'll be in touch."

Austin helps me onto his back, and my cousins sandwich the both of us one more time. If Austin didn't move to stand on the ledge of the building, I don't think I could leave on my own.

I want so badly to bring them with me, to keep them safely at my side, but I'm not sure how safe anywhere near me really is. Not with the board so close. Not with Mitchell Divine trying to manipulate me.

"Brace yourself, Jewel," Austin says. "And don't let go."

I squeeze him tighter. "Fuck, it's a long drop."

Kingston chuckles. "It's a good thing we can fly."

DRASTIC MEASURES

AUSTIN PLAYS WITH MY HAIR, combing his fingers through my knotted tresses to untangle them the best he can. I turn over and run my fingers across his healing stomach peeking out from his unbuttoned shirt. I offered more blood to all my guys, but only Austin accepted my offer. I wasn't sure how good he'd be at a blood draw with how shaky his hands were, and thankfully neither Diego nor Kingston mentioned anything when I allowed Austin to drink right from my body in the backseat despite my stupid mouth making all sorts of noise. My embarrassment was worth it, because Austin seems to be much better.

"Why don't we switch spots so you can lie down?" I ask, shifting onto my back to look up at him.

I was attempting to sleep on the drive home, but there's no way I can even close my eyes. Every time I do so, I see Ramona and the stupid-weird, silver stake aimed at me. Her angry eyes, identical to mine, haunt me. I feel so helpless to our situation. There's nothing I can do short of kidnapping her, waiting for the vampire blood to leave her system, and then having Diego manipulate her mind. While either Kingston or Austin could do it, I'm most comfortable entrusting Ramona's mind to my personality match who I entrust my own mind to.

"I'm good," Austin says, pulling me from my thoughts. He runs his fingers from my hair and down my arm, brushing them over the healing bite marks he left on me. "We're almost home."

"You couldn't even fly, though," I murmur. "Scared the crap out of me."

Kingston laughs from behind the wheel. "You should've seen your face, babe."

Austin leans forward and flicks his brother. "I've never been able to fly. Kingston was messing with you, Jewel."

"What? Kingston, you asshole," I say, twisting my lips. "I was going to ask you to take me some time."

He grins at me. "Don't be so disappointed. It's almost like we can fly."

I groan and sit up to play-slap his shoulder. "Huge difference between flying and falling without splattering, dude."

Snatching my hand, he yanks me between the seats, kissing me softly until I stop glaring at him. I snap my teeth at him, making him chuckle, and then plop back next to Austin who leans on me. I nearly fall over from his weight but brace myself against the seat. He usually makes an effort to keep his weight off me, but now he doesn't, and he's heavier than I expected.

Diego swivels in his seat and gives both me and Austin a once over, probably noticing that I'm holding my breath in an effort to support Austin. "Why don't you come sit with me, beautiful? Having my arms around you will make me feel better. I'm still kind of shaky over the whole ordeal."

I tilt my head and study him. He doesn't look shaky, not like Austin was before he drank from me again, but Diego's pleading gray eyes beg me to give in. "If it's okay with Austin."

Austin bobs his head, motioning for me to climb between the seats. Diego piles his jacket over the center console to fill the gap. Leaning the seat back slightly for more room, he wraps his arms around me, and I sprawl my legs over Kingston's lap to lie sideways so I don't crowd Diego's long legs.

I turn to watch Austin slump down in the seat to lie across the back and realize why Diego asked me to come up front with him. Austin would have never admitted to me that he's still hurt. It's like when we were in the room at Haven Springs and how I nearly had to shove my arm in his mouth to get him to drink my blood. I feel awful I didn't realize it sooner. I just wanted to be with him to make sure he was okay, but it seems he needs space from me because he'll always put me before him.

"Thanks, beautiful," Diego whispers into my ear, so only I can hear. "He'll never let on how bad he feels. He accepted the majority of the injuries because Kingston's faster than him at mind manipulation." So I was right. Austin doesn't want me to know he's struggling.

Reaching back, I take Austin's hand. He offers me a smile, though he keeps his eyes closed until we arrive at the familiar gates of the Divinity Estate. The guards take notice that we're alone, and Kingston murmurs that we lost our entire security detail. It's then that I realize how awful it must be for my guys. Kingston's voice cracks and the guard looking in the window blinks a few times to control his expression as I stare at him. They allow us to pass through the gate after Kingston assures he'll handle everything.

He warned me that there would be repercussions for the events that took place tonight, and I already feel them deep in my bones. Another shift in the world between humans and vampires will take place, and I don't know how on earth we're going to manage.

Kingston puts the car into autopilot and shifts in his seat to look at me. "As soon as we get home, we're going to have to call Mitchell."

"After I check Jewel out," Austin murmurs from the backseat. "I don't like what Mrs. Diggs said about Jewel being inoculated."

"I know you're worried, Austin, but that's going to have to wait," Kingston says.

"But if it turns out to be true, we'll..." Austin lets his words trail off.

"We'll what?" I ask.

Diego nestles his chin into my neck. "Nothing, beautiful. Don't worry about things we don't have to think about just yet."

"And now you freaked her out. She's not going to think about anything else," Kingston says. Reaching out, he laces his fingers to mine, meeting my gaze. "Babe, Austin's worried that if it turns out that you were vaccinated against our venom, then you won't ever transition with our Blood Vows."

I furrow my eyebrows, my eyes watering at the thought. "That would mean...no forever. With you."

Kingston tightens his jaw. "I promised you forever. I intend to assure it."

"If it is true, it would make sense as to why you've experienced side effects from Katherine's venom, but I won't know more until I find out exactly what was done. I just need to figure it out, and I can fix it," Austin says. Not to mention Kingston's venom. I know Austin doesn't think Kingston released his venom, but I might have triggered it. The thought that there's a possibility that my dad ruined my future with his intent to save it leaves me all sorts of confused and angry.

"And he will fix this," Diego says. "We will." His certainty gives me a spark of hope, pushing away my worry.

"But first, the pressing matters," Kingston says, releasing a small growl. "That we won't have any time to prepare for."

Diego swears, holding me tighter.

I turn my gaze away from my guys and peer out the windshield. My heart sinks into my stomach at the sight of Mitchell standing outside the massive doors to the main house. Kingston stops the car and cuts off the engine, swinging his door open to exit the car first. Diego waits for a moment, letting Kingston share words with Mitchell much too quietly for me to hear.

The door swings open, and cool air engulfs me. Kingston keeps his face expressionless as he helps me off Diego's lap and stands me on my feet. Mitchell assesses me, taking in the bite marks up my arm and nods his head like he approves of my condition, of the marks, or the fact that I'm not a blubbering mess after what happened.

"Welcome home, Jewel," Mitchell says, stepping closer. Both Kingston and Diego close in on me at the same time. "My apologies for what looks like quite the troubling night. Are you okay?"

I'm thrown off by his question, the seemingly authentic concern lining his words, but I can't be certain. I bob my head, rubbing my lips together. I don't even know what to say or if I should say anything. Kingston takes my hand and subtly nods.

"Yeah, I think so. Just a little shook up. Haven Springs was not what I expected it to be," I say, keeping my eyes on Mitchell. "It was...enlightening."

Mitchell's eyebrows peak on his forehead, nearly touching his hairline. "Why don't we move our conversation inside? Best to not discuss important matters for all curious ears."

"We can move to my suite," Diego says. "Say in ten? We could all use a moment to get cleaned up."

"Very well. I'll arrange dinner," Mitchell says.

As quick as his words touch my eardrums, he disappears at a speed I can't follow. Diego helps Austin from the car, patting his brother on the back. All three of my guys look me over, making sure there isn't an injury on my body they might have missed.

I reach out and touch Austin's cheek. "Do you need more blood?"

"I could use your blood," Kingston says, flashing his fangs at me in a smile.

Raising my eyebrows, I slowly shift my hair from my shoulder to drape it down my back to meet his tease with my own.

He practically purrs deep in his throat, his eyes flashing silver.

Austin turns and punches him in the arm, making Kingston growl and fake snap his teeth at me from over his shoulder. "There's plenty gen. pop. here for all of us. It'll suffice," Austin says, leaning in to kiss me. "I drank more than all of our share tonight. I'd rather play it safe. Thanks, though. You saved me, Jewel."

I smirk. "You would've been fine. I just didn't want to have to ask your brothers to carry you around. Their arms are for me."

They all chuckle, and Kingston spins me into an embrace I immediately sink in to. "He's probably right, though I want you to know I'm incredibly jealous."

"I'll keep that in mind next time before I decide to protect your ass and take the majority of the injuries," Austin says. "Since you're jealous."

I smile at his words. When they admit their loyalty and love of one another, it gives me all sorts of warm fuzzies. "Aww, Kingston. You should thank him."

Kingston releases me and wraps his arm around Austin's shoulder. "Don't worry, babe. I have. Austin's always been the better fighter, and he'd never let me forget it, so don't think for another moment that you have to thank him for me as well."

"I know I don't *have* to," I tease, looking at Austin. "But I'm gonna."

Kingston shakes his head, smiling. "How about I show you my appreciation? I mean, you are our hero."

I laugh. "Hardly."

The four of us head into the building through the private door that takes us straight to the elevator. Diego and I step on alone while Kingston and Austin take the stairs down. They don't say it, but it's safe to assume they're heading to the kitchen despite Mitchell supposedly arranging dinner.

Diego locks his room door behind us and rushes me toward the bathroom, locking that door too. He hits a few buttons on the wall display, turning on the shower and music at the same time and returns to me, leaning in close to press his mouth to my ear.

"We don't have a lot of time to prepare, so if Mitchell asks you what happened tonight, do not mention the Blood Rebels unless one of us does. You shouldn't know what those are. Don't tell him anything about the supposed vaccine or about Ramona killing Laurel. Let Kingston handle most of the talking. Spinning stories to fit our needs is his specialty." Diego leans away from me to study my eyes to make sure I understand everything he's asking of me. "And Jewel, as hard as it might be, you need to do your best not to react. Mitchell thinks he manipulated your mind to cut ties to your family, remember?"

"Shit balls," I whisper. "I forgot. Are you sure I have to be present for this?"

He scrunches his mouth. "I wish you didn't, but you were the liaison and have been welcomed into our family. These sorts of matters are a family affair."

Family. It's still a strange notion. Because family to me are my cousins and sister. My guys? They're more than that. They're my everything. But Mitchell? He's not even close to being my friend. I accept him because I have to.

"Mitchell insists we immerse you more in our world," he adds.

Unease trickles through me in a cold stream in my blood, making me shiver. What if I mess up and say something I'm not supposed to? What if Mitchell orders Haven Springs to be eradicated to deal with the problem? Donor Life Corp could spin it all sorts of ways and still continue the Blood Match Program. Towns can be rebuilt. Donor Life Corp has a history of recreating places to fit their needs like with The Divide.

"Hey, beautiful?" Diego says, running his knuckles over my

cheek, bringing my attention back to him. "Your pout is making it incredibly hard for me to make you do this."

"Good. Because this sucks. All I want is to take a shower and snuggle in bed with you," I whine. And I mean a full on annoying, nasally whine that makes even me frown. What the hell? It's not like it's his fault.

Leaning forward, he brushes his lips to mine and swears a breath against my mouth. "I'm not denying you showers or cuddles now. But we have to hurry."

I release a loud ass laugh the second my back hits the warm shower wall. Diego grins at me, standing soaking wet in his dirty clothes that stain the water red. I take him up on his offer of distraction and clumsily unfasten the buttons on his shirt.

I don't even get halfway down before he slides his hands under the hem of my dress and up my body to slip it over my head. His eyes rove over me, taking in my curves. And then he pulls me against him, kissing me like he's starved for my love, for my body against his, for a moment with me without having to think about anything but each other.

Roaming my fingers into his shirt, I map the hard muscles of his chest, working my way lower. He sucks in a sharp breath, causing me to jerk back. I attempt to unbutton his shirt more, but he stops me, taking my hand to pull up my arm with his as he leans on the wall.

"Diego, you're hurt," I murmur.

"It's nothing."

I sigh and touch my hand to his stomach to keep him back,

making him wince again. "Seriously? Let me see."

He sighs and unfastens his shirt for me but doesn't move to open it. "It looks worse than it is."

"What is it with you guys trying to hide this shit from me?" I ask, stepping closer. I carefully tug open his shirt and freeze, staring at what looks like a dozen gaping, bloody holes. "Ah, hell." I sweep my wet hair over my shoulder. "You need blood. Here."

Diego releases a breathless laugh, running his fingers over my hair to bring it forward to hide the same spot I let him bite me before. "I can wait."

"You know, all I want to do is take care of you, so why won't you let me? Why hide that you're hurt? Austin nearly passed out on me in Haven Springs. I'm pretty sure you're not far behind from where he was." I wave my hand at his stomach. "I mean, ouch."

Cupping my face, he kisses me again much more fervently this time, sliding his tongue into my mouth, his hands wandering down my sides to hold onto my ass to pull my hips into his. I react to his attempt to distract me, heat traveling from my torso and through the rest of me. I gasp as he lifts me up to curl around him, making it hard to remember why we had stopped kissing to begin with.

"Diego," I whisper. "Bite me please."

He groans and pulls back slightly, meeting my smirk with a fake glare. "You're sneaky."

"And you're stubborn."

He kisses me once more before setting me on my feet. "I'm sorry, beautiful. I don't mean to be. I was trained never to show weakness, and I especially never want to show it with you. How can you trust me to take care of you if I do?"

I grimace. "Admitting you're hurt does not mean you're weak, Diego. I don't think any less of your strength. I think you're incredibly brave and powerful. And you should know that I want you to feel the same about me. I want you to trust that I can care for you, too."

"Oh, I do," he says, smiling. "But no blood right now. Austin's orders. And he'll never let me hear the end of it. He and Kingston are waiting outside."

"They are?" I ask. "I can't hear them." Closing my eyes, I try my best to tune out the music and running water. It takes me a good minute, but I finally catch their muffled voices, though I can't pinpoint what they're saying. I sigh. "You turned on the music so I couldn't hear. And you call me sneaky."

He kisses my pout until I give in and smile before he helps me out of my wet undergarments before completely undressing himself. If I didn't know Austin and Kingston were on the other side of the bathroom door with the possible arrival of Mitchell at any moment, I'd get lost in more of Diego's kisses. But Diego keeps his back to me as he soaps up, and I can tell he's nervous. Much more than I am. And I don't want to push him after his revelation about needing me to always see him strong. So I turn around and stick my face in the stream of warm water, just letting it rinse the night away.

"Mitchell's here, Jewel," Diego says. "Stay in as long as you want. I'll bring you something to wear."

Cool air steals away the warmth of the steam as Diego exits, leaving me alone. Not even a moment later, he returns with a pair of my cotton pajamas, and I'm utterly grateful I don't have to slide into another dress for the night.

I contemplate taking him up on remaining in the shower for as long as I want, but I don't want to miss any of the conversation my guys have with Mitchell. It involves my family. Everyone in Haven Springs.

Shutting off the water, I quickly dry myself and dress, my clothes clinging to my damp skin. I wrap my hair in my towel and exit the bathroom to find everyone sitting in Diego's entertainment room. My stomach roars at the sight of the food arranged for me on a tray resting on the ottoman.

Everyone glances at my stomach, making me blush like crazy. I hadn't realized how hungry I was. I was expecting to eat with my family in Haven Springs, but that obviously didn't happen. It's not like my guys could whip up something for me on the way home, either. All human establishments close before sundown in every town.

"Damn, babe. Next time we'll pack something for you," Kingston says, motioning me to sit between Diego and Austin.

Mitchell reclines back in a chair he rolled from Diego's desk, and Kingston perches on the edge of the ottoman with his tablet on his knee, tapping away at the screen. Austin leans forward for the tray of food and sets it across my lap. He cuts the burger through the middle before holding it up to my mouth.

I smirk, taking a bite. He would probably hand feed me everything all the time if I allowed it, but he mostly only does it out of nerves. He's more worked up than I have ever seen him. I can tell. And I really wish I could have a moment alone to talk to him to see if I can say anything to make him feel better.

"So Jewel. Kingston updated me about what happened tonight in Haven Springs," Mitchell says, getting straight to business. I'm glad for it, because I don't know how much longer my anxiety could handle waiting for him to get to the point.

I nod. "Yeah, I don't ever want to go back. I don't even know why I had to go in the first place. I accepted a Blood Vow into your family."

His jaw tightens as he refrains from giving anything away, though I can tell he wants to pat his own friggin' back because he thinks he's some badass mind manipulating superstar. What I wouldn't give to high-five myself. I'm the one who should get an award for my average acting skills. I'd rock in an old B-rated classic.

"I'm sorry for that. As you know, one of your heirs made a grave accusation against our family. The board takes those instances seriously, so I had no choice but to make it clear that false accusations from the community would not be taken lightly. I suspect your family was coerced into it." If only.

I lift and drop my shoulders. "Don't know. Didn't get a chance to ask, but it doesn't matter. Like I said, I don't want to go back."

"And you won't have to," Mitchell says. "My sons informed me that our problem was handled appropriately. I do apologize that your sister is having a difficult time adjusting to everything."

I grab the burger from Austin's hand and shove it in my mouth, biting a piece so big that Mitchell glances away. Even Kingston looks up from his device and raises his eyebrows at me. I can hear him silently saving this moment to tease me about my savagery later.

Diego squeezes my knee. "Ramona acted as to be expected. She was upset about the Blood Vow because she fears she'll never see her sister again."

"She won't. It's better for everyone that I cut my ties," I mumble through chewing. It's easier to say the words than I expected. The fact that Ramona nearly shoved a stake through my chest helps add to the bitterness rushing through me. I just hope no one mentions...I suppress thinking about Dana and Fallon.

Mitchell nods his approval, and I imagine him patting his back again. It takes everything in me to keep my emotions in check. It helps that I can shove all the food in my mouth to mask everything rushing through me. "I do have to agree with you, Jewel. Especially after what I imagine was a lot of unrest. Can you tell me about it?"

I chew and swallow. "It's kind of a blur. A lot of the security in Haven Springs was hostile. I think something happened between my guards and the gathering people waiting on the young guy I was meeting with. Weapons went off and people slaughtered my security team. The new guy tried to instigate everyone to think I was out to get them all. It was scary and..." I shudder, not wanting to get into more details or my sister's involvement.

"Which is why we were forced to out ourselves," Diego says. "We were afraid for Jewel's life."

"You did the right thing, son. I couldn't forgive myself if something happened to your possible futures with such a marvelous young woman."

I grin like an idiot at his words and could seriously use a good whack over the head right about now. He's supposed to forever be the annoyance of my life, not making me happy with compliments.

Mitchell meets my smile with his own. "Your courage to stand up for what you want from this eternity is a quality I respect. It looks like you also put in an effort to aid my son. I'm grateful for that."

I nod. "I'd do anything for...our family."

"You should have seen Jewel sucker punch the asshole responsible for this shit show," Kingston says, his chest puffing with pride.

"That's something I'd have enjoyed seeing, but what concerns me about all of this is that you were supposed to have a meeting with the council. None of them are under the age of forty. We at Donor Life Corp find that the community runs more efficiently when handled by those who are wise with experience." Or good sense to remain compliant.

I flick my gaze to Kingston, and he sets his tablet down, turning serious.

"It seems that one of the newer arrivals thought an uprising was necessary," he says. "And unfortunately, he's managed to snake his way to use the Jordans' good fortune and resources at his own disposal."

I take another bite of the burger, trying not to react to the fact that Kingston brought up my sister when she's the last person I want Mitchell to focus on. Diego slides his hand around my knee, reminding me that Kingston knows what he's doing. It's just—mentioning Ramona puts me on guard.

"How old is Ms. Jordan?" Mitchell asks.

Kingston hands Mitchell his tablet to look over. "Almost of age."

"Extremely sheltered," I mumble. I can't help it. "I provided her an isolated life, thinking it was for the best, but I was clearly wrong."

Kingston nods his approval. "There were only a few exempt bold enough to take a stand. We chose a more peaceful approach to hopefully ensure that we could eliminate the unrest quietly and quickly."

"Good," Mitchell says. "Now, about your heir, Jewel."

I sit up straighter, remembering exactly what my guys discussed about how to handle Ramona while we were on the rooftop. "If you don't mind me interrupting. I have an idea."

"Go on."

"I want to separate my cousins' inheritance from Ramona's and cap hers to cover basic living expenses only. I don't want to punish her for her naivety, but I can't trust that she won't continue acting out for this particular guy. I'm certain she likes him," I say, setting down the rest of my burger to stop myself from automatically shoving it into my mouth.

Mitchell reaches out and touches Diego's hand on my leg as if he were actually touching my knee. "That's a rather brilliant idea. I'll have the paperwork drafted to put it into effect come next sundown."

"Sounds good," I say, bringing my gaze to Kingston.

Kingston raises his eyebrows and sticks his tongue out at me, making me smirk because I totally ripped off his idea and made Mitchell believe it was my own. I blow him a kiss and silently promise to thank him later, and he nudges my bare foot with his socked one.

There's something I love about sitting with my guys while we're all in pajamas despite the fact that Mitchell is here. I should get used to it. This is his family after all, and I'm the outsider who's been asked to join.

"Now, there's one more thing I'd like to discuss, but with my sons in private," Mitchell says, turning to me. "I hope you don't mind."

I keep my face even as much as I want to frown. "Of course not. Thank you for taking the time to visit tonight. I'll eat the rest of my dinner from the comfort of my bed." I glance at Diego. "Mind helping me?"

Mitchell smiles, watching Diego grab my tray for me. My acting totally deserves an A-rating. Both Kingston and Austin remain expressionless, and I don't try to push them with my silent worry to give me something to go on. Whatever it is, I know I won't like it. This is exactly what Diego warned me about. And I'm thankful I don't have to sit and grin and bear through it.

Diego leans into me and brushes his lips to my ear. "It's going to be okay. Please, try your best not to react. We can still hear you."

I nod, crossing my legs to pick at the fries on my tray, no longer hungry but doing it just to occupy my attention. From my spot, I watch Diego turn on the TV for me and then return to take his seat on the end of the couch, but Kingston, Austin, and Mitchell remain out of my view.

I slowly take a bite of a fry, trying my best not to make it obvious I'm listening even with the blaring TV.

"I need to know how many were involved in trying to take you out," Mitchell says.

"Maybe two or three dozen out of a thousand. Most never left their homes," Kingston says. There are a thousand people in Haven Springs? I had no idea so many people Blood Matched for a population that size. Of course, they might not all be heirs. Laurel wasn't.

Mitchell sighs. "And the council?"

Diego leans back on the couch, flicking his gaze to look at me. "Niall's dead."

I shove another fry in my mouth, studying Diego. He never reacts, just occasionally glancing at me, but not in an obvious way. It's normal for my guys to check on me when I'm not in the same room as them. They're all a little bit paranoid.

Mitchell's chair creaks. I can nearly imagine him leaning forward to rest his elbows on his knees. My keen hearing has made me more aware of people's body language, and even if I can't see him, I can guess what he's doing. "How do you suggest we handle this?"

"I think we let it slide. They were only reacting to our threat to change exemptions," Austin says. "If we let it go, they'll see there is nothing to rise against."

Mitchell growls, and I hear his fangs extend. It's a click I'm familiar with because my guys do it so often. "Or they'll think they can continue to rise. I want to put a stop to this *now*. I think we should send in security to reform the city and put those ungrateful of what we've provided them in their places."

Oh, God. Security? Reformation? Without having to ask, I can tell Mitchell's reformation of Haven Springs will involve murdering all who try to protect themselves. All who stand up. Hayden said they were prepared to fight. And Ramona will stand up with him. I know it. If she does, there would be nothing I could do.

Kingston sighs. "No, Dad. The last thing the Blood Match Program needs is for word to get out that we've gone in and killed anyone who fought the changes. It's in their right to fire on sight, remember? It's the biggest allure to get donors to apply to be matched. Donors love their sense of entitlement, and it helps keep order. What you suggest would cause chaos. They're armed. Well armed. We couldn't guarantee one of our own wouldn't get hurt. Pedro fell only minutes after Jewel's security detail had. They not only had guns but a few explosives."

A deep growl sounds from the room. I'm sure if there were any humans nearby, they'd have heard Mitchell's displeasure as well. "Then tell me how you'd handle it. Explosives of our own? Send in human staff? Pay extra to get those placated to turn on those who want to fight?"

Tears burn my eyes at every one of his suggestions that would surely be the end of so many innocent people.

Kingston clears his throat. "We can drug the water and corral everyone for a peaceful interrogation."

I plop another fry in my mouth, hoping my loud ass chewing will drown out my racing heart. While Kingston's suggestion is far better than any of Mitchell's, the thought of caging people sends my stomach reeling. It sounds like how The Divide happened. I can just imagine how traumatizing that'll be on my cousins. On everyone.

"Now, that's a plan I like," Mitchell says. I think he pats Kingston on the back from the hard thuds. "We'll pump a slow acting sedative into the water tanks. It should take care of enough people to lessen any chance of bloodshed. It should be effective enough to get in and manipulate people's minds."

I audibly groan, bringing Diego's attention to me.

So I groan again and say, "Hey, Austin. I think something

was wrong with my food. I don't feel so well."

"Just a minute, Jewel," he calls.

I take a breath, clenching my fingers into my palms.

"That sounds like a reasonable plan," Kingston says, carrying on the conversation. "But I should warn you."

OhmyeffinG. I release an audible gasp before Kingston even says anything.

Austin peeks his head out from the doorway, checking on me.

"Yes?" Mitchell says, not even paying attention to the fact that I'm losing my shit.

Kingston clears his throat again. He's nervous. I don't have to see him to know so. But it's not Mitchell making him nervous. It's me. "I can't be sure, but I suspect some residents have been consuming vampire blood."

Mitchell growls. "From where? You don't mean?" He doesn't finish his question out loud.

Kingston hums under his breath. "Possibly. I suspect the guy who threatened Jewel is their leader."

"Then we'll take care of the matter appropriately. I will not risk anyone slipping through. Those who can't be manipulated will give their final donations, understand? We have to make a point."

I startle at his words, accidentally knocking my tray of food from my lap. Everyone emerges from the entertainment room at once, and I stumble to my feet, accidentally stepping in the broken glass of my shattered dishes.

"I'm sorry," I say, hopping on my foot, blood dripping to the rug. "I need to—" I cover my mouth with my hand, my stomach twisting the second my gaze meets Mitchell's. This time, I'm really going to be sick.

Austin rushes to my side, picking me off my feet to race me to the bathroom. He clicks the door closed, and I hang my head over the toilet. My whole body convulses as Mitchell's words sink in. How could this be happening? I feel so helpless.

"I'll arrange the contamination today," Mitchell says. "We'll send a team in at sundown."

"Sundown," Kingston and Diego repeat.

Oh, God. Ramona will be caught up in this mess. They'll know immediately that she was part of the uprising. And as much as she hurt me, as much as she broke my heart, I can't let that happen.

If she's caught, she'll die.

THE BACKUP PLAN

DOZENS OF VOICES MURMUR THROUGH the air, drawing me through the arched doorway and into the dining room. Shadows dance around me, touching my flowing dress, cool fingers gliding across my bare shoulders, a sweet kiss to my cheek.

Someone slides their fingers through mine, and I turn and smile at Mitchell. He guides me forward to a cushioned seat at the middle of the table and pulls it out so I can sit down. Figures materialize all around me, and I tilt my head back and smile at Kingston hovering over me. He flashes his fangs and bites his wrist, dripping his blood into my open mouth.

"I hate you!" A screech rips through the air, drawing the shadows dancing around the room closer. "I'll kill you for this."

Diego and Austin drag Ramona forward, holding each of her arms in their hands. They offer me brilliant smiles, the sight of their fangs flashing sending desire through me. They toss Ramona onto the table, and the shadows drag her across, ignoring her screams ripping through the air.

"Here's to you, Princess Jewel of the Divinity Estate," Mitchell says, raising a golden goblet toward me. "And the satisfying end of your legacy."

Blood rains down from the ceiling, splashing over Ramona. Her blue eyes burn invisible daggers at me. She pushes to her knees, snarling. She looks feral, dangerous even, but she doesn't scare me.

I laugh and reach out, grabbing the front of her bloody shirt to drag her closer. "To the end of a legacy."

Ramona screams, launching at me.

"Jewel, wake up."

I startle, the room spinning out of control as it rushes around me. Diego yanks the back of my shirt, stopping me from smashing into the ground. He tugs me up into the air to catch me in his arms.

"Shit," I say, burying my face into the soft cotton of his shirt.

"That was some dream," he murmurs, rubbing his hand down my back.

"Why did you let me sleep, Diego? You know I have to call my cousins and let them know. They're going to be so scared," I say. I haven't been able to reach Ramona to warn her either.

The silence has me on edge. "I want to try to call Brayla again too. She needs to know what's going on, so she can warn her family."

"Dana and Fallon are fine, beautiful. I already talked to them. We also put out special instructions that no one is to touch the Diggs household. Calling Brayla isn't a good idea right now, but later, I promise. We have to deal with this before Orlando. Her family will be safe and will remain inside until we tell them otherwise. They'll call once the team arrives."

"What about Ramona?" I ask. "Did you reach her?"

He grimaces, his expression speaking volumes. "Jewel, we can't tell her."

"So, you're responsible for blocking my call to her," I say, turning away from him. "Diego, how could you? I know you have hard feelings toward her, but she's my family."

"She will be the death of you, Jewel," he whispers.

"So you expect me to be the death of her?"

The door to our bedroom swings open and both Kingston and Austin appear right on cue to back up Diego's decision. Something dark snaps in me, and I push away from Diego to get to my feet.

"Great," I mutter. "Now, you're all going to gang up on me."

"Babe," Kingston says.

I shake my head, tears spilling from my eyes without my permission. Nothing they say will make me feel any better about the possibility of them agreeing to let Ramona stand in the line of fire.

I can't handle the look of pity crossing their faces. I'm usually okay with them smothering me, but my chest heaves as I gasp for breath that doesn't come. A mixture of emotions battle it out inside me, and I feel like I'm being ripped at the seams between what I know has to be done to keep the majority of Haven Springs safe and what I want to be done with them. I just want Donor Life Corp to leave everyone alone. This is my fault. Hayden was right about me being responsible for the soon-to-be devastation of humankind.

I take a few steps toward the balcony door. "I need air."

"Jewel, please," Austin says. "It's going to be fine. Just come here and hear us out."

"Air first," I mutter. "Now stay back. I'm just going to crack it a little."

I hook my fingers to the doorknob to the balcony and push down, but nothing happens. Of course it wouldn't. I never once tried to open one of the balcony doors in my guys' rooms, and it's locked to prevent such an occurrence from happening with my guys' light sensitivity.

I react by kicking the door, sending a zap of pain into my already tender foot from stepping in glass. Diego reaches me first, lifting me off my feet and taking me back to the bed that I don't even have time to protest.

"Damn it," I snap. "You guys are—"

Kingston presses his hand to my mouth, silencing my words. "Stop, babe. You're making us nervous. I know you're scared and pissed off about everything, but—and I'm saying this as nicely as I can—you need to chill the fuck out. Despite my feelings for your sister, I'm not letting anything happen to her."

Narrowing my eyes, I glare at him before licking his palm. He doesn't react, studying my eyes, waiting for me to release the breath I'm holding to stop myself from screaming into his hand. I'm so antsy. I feel like I'll combust at any second if I stay in this room a minute longer.

"Why?" I murmur into his hand.

His jaw twitches. "She's your sister, and you love her. We don't want to risk you hating us."

I lock my fingers around his wrist and pull his hand from my mouth. "You know I wouldn't blame you, so tell me the truth. What other reason do you have?"

Kingston doesn't react.

Turning my gaze to Diego, I meet his gray eyes with raised eyebrows. He gives nothing away, his lips hidden in a line. I shift and look at Austin next, and he gives everything away with his pouty mouth and sad eyes.

"Austin," I say.

"Stay strong, brother," Kingston says.

I throw a pillow at him, and he lets it hit him in the face. His words make me feel guilty that I was going to totally attempt to use Austin's love to get an answer, but he already beats himself up over this entire situation. He's acting worse than Kingston, and I can't figure it out. He's always so stoic.

Staring at his sad face strikes a nerve inside me, and a sob escapes my mouth. My shoulders shake, and I cry, everything awful in the world suddenly weighing heavy on me. My chest tightens, my gasping making things worse.

"Damn it," Kingston says, wrapping his arms around me. "I'm sorry, babe. Please, don't cry. I don't like what it does to me."

"Instant boner killer," I mutter, reminding him of the first night we met and what he told me that made me laugh.

"Worse. It's tearing my insides out," he says, rubbing his hand in circles over my back.

"Then tell me," I say. "We're supposed to be a team. And I don't feel like we are right now."

Diego groans. "Screw it. I'm telling her," he says to Kingston.

Kingston growls.

"Ramona is our backup plan, beautiful," Diego admits, turning his gaze from mine before he can catch my gaping stare.

"What?"

"Babe, don't get mad. You know we don't like your sister, but we know you love her, but we kind of need her in case."

Effin' A. Of course this would be their reasoning. If something were to happen to Ramona, the blood debt can go two ways—to me or to my cousins—and we all know that I'd accept it for my cousins despite them still being four years away. But Ramona? I don't even know now. I hate myself for even thinking it.

"Please forgive us," Austin says, finally braving my emotional state. "It won't come down to it, but I'm not risking losing you. Just the thought that something might stop us from our Blood Vow is killing me. I couldn't stand it if...I'll kill Orlando if he came after you."

"Except Austin would most definitely not survive if he's who I think he is," Diego says.

I start bawling my eyes out, snot and everything, while hiding my face in my hands. I can't take thinking about any of this anymore. All I wanted from today was to cuddle with Diego, have a nice date, maybe work on my fighting skills, and then to tease Kingston come dawn and see how long it would take for us to finally give in to our body match. I didn't want to deal with any of this bullshit.

Three pairs of arms wrap around me as my guys sandwich me between them. Kingston kneels in front of me, pressing my knees into his stomach, getting all up in my space that I'm nearly certain he has X-ray vision to peer at me through my hands. I nudge him away with the back of my hand, and he links his fingers through mine, breathing a cool breath against my lips.

"Kingston, stop smothering her," Austin says.

Kingston brushes his nose against mine. "Babe, the only way I'm going to stop smothering you is if you look at me."

Heaving a breath, I open my eyes and peer into his blurry face. He scrunches his nose while crossing his eyes, and then he sticks out his tongue. I surprise the hell out of him by biting it—not hard, just firm enough that he resists from jerking away from me. And then he laughs. So do Diego and Austin.

"Careful, Kingston," Diego says, "she doesn't know her own strength."

I laugh, letting go of Kingston's tongue in the process, and he puts space between us but still holds onto my hand. Austin sits beside me, resting his head on my shoulder. I slide my free hand into his and bring it to my cheek to feel his skin against mine. Diego doesn't take his arms from around me. He just hugs me—and Austin too because he's so close—and waits until I pull myself together.

"I wasn't sure I'd ever hear you laugh again," Austin says, turning slightly into me, begging for me to kiss him without having to ask.

I caress my lips to his for a moment. "That's how I feel about your smile."

He offers me a small one but his heart isn't in it. Kingston and Diego must sense my sudden need to be alone with Austin because they both stand up and make excuses to step out of the room for a moment.

Austin engulfs me in a hug the second Diego closes his door, and I freeze at the warmth of his tears soaking into the cotton of my sleeve. Fear steals my voice away, and I can't even manage to whisper his name. So I hug him tighter, shifting onto his lap to put my whole body into it.

"Jewel," he whispers. "I'm sorry."

I pull back and get him to look at me, his green eyes shining in the light. "It's okay. You don't need to apologize. I'm fine. You're fine."

He bobs his head. "I keep telling myself that."

"So, what's wrong?" I ask. "Is this about the Blood Vow?"

He shrugs without responding.

"Because we'll make it work no matt—"

"I killed someone in Haven Springs," he blurts, his whole face morphing with a pain that steals my breath and makes my whole body hurt. "I'm so sorry. I couldn't stop myself. I was just—"

I cut his words off with a kiss, clutching his face in my hands. I knew something had been bothering him, but I had no idea this was the reason. And then I remember that Austin told me he had never killed a human. He cares for the human race and doesn't see them the same as other vampires. He even sees donors differently than Kingston and Diego.

"You don't have to apologize to me," I whisper into his lips. "And I hate that you found yourself in this position. I know what it's like. Don't you remember that I killed someone, too?"

"You were protecting yourself," he says.

"And so were you."

"It's different."

"It's not," I say, resting my head on his shoulder. "We do what we have to do to survive."

"But we should do more."

His words sink into me. He's right. I've always used the excuse about doing what it takes to survive, but life isn't about surviving. It's about being aware of our actions and how they affect others. Like what Mrs. Diggs said about Ramona and how she knows what she's doing. And Austin's right. We should do more. I should do more.

"Jewel," he says, bringing my attention back to him. "I promise you that I'll do more. I want to change things for you. For us."

I kiss him. "And I'll help you."

"So will we," both Kingston and Diego say through the door.

Austin groans before releasing a breathless laugh, and we find ourselves squished between his brothers. I kiss and hug each of them, my heart already feeling a thousand times better than it did. It gives me hope that everything will be okay.

Diego's phone rings from his desk, drawing our attention to it. He crosses the room first and glances at the screen. "It's your cousins. They're calling earlier than expected."

I release a breath. "Do you think Ramo—"

Diego answers the phone before I have a chance to spit the words out. He leans down to look at his monitor, and I scramble to get to my feet. Kingston picks me up and races across the room. Austin slides up behind us.

"Jewel," Dana whispers. But I can't see her. The video screen is completely black. "Ramona's making us leave Haven Springs."

"Hayden has a car," Fallon adds. "I'm scared. I don't want to go."

"Fallon, hang up. They're coming."

The line drops, and I spin, combing my fingers through my hair. "Oh, God. What the eff is she thinking? Leaving Haven Springs? Why? What would make her possibly do that?"

Kingston slaps his hand on the desk. "She knows."

"A traitor."

"What do you mean a traitor?" I ask, bouncing on my feet despite my aching foot. I can't stay still.

All three of my guys look at me, but it's Diego who steps forward to hold his arms open for me. "Could be a human member of the staff or a vampire. Hard to tell. Blood Rebels can be either."

I twist my fingers together. "Why would a vampire be a Blood Rebel?"

"The same reasons humans are," Austin says.

Kingston huffs a breath. "To rise."

Diego releases a low growl. "So we can fall."

DIVINE AFFAIRS

"I'LL PARK THE CAR UNDER the tree by Kingston's balcony. It's not in the direct sunlight, so you all can jump," I say, peering through the tinted glass of Diego's window at the sun lowering in the sky. It's still two hours until sunset, and I'm afraid if we don't leave now, Ramona will disappear with my cousins, and I'll never see my family again.

Kingston paces around me so quickly that his form blurs. "That would require you to go outside alone."

"I'll be fine."

"But what if you're not. Last time—"

I extend my arm out, concentrating on Kingston's figure every time he comes back around. Jerking my hovering hand forward, I snatch his arm. His quick movement drags me off my feet in the process. He catches me before my ass collides into the rug. "I'm better than last time. Faster. Stronger. I can hear any threat coming."

Kingston squeezes me so tightly into a hug that I gasp. "Babe, I don't care. You...you could get hurt."

"Is this what the rest of eternity is going to be like? I can't even step ten feet from you outside these rooms?"

"Kingston, if you're so afraid, then go with Jewel and move the car yourself," Austin says. "Because according to the tracker, Ramona's on the move. Heading south."

"No one is coming with me into the sun. I need you all in the best condition in case. It already freaks me the eff out that you're going to be in the car. I mean—anything can happen," I say.

"We can all go in the sun covered," Diego says, tossing a hooded jacket at Kingston. "No need to move the car to the shade because Kingston doesn't like the heat. Our clothes should suffice long enough. If we can't handle this, we have bigger problems."

I puff air through my lips. "I'm so glad you all don't explode in the sun."

Kingston lets me go to shrug into his jacket. "Yeah, because we would've all been dead weeks ago."

I frown.

"Shut up, Kingston. Your smartass remarks aren't helping." Austin turns to me. "Don't let Kingston's dramatics get to you. You're strong and plenty capable of keeping us safe. There also happens to be thousands of sun protectors all over the place to provide relief if something goes wrong."

"Oh." I don't know what to say. I never thought much about vampires traveling in the sun. If I had known this growing up, I'd have probably been scared to death. Now? I'm so friggin' thankful I don't have to wait for the sun to set. "Well, nothing is going to happen. You're right. I'll keep you all safe."

"Because we're all dead if you don't," Kingston says.

Austin punches him in the shoulder, but Kingston spins with the motion, taking me with him. I press my hands into his chest and shake my head at him. All he does is smile at me, flashing his fangs.

I snuggle close to him. "You really are dramatic."

"I can say the same about you."

Before I can lose myself in Kingston's dark eyes, Diego pulls a mask over Kingston's head, making him growl. I laugh and poke Kingston's hidden nose before scrambling away. Austin catches me, twirling me out of Kingston's reach. He flips me over his head, making me screech, and I can't stop laughing as he plays keep away with me from Kingston.

"Okay, okay. As much as I love hearing our girl laugh like crazy, we gotta go," Diego says, tossing Austin a mask.

Austin sets me on my feet, and I slip into the jacket Diego hands me to wear over my long-sleeved shirt the same black as my pants and boots. I'm definitely dressed for the cover of night. I even get my own beanie to tame my hair and keep it hidden. We're dressed nothing like I'm used to—even Kingston doesn't wear the suits he seems to favor when we leave. It freaks me out that we're dressed for whatever battle the guys imagine, but I hope it doesn't come to it. All I want is to get my family away from the Blood Rebels.

Each of my guys loads themselves with weapons, and Diego hands me a small dagger—just in case—and we take the elevator down. The guys make it inside the car faster than me, letting me get behind the wheel. I double check to make sure everyone is okay and that the tinted glass holds up the minute we sit in silence, and then Diego programs Austin's com device into the navigation system, and the screen lights up to display where my cousins are.

"Inform Jewel that she will not be driving wherever it is you're going rather early." A familiar voice drifts from outside, making me stiffen in my seat.

"Shit," Kingston murmurs from the backseat. "Crawl back here, babe."

I swivel in the seat and catch sight of a figure hovering in the short line of shade created by the protruding statues carved into the stone façade of the building. Shielding his eyes with his gloved hand, he waits for me to react.

Mitchell sweeps his fingers at me to move. I'm afraid if I don't, he'll come and open my door anyway, and the last place I want to end up is on his lap. I do as Kingston asks and crawl into the backseat. All three of my guys put their masks back on just in time for Mitchell to swing the door open and slide behind the wheel. He removes his hat and twists in the seat to get a better look at all of us.

"Let me guess. You're heading to Haven Springs to oversee the task at hand?" he asks, meeting my eyes directly to assess my reaction.

"No," I say, crossing my arms over my chest. I stare at his pink-tinted nose. He obviously cares less about the sun than my guys.

Mitchell raises his eyebrows and turns to the dash to mess with the navigation. "You're tracking someone."

Before I can even move, Mitchell leans between the seats, hooks his fingers to my chin, and attempts to lock me in his gaze. I nearly give myself away because of the collections of growls coming from all three of my guys.

Diego surprises me by yanking Mitchell by the shoulder and jostling him hard enough that he lets me go. I bring my hands up to the ache in my chin created by the pressure of Mitchell's fingers and gape in shock at his nerve to try to mind manipulate me without my guys' permission.

"Don't do that again," Austin says lowly, a threat in his voice I've never heard before. "You want answers, you ask one of us."

I'm pretty sure if we were back inside, Mitchell would attack Austin like he did Kingston the other night. His eyes shift from Austin to me, and I sink lower, my heart racing and giving away my fear. My uncontrollable quivering lip doesn't help either.

Summoning my courage, I say, "Please, stop it. We're wasting time. My sister is on the move, and we have to get to her before sunset."

"Your sister?" Mitchell asks.

I hate myself so much in this moment that I start to cry, the hot tears streaking down my cheeks to brand my skin pink like Mitchell's. The last thing I wanted was to place the blame on Ramona, but I know things I shouldn't, and I don't know what I can say or not about the Blood Rebels.

I nod my head. "She kidnapped my cousins from Haven Springs."

"We think it was the rebel leader," Kingston adds, arching forward in the seat, inconspicuously leaning in front of me to semi-shield me from Mitchell.

"He has an informant," Mitchell says, his eyebrows lowering on his forehead.

All three of my guys nod, and then Diego says, "It's why we've turned matters personal. We don't know who to trust, and even if Jewel is ready to cut ties to the Jordans, we'd like to see to it that her heirs remain safe."

Mitchell taps a few buttons on the dashboard and adjusts the seat. Glancing in the mirror, he says. "You're right. This is now a family matter. But boys? Next time you better include me. You're not the only ones to find Jewel important. She's important to me and all of Donor Life Corp."

Something about his words bothers me.

And after looking at each of my guys, I can see that his words bother them, too.

The sun dips low on the horizon, turning the blue ocean gray. Sundown will come in less than ten minutes according to the navigation screen that displays everything we need to know about the conditions outside the safety of this car built to withstand even a hundred raging vampires. Possibly two hundred armed humans...at least, that's what I keep telling myself.

I bounce my feet up and down on the floor, shaking both my knees. My behavior lasts all of two minutes before Kingston slides his hand under me to plop me on his lap while Austin adjusts my legs over his knees to keep me from fidgeting.

"I'm nervous as hell, dude," I whisper to Kingston. "What if they attack us on sight?"

"They probably will," Mitchell says, butting right into my conversation. The whole trip so far, he's been putting his annoying opinion or thoughts into everything I say like I'm personally having the conversation with him and not my guys. It doesn't help that we're too close to each other that I don't want to risk whispering to have him realize I'm even more awesome than I look, super-hearing, amazing regenerative blood, backworld dialect and all.

"Shit balls," I say, squirming on Kingston's lap to shift to peer out the window.

He grips my legs, digging his fingers into my thighs to hold me in place. "Babe, please. Now's not the time to be antsy. I need to stay focused on our surroundings and not your cute ass wiggling on my lap."

My cheeks burn with what is surely fire summoned from the pits of hell, because I know everyone, including Mitchell, heard his comment.

I elbow him in the ribs, making him oomph. "Get your mind off my ass, and maybe I wouldn't be so squirmy."

Kingston releases a loud laugh and relents to nudge me back into my seat. But he's right about distractions. As much as I want to joke around and tease him, our green dot on the navigation system draws closer to the red dot that has finally stopped moving.

Mitchell's gaze catches mine in the mirror, and he smiles at me, creeping me the hell out. The more I'm around him, the more uneasy I feel. I have to keep reminding myself that I have three badass, powerful, and occasionally pouty—like now—vampires who'll rip someone apart to keep me safe. And after Mitchell's actions toward me, I'm nearly certain he'd be included.

Austin massages my legs, drawing my gaze to him. I can't stop myself from shifting closer to him and out of Mitchell's line of sight. I twist my body, resting my feet on Kingston's lap instead. He grips my feet and begs me not to startle and kick him, making Diego laugh from the front.

"You hungry at all?" Austin asks, talking into my skin because he presses his face to my arm.

I rub my lips together, knowing there is no way I can eat, but my guys might not if I don't. "Are you guys?"

Kingston sighs and reaches for a box under the seat to pull

out what looks like three thermoses. "I have enough for three. Sorry, Dad. Didn't know you were joining us on our road trip."

"He can have Diego's," I murmur, not wanting to leave myself vulnerable in front of Mitchell, but he might think it weird that I don't offer to provide blood for the son I'm technically supposed to feed tonight.

I don't have to hear Kingston to know he's inwardly groaning to himself because he's become spoiled that I usually give my blood to all three of them but can't do so in front of Mitchell. He freaks me out enough to fear that if he were to discover our secret, he'd cancel my Blood Vow and put me in a cage and on permanent tap to turn my life into my worst nightmare as a donor on the dining room table for all to taste.

Diego touches my knee, and I look up at his beaming smile. "Thanks, beautiful."

I rest my hand over his. "You don't have to thank me."

"But I like to."

Kingston slides closer to us, using his body to shield me the best he can as Austin draws my blood using the medical kit he keeps under the seat. I cringe at the small murmur Mitchell releases, and Kingston meets my frown with his own disgusted grimace, but none of them remark on something I shouldn't be able to—and I really wish I couldn't—hear. Seriously gross. I mean, Mitchell isn't hideous by any means, but come on. It's rude as hell. I'm the love of his sons and I love his sons back. He needs to stay far, far away from me.

Austin applies synthetic skin to my arm to stop any extra

blood from spilling and hands over the vial to Diego. Gulping his thermos down in one swig, Austin drops the container to the floor and then pulls out another one from his kit and hands it to me.

"You packed breakfast?" I ask, smirking at the contents.

He smiles and kisses me. "You know how much I love to feed—"

The car jolts, bouncing over something in the road, sending us fishtailing back and forth. Austin locks me in his hold, and Kingston braces his arms around the both of us, stopping us from jerking around the backseat. Blood cascades through the air, splashing over all of us, coating the windows. Mitchell regains control of the car, and after spinning once more, we come to a jerking halt. A cloud of dust engulfs us, turning the world around us a hazy orange.

Nobody moves to get out.

My guys couldn't even if they wanted to.

"Duck!" Diego yells, bending forward to cover his head.

Both Austin and Kingston shield me as the windows explode, sending glass shards shooting through the air. Bright sunshine lights up the world around us, warming even my skin with its intensity. But I realize it's not me at all. My guys are all lying here exposed.

And then someone outside the car screams.

SACRIFICE

"JEWEL!" A FAMILIAR VOICE CALLS my name, breaking through the ringing in my ears. "Oh, my God. Jewel!"

I squirm under Kingston and Austin, both groaning and unable to do much with the blinding sunlight streaming in through the broken side windows. I quickly yank my jacket off and do my best to cover them while I move around the car as fast as I can, grabbing whatever I can use to protect them.

I manage to find both Austin and Kingston's masks wet with blood under us on the seat, and I pull them out and place Austin's on first before I help Kingston with his. Crawling into the front seat, I take off my shirt and cover Diego as he cowers against his window. I find Mitchell's hat first and hand it to him. Bending between Diego's legs, I manage to grab his mask and help him get it on.

"No, don't!" a feminine voice screams from outside.

A strange hissing sound tickles my eardrums, breaking through the ringing, and then Diego grabs me and shields me with his body as the windows on his side of the car explode in a shower of glass. Pieces sink into my exposed side, and I release a cry as pain shoots through me.

"Everyone out," Mitchell says from behind the wheel. "Three minutes to sunset. Split up and wait it out."

"Kingston, take Jewel," Austin says.

I don't even have time to orient myself to what's happening before the world blurs again, and I find myself in Kingston's arms, standing in a crevice within a tall cliff. Kingston presses himself into the rock, the shade not even enough to completely cover him because of the position of the sun. If I hadn't managed to grab his mask, the side of his face would be burning.

I hold my hands up and shield him the best I can. "You okay?" I ask.

He hugs me tighter. "I've been worse. You?"

"I'm okay. Shirtless with glass burning my side, but okay."

Puffing a breath through the mask, he says, "How come I can't ever get you to take off your clothes that fast at home?"

"Kingston."

"Sorry, Jewel. I joke when I'm nervous, and I'm a fucking wreck," he admits, surprising me. "Fucking Mitchell. This is his fault."

I groan. "Be quiet. He might hear you."

"I don't care!" he shouts.

Bringing up my hand to his mouth, I silence his words through the mask. Not only am I worried Mitchell will hear us, I'm afraid—

"Shit, someone's coming," Kingston whispers. "You got the dagger still?"

I touch my finger to my hip, feeling the cool metal. "Yeah."

"Give it to me."

Quietly setting me on my feet, Kingston motions me to get next to him and away from the opening of our narrow hiding place. Gravel crunches under shoes. The slow, purposeful steps indicate that whoever approaches knows we're here. They try to muffle the sound of their movements, but they underestimate a vampire's ability—my ability. It's this type of behavior that gets people attacked from the shadows in Dark Terrace Ranch. Unfortunately for whoever approaches us, Kingston's about to channel his inner shadow dweller.

Everything happens so fast. A gun fires and a bullet ricochets above my head to send fragments of rock raining down on me. A small gun falls at my feet, but I couldn't squeeze down to pick it up if I wanted to. Kingston drags a man forward into the small space with us, shoving his back into the rocks. Holding up the dagger I gave him, Kingston aims it at the man's throat, poking him hard enough to send drops of blood down his neck.

The guy snarls, darting his eyes from Kingston to me. If I were him, I'd be a sobbing, freaked-the-hell-out blubbering mess. But the man remains steady on his feet, his veins bulging as he glowers at Kingston without an ounce of fear. His hatred gives him the confidence to look Kingston straight in the eyes no matter how idiotic I find his bravery to be.

"Tell me where you're heading," Kingston asks.

The man spits in Kingston's face, making him growl.

I touch Kingston's arm to stop him from reacting. "Please, if you tell us, we'll let you go. You can run."

"Traitor to humanity," he says at me, his throat deep with fury. "Noah would be disgusted with you. Ashamed you gave up the Jordan name. And for what?"

Anger bursts through me at the mention of my dad, and it takes Kingston blocking me to stop me from raising my hand to the man. "For my family," I snap. "My dad left us. He left me in this position. And you know what? I'm fucking glad."

"Traitor," he says.

More gunfire rings through the air, and people scream out. My heart races, sending adrenaline coursing through me. The man glances toward the opening of our crevice, and I follow his gaze, watching the sun dip into the horizon.

Kingston pokes the dagger deeper, making the man's eyes widen and return to focus on him. "You have seconds to tell me. I'll stay true to my match's offer, but once the sun sets, time is up. But don't worry. I won't kill you. You'll only wish you were dead."

"Just tell him," I plead.

The man tightens his jaw, and I expect him to give in.

People do what it takes to survive. I know this.

"Babe, close your eyes!" Kingston yells.

But it's too late.

Throwing himself forward, the man forces Kingston to stab him through the neck with the dagger. Blood pours from the man as he slumps into Kingston, who quickly shoves him from the space but not before the man's blood splashes across my chest and stomach, soaking into the soft pink fabric of my bra.

I release a strangled sob, swiping at the blood, just making it worse. But I want it off of me. I want out of this crevice and away from the dead guy.

"Why did he do that?" I ask, shuddering as my stomach twists.

Kingston yanks his mask off, the sun no longer a threat to him as twilight grabs hold. He uses it to wipe off the blood from my body the best he can and then shrugs off his jacket to put on me.

"I'm sorry, Jewel. I tried to pull back but the space—"

I groan and bury my face in his neck. "It's not your fault. He came after us. I just—I don't understand." All my life I thought that people do what it takes to survive, and this man's actions go against everything I know. Everything that makes sense to me. He could have told Kingston what he wanted to know, and he would have let him go. But he didn't.

He brushes the stray strands of my hair coming out of my beanie back to look into my watery eyes. "Jewel, some people aren't about self-preservation. This man sacrificed himself to assure whatever—whoever—he's protecting gets out alive."

I search his dark eyes, taking in his puckered pout. His words make utter and perfect sense. And I realize the man isn't any different than me. Because I don't live my life in a state of self-preservation. I've lived my life in a state of sacrifice for my family. But I'm changing. Ramona saw it before I did. She's spent all her life living under the care of people who would do anything for her, who always put Ramona's needs before their own. But I stopped. I gave into my own wants and desires for my life, and she turned to people I used to be like—people who are willing to sacrifice their lives for something bigger.

Now, I don't know how I feel or what I should feel. "Kingston, I—"

More screams rip through the air, cutting off my words. The chaos kicks me into action, and I manage to wriggle free of Kingston's embrace. I slide past him, rushing to the entrance to get a better view.

I don't even get a foot out of the crevice before he yanks me back by the over-sized jacket. Spinning me around, he wraps me in his arms to hold me against him. "You can't go out there, babe. It's too dangerous."

I hit my hands on his shoulders. "It sounds like they're being massacred!"

He only squeezes me tighter. "Please, you have to trust us to handle it."

"Not like this. I have to get out there," I say, my voice hitching. A few yells cut off, the silence making me woozy. "I can fix this."

"Babe," Kingston begs, hugging me despite my struggling. "They'll try to kill you."

"I don't care!"

"Jewel, please."

Sucking in a deep breath, I yell, "Austin, Diego!" I can't help it. All I can think about is what they might be doing. I can't get my conversation with Austin from my mind and how devastated he was about ending a human's life, something I hadn't thought about until this moment, a life he seems to put above vampires. He once told me that he chose to Blood Match for that reason despite asking me to be like him with a Blood Vow.

And I'm afraid. I'm afraid tonight might change him. Change Diego and Kingston. What if this group of Blood Rebels turns them against humanity? What if they change into vampires like those on the board, like the shadow dwellers...even like Mitchell, who Diego told me loved humans—loved to be worshipped by humans. Holy shit balls.

Mitchell isn't here to stop some sort of threat against the foundation of Donor Life Corp. He's not here because he's scared of an uprising despite what my guys think about what an uprising can lead to. Mitchell is here to punish those who've turned their back on a Divine. Those who no longer idolize him, who possibly idolize another.

Kingston covers my mouth. "Babe, please. They're okay. They won't hurt anyone if they can help it. But you're going to draw more attention to us."

"I don't care. I need them. I'm scared for them. What this will do to them." I struggle to get him to let me go. "Kingston, please. Let me go. If something happens, I'll—"

Kingston releases me, his dark eyes flashing silver and lining with panic unlike anything I've seen before. I step away from him, but he doesn't allow me to exit first. He peeks his head out, making sure it's safe.

"Kingston, don't let her see," Mitchell commands.

Kingston growls, fisting his hands. "I'll not risk her never forgiving me!" he shouts.

Stepping out from behind him, I search the landscape. "Austin? Diego?"

I catch sight of them binding the hands of humans by the side of the road where our car rests askew and burnt with no glass in the windows. The two of them abandon their task and rush to me with the same expression as Kingston. They look at me like I'm the one who shatters their hearts when it's me who's trying to save them.

Before they can reach me, Mitchell materializes between us. He swings his arm and clocks Diego in the face, knocking him a dozen feet back. Austin ducks and collides into Mitchell, sending him crashing into the rocks of the cliff side. Mitchell pushes off, ramming back into Austin, knocking him off his feet.

Kingston hooks his arm around me, dragging me back. Everyone moves too quickly. The only time I see any of my guys clearly is if Mitchell manages to knock them to the ground or into something.

Something smashes into Kingston's back, sending us sprawling forward. I scream as strong hands grip my wrists and rip me away from him. I fly through the air and land in the sand, heaving a breath. Mitchell stands over me, flashing his fangs, sending fear through me.

"Stay back," he commands to my guys.

Something in Mitchell's tone makes them hesitate. Mitchell extends his arms out to me and tugs me to my feet, spinning me away from my guys and the group of people screaming and crying, still trying to get away even though they've been disarmed. I shove my hands into Mitchell's chest, pushing him back. He lets me and watches me scramble a few feet away toward my guys on the other side of the road.

I shift my gaze from them to the people, looking at each of them for my family. But they're not there. Fear steals my breath, and I can't stop myself from wailing.

"Where are they?" I scream, asking no one in particular.

Swiveling on my feet, I turn back to Mitchell. He charges me, cupping my face in his hands to lean in close. A strange sensation crawls over my skin. Fear erupts from my heart as my muscles start to relax.

All three of my guys swear at once. I never had the chance to drink their blood tonight, and it only lasts so long. I would have drunk it in the car with my dinner but...

"Jewel, do not take your eyes from mine," Mitchell says.

My fear turns into full-blown panic at the realization that

Mitchell cracks into my mind without my permission. I try to summon the strength to break his stare, but his eyes lock me in place. I can't do anything as he holds me to him close enough that I can feel his breath blowing the strands of hair spilled from my hat.

"Dad, don't," Kingston says. "Please. I'm begging you. We'll do what you want. Just don't do this to her."

Mitchell runs his finger over my cheek. "Relax, Jewel. No harm will come to you, but I need you to stay still. This must be done for your sake and the sakes of the Divine."

I manage to twitch my fingers, fighting against his mind manipulation. My guys' blood hasn't worn off completely, and I cling onto control of at least some of my body. If only Mitchell would look away. If only my guys could get to me.

"Dad, let her go," Austin says. "She doesn't need to see any of this."

"But I want her to. I want her to know what lengths I'm willing to go through to protect our place in the world. I want her so see what lengths you will go through to protect her." Mitchell twists me back toward the street with the Blood Rebels. "These people sought to corrupt your heirs. They sought to turn them against you. They won't stop."

Tears burn my eyes, and I silently plead with Kingston, Diego, and Austin to do something, anything. Because I can't. I can't even open my mouth. I can't blink away the tears blurring my eyes. I can't stop my heart from breaking as Mitchell's words burrow inside me to take root and twist around my insides, squeezing me so tightly that I struggle to breathe. If this is what my eternity becomes, I'm not sure I can face it. I'm not sure I want to be a Divine.

And all my guys see the thoughts cross my eyes. They feel them as deeply as I do.

Mitchell extends his arm to point at the car on the side of the road. "But I will stop them. I've saved your heirs. See?"

"Girls," Mitchell calls. "Sit up, please. Let Jewel get a good look at you."

Three figures appear in the backseat of the car as they all sit up higher under Mitchell's command. A baby cries out, and my heart falters as Dana adjusts Dougie from her lap and onto her shoulder. Fallon leans over her, dirt smudged on her face. Ramona glares once and turns her attention in the other direction.

I try to do everything I can to scream out at Ramona, to run from Mitchell, to do what it takes to break his control over my mind. A dozen thoughts swirl through my head, and fear suffocates me, making me convulse in Mitchell's arms. He releases me, letting me fall to my knees in the sand.

"Jewel, your heirs will be fine. I have everything under control now. The rebels will get the message that they cannot mess with your family. They cannot use them to get to you."

His words strike me to my core, igniting something dark inside me that manages to sever his control on me. I dig my fingers into the sand, turning my gaze away from my cousins to the people bound on the road.

"Do it, boys," Mitchell says from over me. "Show Jewel

what your vows entail."

None of my guys move. They stand in shock and confusion.

"This wasn't the plan," Kingston says, speaking out.

"There are other ways," Austin adds.

Diego takes a step forward. "We still need to get the information we're looking for."

Mitchell growls. "I'll extract it myself from the heir since it seems her influencer has miraculously disappeared."

My lip quivers. "Please, don't do this, Mitchell. Don't make them do this."

Kneeling down, he gets into my space, touching my shoulder. I refuse to look at him and yank my body away before he tries to lock eyes with me again. He hums lowly from his throat. "You're stronger willed than I thought, Jewel. A great asset for our family if molded correctly. But I fear it's not you my sons change. They're changing for you. Something we can't have. They must remember their place, and you must remember yours."

I sneer. "My place? My place is with them not with you. I chose them. My vow is to them!" My voice echoes through the air, and Mitchell thrusts me back.

He shoves his hand against my chest, holding me down. I struggle underneath him, his fangs flashing, his power strong enough to kill me if he chose to.

"We'll do it!" Kingston yells. "Just let her go."

Pulling away, Mitchell looks over at his sons. Kingston

drags a man to his feet, spinning him to face us. The man thrashes in his hold, and Kingston forces his head to the side, flashing his fangs. His silver eyes never meet mine, stealing the beautiful darkness I love to lose myself in.

My heart rams against my ribcage, watching as Mitchell pushes Kingston toward doing something I might never forgive myself for. Because he's doing it for me. He's willing to jeopardize himself to see to it that Mitchell doesn't manipulate the parts of me that make me who I am. The girl I thought long gone. The girl who can't sit here and do nothing. Because Jewel Jordan doesn't do what it takes to survive. I do more. I'm willing to sacrifice myself so others don't have to.

I might have taken on the Divine name, but in this moment, I realize if my dad was a Blood Rebel like people claim, then he passed down everything that made him who he was—his strength, loyalty, and fearlessness—to me. And I'll never let them go. I'll never let anyone take them from me.

Kingston yells out his anger and frustration, struggling to go through with what Mitchell claims has to be done. I glance away, bracing myself. Mitchell doesn't take his eyes away from Kingston, his incisors poking out from beneath his lips, his pleasure over pushing Kingston to bend to his demands obvious.

I take advantage of the distraction.

Scooping up sand, I jerk my hand at Mitchell and throw it in his face. I bolt from the ground, completely free from Mitchell's mind manipulation. My feet sink into the sand as I rush as fast as I can toward the street with the people. But I'm no match in speed or strength to Mitchell. I don't even get a dozen feet away.

Grabbing the back of my jacket, he lifts me off my feet and tosses me in the air. I screech as the world blurs, shocked by his actions. I close my eyes and brace for the impact that never comes. Kingston catches me in his arms, muttering a whole slew of swear words into my hair.

Diego and Austin come to our sides, surrounding us. Austin runs his hands over my body, quickly and gently, assessing me for signs of injury.

"I'm okay," I whisper. "Are you?"

"I'm going to kill him," Kingston whispers, handing me to Diego. "Protect Jewel."

I reach out and grab Kingston before he can race away. He reacts to my touch, closing the space between us. I twist in Diego's arms to cup Kingston's face. "You can't. He will kill you. I know he will. Please, Kingston."

"He's ruining everything. I don't understand," he says, his dark brows lowering on his forehead. "He's going against everything he taught us. I don't recognize him."

"It's the Blood Rebels," I whisper.

"It doesn't matte—" Screams pierce the air, cutting off Austin's words.

Another wave of fear washes over me, and I wiggle in Diego's arms. But he doesn't let me go. Both Kingston and Austin block me. Convulsions start deep in my core and shake through me the louder the screams get. I can't believe this is happening. I can't believe that what started as a rescue mission to get my cousins from Ramona turned into a massacre.

"Oh, God," I cry, hiding my face against Diego's chest. "You have to do something. He's going to go after my family."

Diego tosses me back to Kingston, and I watch as Diego and Austin run toward where Mitchell bites the throat of a woman. She doesn't move, standing as fearless and brave as the man who killed himself on Kingston's blade. The two close in on Mitchell, but he's too powerful. All it takes is a few blurry moves to knock both Austin and Diego away.

Kingston zooms us forward, drawing Mitchell's attention to us. He grabs a yelling man from the ground and tears into his shoulder, turning his shouts of anger into horrifying wails. Diego attempts to get close to Mitchell again, but he thrusts the bleeding body of the man at him, knocking him back.

Mitchell realizes the direction Kingston takes me, his eyes flashing silver.

Faster than we can move, he closes the distance to our car where my family remains. Ramona screams as Mitchell grabs her dark hair, trying to pull her out. Loud pops sound through the air, startling me. Mitchell's body jerks as someone fires a gun from a place I can't see.

Bright flashes light up the night, and a strange rumble echoes through the air. More pops ring out, and Kingston tosses me into the front seat of the car, falling on top of me, nearly squishing me with his weight.

Dana and Fallon cry from the backseat, shoved the best they can on the floor. Dougie wails his lungs out, sending another wave of panic through me.

"It's almost over," Ramona says, her voice remaining even. "Just stay down like I showed you. Hayden will get us. He promised. Just a couple more minutes. They'll leave or die."

She's talking about my guys and Mitchell.

"Ramona," I say. "How could you do this? Dana and Fallon didn't want to come. If you'd have just—"

"Fuck! You're the ones who called the Divines? Hayden's going to flip his shit. He's—" Ramona releases a low scream of frustration and takes a breath. "Whatever. It doesn't matter. We still have Jewel. Hayden was right that she couldn't turn."

"Have me?" I ask, ignoring the fact that she says the same thing as Mrs. Diggs did. Somehow, Hayden knew it. We really did only get them by surprise. "You're going to get yourself killed."

"Hayden won't allow it. He protects me unlike some people. You're lucky we need you, Jewel. We could use your asshole master too. Obviously he's not sharing the benefits with you or else his creator wouldn't have gotten in your head. But you probably like that shit."

"Babe, I'll make it quick."

Balking at Kingston's comment, I hold him tighter. "No. Stop it. She's brainwashed."

"You are, Jewel. Hayden thinks there's no help for you."

I frown. "Then what use am I? I told you I'd fix the blood

debt. Dad is still alive and even if he wasn't, you have a year."

She doesn't respond.

"Jewel," Dana says.

"Shut up, Dana," Ramona says.

"No!" she screams. "Hayden is an asshole, and I hate him. I'm not letting him do this to Jewel. Uncle Noah wouldn't want this."

"He would if he saw her," Ramona snaps.

"Wouldn't want what?"

"Hayden thinks that they can trade you for Uncle Noah," Fallon says, speaking for her sister. "That's why we have Dougie. Hayden thinks Brayla will give up her master's location for her brother and they can make a deal."

A shiver rushes down my spine.

"We won't let that happen," Kingston says. "It doesn't work like that. Trust me."

"Trust him?" a familiar voice says. "That would be the stupidest thing you could do, Jewel."

Sudden silence leaves my ears ringing. The crunch of shoes on glass and gravel breaks through the sound of the calamity my life has become. Kingston shifts up, trying to drag me out of the car, but he stiffens.

A familiar figure appears in view through the passenger's side window, and Hayden aims his gun at me. "You okay, Mona?" he asks my sister. "Dana and Fallon, you?"

"You're making a mistake," I say. "You're going to get yourself killed."

"By whom?" he points his gun at Kingston. "Him?"

With a twitch of his finger, Hayden pulls the trigger.

I can't hear anything over the sound of my piercing screams.

BRAINWASHED

KINGSTON'S BODY CRUSHES ME INTO the seat, muffling my screams. His warm blood pours over my shoulder in a hot stream. I cry, my lungs struggling to gasp in a breath, and I inhale his blood into my nose and mouth in the process, making things worse. My cousins' sobs sound louder than my own, and I listen to someone open the back door and pull them out.

I wiggle underneath Kingston, trying to free my arms. "Kingston, please," I plead. I manage to get my fingers free and squeeze his hip because it's the only part of him I can reach. "Please."

"Fuck, babe. Stop squirming." Kingston's low whisper tickles my ear. "My cock doesn't know I'm supposed to be dead."

His whisper of breath on my neck ignites a flash of relief

inside me. Freezing at his words, I focus on him, just listening and feeling the subtle sounds of his body still very much alive despite the gush of blood. His heart thuds against my back slower than mine, and his breath tickles my skin, but he doesn't move a muscle—I take that back. He flexes one bulging muscle against my thigh, and it makes me squirm again.

"Shit, Kingston," I whisper. "I thought…"

"Some asshole isn't going to kill me with one poorly aimed bullet, but it hurts like hell."

I can't stop myself from crying at his words, a rush of anger and relief racing through me. If Kingston fooled me, he fooled everyone. And the Blood Rebels want me to suffer under him because I hear them surrounding the car but no one attempts to pull Kingston off me to get me out. They're too busy strategizing and caring for their wounded.

"Jewel, I need you to be strong for me right now. I'm weak and can't move as fast, and as soon as we get the chance, we're going to run…somewhere private." His words of encouragement and playful banter manage to clear my foggy head and calm me down so I can keep my shit together. Kingston's fingers curl through mine as he risks subtly moving. The second our hands touch, I gasp a few deep breaths.

I swallow the burning in my throat, my tears still threatening to spill. "We better," I manage to say. His admission makes me push my panic away. Because Kingston needs me. His revelation about his condition digs into me to pull out my strength for him. His honesty about his vulnerability—something his brothers struggle sharing with me—reminds me of the many reasons I love him. "But first, bite me. You need blood. I'm pretty sure I'm wearing all of yours."

"I can't reach your arm."

"Doesn't have to be my arm. Just be gentle, okay?"

Unlike with Austin and Diego, Kingston doesn't argue. He whispers for me to relax the best I can and take a breath a second before his incisors pierce the sensitive skin of my neck. I release a loud-ass strangled moan that I muffle by pressing my face into the leather seat, nearly suffocating on Kingston's sticky blood pooled beneath me.

"What is wrong with you all? You can't leave her like that." It's Fallon reacting to the weird noise I made that makes Kingston softly hum as he drinks from me, sucking my neck hard enough to distract me from the fact that we're about to face a shit show.

"She deserves to suffer for being a traitor," one woman calls. "Half of us are dead because of her."

Me? Of course they blame me instead of Mitchell. Or the fact that *they* attacked *us*, initiating a fight. They basically tried to stake four powerful vampires with a fork, and they don't even realize it. I'm thankful for their carelessness in handling Kingston, but these Blood Rebels have no clue who they're dealing with. The Divines are responsible—Mitchell is responsible—for taking control of humanity in the divisions. The history of Dark Terrace Ranch shows it takes more than courage and weapons to change the world. If it were so, humans wouldn't live in places like The Boxes.

Humanity needs someone to speak on their behalf who understands them. And my guys were trying. They wanted to do it for me. But now? I don't even know if I should care. These people despised Jewel Divine, but they don't give a shit about me as Jewel Jordan either. Hayden proved it. Trading my life for someone he feels is entitled to freedom, even if that someone is my dad, shows that he doesn't care about all of humanity. He only cares about those who follow. And me? The only people I ever want to follow now are my guys. But they see to it that I lead.

Kingston kisses my neck before pressing his chin into the puncture holes in an attempt to staunch the bleeding without moving. I groan, so mixed up by the emotions flooding through me, sending my body tingling. It doesn't help that I accidentally consumed Kingston's blood, and I can already feel it rushing through my system.

"Jewel! Jewel!" Dana yells, misinterpreting the sounds I can't stop coming from me. "Please! Get her out of there. This is cruel. She was in love with him."

"She was brainwashed," Ramona snaps.

Dana takes a shuddering breath. "Brainwashed? Are you kidding me?"

"How could you do this to Jewel, Ramona?" Fallon asks. "She saved us. If she didn't Blood Match, we'd have ended up on Starlight Row. You think we're dumb or naïve, but we listened to Uncle Noah, too. Jewel was giving us a better life and you ruined it."

"We don't even want to be here!" Dana adds. "Especially not with *you.*"

"Whatever. You'll understand and thank me when you're older," my sister mutters.

"Fuck you, Ramona!"

An audible slap sounds through the air followed by a whimper, and then Fallon starts crying. I struggle under Kingston even though there's no way I could push off his weight, even if he did let me try. My choked sob morphs into a yell, and people laugh—friggin' laugh—at my suffering. At my cousins' pain as Ramona breaks their hearts. As she obliterates mine. Any ounce of mercy or regard I had toward these people drains from me like a blood spill. All I can think about is...

"Babe, I know you don't want me to kill the—"

"Do what you have to," I say, not even trying to muffle my voice.

"Did you say something, *Ms. Divine?*" Footsteps crunch as Hayden's voice sounds from behind me. I see what he's trying to do, saying my chosen name for the other rebels to hear. He thinks he's belittling me in front of them, but hearing my name gives me strength to remember that even if Mitchell tried to ruin the name I love because it belongs to my guys, that Jewel Jordan picked it. And no matter the name I choose, I'm still Jewel regardless. And every part of me is fed up and pissed off.

"Yeah, asshole," I mumble into the seat. "I said I'm going to kill you."

Hayden erupts with laughter, his voice wild and demeaning even without having to say any coherent words. A few people grunt, and Kingston's weight slides off me. He doesn't make a sound or move or anything to give himself away as they drop him to the pavement. Someone grabs my ankles, dragging me out of the car by my feet. If I didn't protect my face, I'd have hit my chin on the frame. I land on top of Kingston, my whole body tensing. He releases a low growl that no one can hear.

Grabbing me by the back of my jacket, Hayden hoists me off Kingston to drop me next to him, shoving his boot under my stomach to flip me over. Another growl sounds from my left, and I intake a sharp breath at Diego's familiar deep voice. I knew my guys were okay. I could feel it inside me, but finding out for certain is like finally getting to breathe air after being submerged underwater longer than anticipated.

Ramona stomps up to Hayden to peer down at me, her face twisting, turning her soft features ugly and unrecognizable. "Your neck."

The second the words escape her mouth, Kingston lunges. But he doesn't grab Hayden. He flies at Ramona, knocking her back a dozen feet with the sheer force of his weight and speed. They land in the sand with her on top of him as he takes the impact of the fall, using her as a shield, making the remaining humans hesitate instead of automatically firing their weapons.

"Hayden!" she screams. "Help!"

To my surprise, Hayden reaches for me instead, trying to grab my hair spilled from my hat. I lock my fingers around his wrists and dig my nails into his skin, but he doesn't let me go. Someone screams from the perimeter. A body flies and hits the car, crashing to the ground. Hayden drags me, his eyes wide and wild and dangerous. Releasing one of his hands from me, he grabs his gun and jerks it around, aiming at something moving too fast.

A figure rushes him, and he shoots. My scream pierces the air, sounding louder than even the gunfire. Fallon hits the ground next to Hayden, her body convulsing as blood stains the pavement around her.

"No!" I scream, scrambling to her side.

Hayden jumps to his feet, firing another few rounds, not even taking a second to think about what he did. Diego blurs past me after Hayden, and I beg to the universe for him to do the one thing I asked him not to.

"Jewel," Austin says, dropping to his knees at my side. "You're bleeding. How bad are you hurt?"

"Not me!" I scream. "Help Fallon. Hayden shot her."

"Find my kit," Austin instructs, putting pressure on my cousin's stomach.

Dana calls out my name, and I jerk my attention to catch sight of her holding Dougie in Mitchell Divine's arms.

"The kit, Jewel!" Austin yells. "He won't hurt Dana."

I push myself to move and scramble to the backseat of the car. Austin's medical supplies lie scattered and stomped on across the floor, and I gather up as much as my arms can and shove them in his small box.

Hurrying back to his side, I set the kit down and grab onto Fallon's bloody hand. "Hang on. Austin's got you. He's going to take care of you."

Fallon doesn't respond. Her body trembles, her eyes rolling and unable to focus. My chest heaves as I suppress a sob. I can't lose her. She's supposed to have the future Aunt Dottie imagined. She's supposed to grow up without having to know what it's like to donate blood. Or worry about where our next meal will come from. She was supposed to have the future I traded for another.

Gunshots continue to pop through the air. I bend lower, shielding both Austin and Fallon with my own body. Ramona screams and screams, her voice the only thing I can hear over the fighting.

A loud thud hits the roof of the car, and Diego rolls off and drops next to me, landing crouched on his feet. He doubles the shield over my cousin as Austin quickly works his fingers over Fallon's bloody stomach too fast for me to see.

"Hayden!" Ramona screams. "Hayden! No!"

Tires squeal over the strange rumble of something mechanical. Putrid smoke clouds the air, and I watch as two ancient-looking cars like the ones forever broken on Starlight Row speed away from us.

Fallon starts convulsing in my arms, and Austin swears under his breath. Diego moves to help Austin by holding Fallon still on the ground. Blood pours everywhere—too much blood. It gets over all of us, and no matter what Austin does, it doesn't stop.

"Austin, what's happening?" I ask.

"Diego, get Jewel out of here," he says.

Diego tries to grab me, but I elbow him hard enough to make him pause. Tears burn my eyes, and I pull Fallon into my lap. Austin drops his hands, his eyes glassing over. He stares at us without doing anything, and I take over and press my palms into Fallon's stomach.

"Austin," I cry. "I can't lose her."

"I'm sorry, Jewel," he whispers. "I don't have the right supplies."

"Give her your blood," I snap.

"Jewel, I...I can't," he says. "It's against—"

I release a loud scream, hugging Fallon tighter. She stops moving in my arms, her body slumping. My breath heaves, my eyes burning with tears so hot I'm not sure I'll ever see again. I listen to her erratic heartbeat slow. My chest hurts with my shattering heart, and I'm sure I won't survive this.

A cool hand laces around my wrist, and Austin gently tugs my arm away from Fallon. His eyes flash silver, and a frown pouts his face, reflecting my own pain back to me. He bites his arm without a word. I suck in a deep breath at the sight of his blood trickling down his skin in rivulets. Squeezing his eyes shut, he holds his arm to Fallon's lips without looking. A million emotions cross his face, and I hug my arm around him.

"Austin," I whisper. "You're breaking the rules for me."

He opens his eyes, his green eyes meeting mine. "I'll do anything for you, Jewel. Fallon's your family, which makes her part of my family."

"Our family," I whisper, touching his cheek.

Slowly pulling his arm away, he staunches the bleeding with his fingers. Diego rubs his hand over my shoulders, silently giving me his strength without saying a word. Austin takes off his jacket to remove his shirt and tears it into strips to wrap around Fallon's torso. The bleeding stops, but the wound still looks awful.

"I don't have enough synthetic skin, but this should do until we get her home," he says.

"We're taking her home?" I ask, my eyes widening.

"Yeah, beautiful," Diego says. "At least until everyone in Haven Springs has been evaluated. But we're still not sure about Ramona."

"She's going to wake up with murder on the mind," Kingston says, appearing next to us. He holds Ramona propped on his shoulder, his face poutier than ever like even touching her brings him great pain.

"Jewel, is Fallon...?" Dana's soft voice drifts over to me, and I bring my attention to her now standing beside Mitchell, holding Dougie. Mitchell silently watches us without a word, and it takes everything in me not to jump to my feet to confront him.

"She's stable," Austin says, "but I won't know more until I can evaluate her in a medical setting."

Dana takes a step away from Mitchell, glancing at him to

see if he's going to react to her moving. He remains utterly still and quiet, making me a nervous wreck. I can't read his serious expression, but I'm beyond giving a shit about what he thinks of me. Because I know exactly what I think of him, and that's what matters.

Kingston taps the trunk of the car, opening it, and I gape at him as he sets my sister in it. He meets my surprise with a raised eyebrow and shuts the trunk with a little too much purpose. It's obvious that the feelings I share for Mitchell are the same feelings Kingston shares for Ramona.

"She will be safe enough back there, and that way there is room for the rest of us, though I'm most definitely going to need you to play lapsies with me on the way home." Kingston smirks at me for a second before glancing behind me. "Will you be okay finding your way back to Dark Terrace Ranch?" he asks Mitchell under his breath, so Mitchell thinks Kingston's keeping it for vampire ears only.

"Yes, Kingston. I have quite the situation to handle since Diego let some of the Blood Rebels go," Mitchell says, keeping his response just as low as Kingston's.

Diego growls. "It was three, and I'm sorry, if it wasn't for your rash decision, we could have had all of them in our control."

Mitchell responds with silence, but the silence sounds louder than anything I've ever heard. His displeasure for his sons' actions and decisions tonight won't be let go. I'm sure we're just seeing the beginning of it.

Glancing up, I try to catch one more peek at Mitchell. His figure appears hundreds of feet away before he disappears into the dark night. Diego clears the stray glass from the car, using his jacket to soak up mine and Kingston's blood from the driver's seat. Kingston comes up behind me, wrapping his arms around me. I spin in his arms and hug him so tightly that he laughs and nuzzles his nose right above the bite he gave me on my neck.

"Need more?" I whisper.

He breathes against my skin. "Later. Alone. After a shower. In bed."

"That sounds like the best idea ever," I murmur.

"That's only the foreplay." He kisses my throat, humming against my skin.

I laugh. "Kingston."

Diego manages to start the car, and only one of the headlights blinks on, illuminating the stretch of road in front of us. I pat Kingston's cheek and stroll toward Diego to fall into his open arms. He lifts me off my feet to bring my mouth to his and kisses me sweetly.

"Ready to go home, beautiful?" he asks.

I nod. "Friggin' finally. I'm not sure I ever want to leave again."

After Diego sets me on my feet, Austin hugs me from behind. "I hope to change your mind about that," he says, spinning me around.

"Babe, I'm cool if you don't. I could survive eternity with

you in bed."

I roll my eyes. "I bet you could."

"But we want more," Diego says. "What Mitchell did tonight...it gave us some much needed perspective about how we have to prepare and handle our futures together. And he was right about you. You've changed us. But for the better. With you, we see more options."

"That's right. I know I see more than the world within my reach," Kingston adds. "Though it fucking sucks and not in a good way."

"Definitely not like you," I tease.

Kingston releases what sounds like a purr from his throat. "Damn straight."

I smile at Austin. "Or you." Turning my gaze to Diego, I add. "And definitely not as good as you."

"Way to make me feel special, babe," Kingston says, pursing his lips.

"You are," I say, grinning. "I'll show you."

"On the way home?"

"Not in front of my cousins."

"Definitely not in front of us," Diego adds.

Kingston smacks his hands together. "Fuck then. Let's go home."

Nothing has ever sounded better.

US AGAINST THE UNIVERSE

"YOU'RE ANTSY. I CAN HELP you relax." Kingston kisses my throat, working his way down my body, exploring every inch of me with his fingers. The sun glares through the tinted window of his bedroom. The sun barely rose before he insisted I needed a shower and rest under his care. If it wasn't his day, I'm sure he'd have still managed to convince his brothers to trade.

I sink deeper into my pillow. "I feel like I should be with them or waiting at your desk to see if Brayla calls back. I don't want to miss her."

"It's late. Diego's got it under control. The girls are resting. Austin is watching Dougie. Ten phone calls to Brayla is plenty. She's probably sleeping right now. And if she isn't sleeping, this seems to be the sure-fire way to get her to call. You know, since the universe is against our body match."

I laugh. "Give us a sign, Universe."

"Shhh. Stop instigating and let me take care of you," he murmurs, "and show you how much I appreciate you. Last night was rough."

"I could use some extra love and cuddles." I run my finger down his bare chest and smirk.

"And more?"

"Definitely more."

Lifting my legs faster than I can react, Kingston sneaks his way between them and cages himself in with a smile. Goosebumps travel across my skin, my body blooming with the desire Kingston awakens in me. He brushes his lips across my thigh, occasionally grazing his fangs against my skin until he reaches my lacy underwear.

With perfect precision, he tears the delicate band around my waist with his teeth, undressing me. I gasp in surprise and automatically shut my legs, trapping him. He chuckles at my reaction and gently eases out of my thighs' sudden death grip on his head to shimmy up higher to lay on top of me.

"I was only going to kiss you there," he whispers, tracing his finger down my stomach to touch between my thighs. "Is that okay?"

"I—" Ah, hell. My nerves make it hard to spit out anything coherent. "I don't know. Um, I—"

"We'll take it slow," he says, brushing the hair from my face. "I don't mind. I enjoy every second with you no matter what we're doing."

I rub my lips together, trying to slow my racing heart and suppress my nerves. It's not that I want to take it slow. I was just surprised, and when I'm surprised, I get flustered. With Kingston, it seems to be a constant state of wanting to cross all the boundaries and explore every level of a relationship together. And now, I want to let him touch and taste and know me as his perfect body match. I want to get carried away and to forget the world still spins outside us. I need to forget.

He rests his forehead to my temple. "I know this probably isn't the right time anyway. I just—after feeling like one of us was going to die and we'd never get to experience something that I know will be amazing—"

I shut him up with a kiss and reach down to lace my fingers around the raging boner I gave him—his words, not mine—the second I came out of the shower in lingerie from my wardrobe. Kingston reacts with furious passion, forgetting any notion of what slow means, and I hungrily accept his roaming fingers working over me in a way that makes me moan into his shoulder.

Indescribable sensations ignite through every part of me, heating my skin. Kingston whispers my name into my hair, flicking his tongue over my neck as he explores my skin with his mouth. The feeling of his teeth just grazing my neck pushes me to a new level with Kingston I never want to return from. His hands roam over my legs and up my torso to cup my breasts through my bra, which he quickly unfastens. He takes his time to familiarize himself with my body, making it hard for me to stay still as I grind against him. Fumbling my hands around, most definitely not as softly or expertly as Kingston, I rush to map all of him and relish how even though I'm still figuring things out, he reacts with murmurs and moans and breaths of pleasure all the same.

"I'm ready," I whisper, making him slow down. "I mean, if you want to or we can mess around and wait for the universe to object."

Chuckling, he meets my gaze with his dark eyes. "Are you sure?"

I nod, channeling my best Kingston impression. "One hundred sexy, undeniable, perfect percent body match sure. I love you, dude—Kingston."

Smiling, he kisses me deeper, brushing his tongue over mine, his breathing quickening to match my gasps. And then I feel him between my legs, the pressure building with my desire. I clutch onto Kingston, digging my fingers into the muscles of his taut back, ultra-aware of what's about to happen, something I've imagined a dozen times over the weeks since the first time he teased me about wanting my body.

"I love you, Jewel," he whispers, my name sounding sultry coming from his pouty, full lips. "But don't forget. Romantic comedy."

Kingston cuts off my breathless laugh with another kiss, and I lose myself to him in the best possible way—to his touch and kisses that leave my whole body shuddering and gasping, exploding with love and lust and everything that takes me to what feels like the edge of nowhere and everywhere.

I feel so out of control yet safe in his embrace. He takes his time to discover what I like, and my loud mouth yells his success in the most embarrassing way. He grins and guides me, only laughing once when I accidentally knock my head into his chin trying to crane my neck to bury my face in the pillow. He showers me with all his love, letting me swim in the incredible emotions and feelings he elicits with the sweet words he whispers into my hair about how amazing and beautiful I am and how perfect we are together.

Kingston cuddles with me for a long while after, our legs entangled, his arms so strong yet gentle as he holds me close with no space between us. And even when he shifts to lie next to me, he laces our fingers together between our heaving chests, our faces still close enough to kiss. He smiles for the gazillionth time, leaning in even more so he is all I see.

"You okay?" he asks, sucking his lip between his teeth. "Be honest...but not too honest. Because this was better than I could have ever imagined."

I nod and smile. "It was more romantic than comedy. Next time I'll have to accidentally knock you off the bed."

He laughs so loudly that he surprises himself, and he covers his mouth with his hand. I bow forward and kiss the back of his fingers until he meets me for a kiss, releasing a sound like a cross between a hum and moan.

"And of course now the universe sends the intervention

squad," he murmurs, playing with my hair spilling around us.

Soft footsteps sound from the hall, and someone taps on the door. "Technically it wasn't the universe to send us, but Mitchell's close enough. Not sorry about our perfect timing."

"Mitchell?" I groan. He's the last person I want to think about.

"Yeah, it's about Ramona," Diego says, his muffled voice sounding through the door a second before it swings open. "And I'm really not sorry about interrupting—"

Kingston quickly pulls the covers up and growls. "Out. We need a minute."

Austin groans. "Not perfect timing, Diego. Terrible timing."

Diego frowns. "I'm sorry, Jewel. I thought because you responded—"

I grab Kingston's hand before he flies from the bed naked to chase his brothers out and say, "It's fine. I've been anxious about all this." I shift to look at Kingston.

"And I'm helping her relax, but you're ruining it," he says, reaching for the remote on his nightstand to turn off the music humming in from the hall.

I knock my elbow into him. "Don't listen to him. We were about to get dressed. You guys aren't ruining anything." Turning to Kingston, I meet his annoyed expression, burning daggers at his brothers who give nothing away. We all know if their places were swapped, Kingston would totally be okay with interrupting. "Nothing can ruin this," I whisper to him, leaning in to kiss him.

He heaves a sigh and stops glaring. "Maybe not them but Mitchell."

"The board wants to meet your family and assess your sister," Diego says. "But don't worry. We will insist she...gets her mind wiped and sent home."

I cover my face with my hands, still too caught up on Kingston and our incredible moment to want to deal with this. So I don't respond. All I do is wrap the comforter around me and leave Kingston to fend for himself with the sheets. He doesn't even bother covering up to follow me into the wardrobe. Diego and Austin instantly turn around, and I can hear them whispering to each other but too quietly to hear over the pounding of my heart.

"So when do we have to leave?" I call. "I want to be there."

Austin clears his throat. "I was thinking it—"

"Let Kingston handle this," I hear Diego whisper to Austin, barely loud enough for me to hear. "How about we talk about this in a few minutes, beautiful? We'll wait outside."

I frown, listening to the door click closed before I can respond.

Kingston slides his arms around me, stopping me from rushing to get dressed to follow them and find out more about what all of this means. "One of them can handle this. Or I can handle this if you insist it be me. They just wanted to keep you informed about what's going to happen."

I shake my head. "I don't want to be informed. I want to

be involved. If the board wants to meet my family, I need to go. Ramona...I need to be there."

"I just don't want you having to deal with this, babe. I'd rather snuggle you for the rest of the day and our night and make sure nothing can—"

I cut off his nervous rambling with a kiss. I might have given my virginity to Kingston today, but he still gave himself to me, and I can already sense it changed our relationship for the better. He's worried something will mess it up, but I won't let it. It's these perfect moments that keep me going and staying strong. It's moments like these with my guys that cement our lives together. These incredible moments are the last threads of anything certain in my life, and I'll protect them with my very being. "We're supposed to do this together, remember? It's going to be fine. I'll not remember this night as...what was all that stuff you were trying to distract me from again?" I ask with a lightness to my voice that makes him smile. "Because all I can remember is you—"

"Deflowering you?"

I scrunch my face. "Dude."

"Poppin' your—"

I cover his mouth with my hand. "Don't you even think about finishing that line."

He licks my palm until I relent and drop my hand to let him speak. Reaching up, he brushes my hair behind my ear and leans in to kiss me. "Showing you how much I love and appreciate you while making you the happiest person in existence?"

I laugh. "That's better."

"And I'll remember it as the best day of my eternity. But only the first of many."

"I hope so."

"I know so."

Diego stands in the hall outside of Kingston's room when we emerge. I pinch Kingston's side to get him to keep himself in check, because I'm pretty sure if I allowed it, he'd shout to the world that we had sex. Diego eyes his brother with an unreadable expression, and we all ignore the obvious.

"I'm sorry again, beautiful," Diego says, keeping his hands in his pockets. "I didn't mean to let Mitchell mess up your day."

I reach out and squeeze Diego's shoulder before sliding my hand up to touch his cheek. "Nothing was messed up. I'm glad you told me now instead of waiting until sundown. Don't let Kingston make you think otherwise either." I eye Kingston. "Everything is fine. Right, Kingston?"

Kingston turns his attention away from me for the first time. "Yeah, everything is fucking awesome, Diego. Next time I'll just turn up the music even louder."

Diego groans and shakes his head. "Now it makes sense."

"Music?" I ask.

Kingston smirks. "Hallway surround sound."

Blowing out a breath, I playfully nudge Kingston's shoulder. "Fuck. Me. This is awkward."

Diego laughs. "There won't be anything awkward if we ever—"

Kingston punches his brother, sending him back. I slide past them and open the door to my old room, knowing that it's probably better to just ignore them than intervene. Machines beep in a rhythmic pattern, easing some of the anxiety suddenly rolling through me.

Austin double checks the machine hooked to Fallon, assuring she's healing and working through his vampire blood. Dana snuggles close to her sister, fast asleep. I shift my gaze to my sitting room and try not to cry at the sight of Ramona. She remains sedated on the lounge chair with an IV stuck into her hand until she can also work through the vampire blood she consumed with Hayden, something I learned she was well aware of.

I sit on the end of the bed and touch each of my cousins' feet through the comforter. "Everything still okay?"

"Yeah, Fallon will be good enough to travel but will still need time to heal. I hope you don't mind that I gave Dana something to help her sleep. She kept waking up to check on her sister," Austin says, perching on the bed beside me. He turns his gaze to me. "I also caught her hovering over Ramona. She's pretty upset with her."

I purse my lips. "Who isn't?"

"Yet you still won't let us handle her," Kingston says, coming inside.

He shares a look with Austin and Diego, and they both turn to me. They could easily band together and decide for me since I'm outnumbered, but all they do is try to use their damn pouty faces to try to get me to side with them. But I can use their own trick against them.

I slump my shoulders. "If you are all seriously against this, then I'll do what you want and stay here. Majority rules in this type of thing."

Austin touches my knee. "Jewel, it's not—"

Flying up beside me, Kingston picks me off the bed and slings me on his shoulder. "Nope, Jewel says we get what we want so it's settled. Call us if it's an emergency."

Diego blocks our way. "Majority rules in Jewel's favor, Kingston."

"You'd rather drag Jewel in front of the board than let me fulfill her every desire? If it was your night, I'd still agree that she shouldn't—"

I run my fingers down his back to squeeze his butt. "Kingston, what if I spend an extra day with you since you're giving up your night again…if that's okay with Austin."

"Actually," Austin says.

I frown at Austin upside down. "I'm sorry. I didn't mean to assume—"

Flipping me off his shoulder, Kingston sets me back on my feet and strolls to the wall to lean against it. Holy shit balls did I not know how ridiculously pouty all my guys could be. Only Diego remains semi-expressionless.

Again, my guys share a look with each other, but this one is loads different from the last. It feels less about me and more about each other. And from their steely expressions, I'll get slapped with a bro-code or some bullshit like with their rule about minding whose night it is or whose room I'm in. But now? Standing in my old room? It's uncharted and undefined territory. Technically, it's neutral and mine even if I don't come in here.

I huff a breath and swing my finger to point at each of them. "Whatever this is needs to get knocked down a notch. I know it's been a tense few days, and I'm well aware of your opinions about my sister and Mitchell and the board for that matter, but I need each of you to please try your best to just be here for me. That's all I need right now. Not more rules or double the protection. I just want each of you to be here."

The three of them surround me so quickly that I startle. Kingston hugs me first, rocking me in his arms for a minute before easing back like it's painful for him to allow space between us. Diego hugs me next and kisses me, meeting my eyes with his gray ones. He bobs his head without saying anything, just letting me know he heard me and assures he's here for me.

Austin opens his arms for me, but Dougie starts crying from the portable crib he brought from the staff housing. I knew that the humans of the Divinity Estate created families, but I haven't seen a single child around, which means they're well protected.

Beating me to the crib, Austin picks up the little guy in his arms to cradle him. Any normal human from Dark Terrace Ranch would freak the hell out to see a vampire with an infant, but Austin's whole face lights up as he talks to Dougie like a tiny adult, asking him questions he knows he won't respond to. I smile, watching him bounce around in place until Dougie settles down and closes his eyes. But Austin doesn't set him down. He just holds him and continues to rock him back and forth.

"You didn't have to do that," I say, stepping closer to curl my fingers over Austin's shoulder to peer down at Dougie. "I'm here. I can handle him."

"You hold him like he's going to explode at any second," he teases.

I crinkle my nose. "He might."

He laughs, leaning in to kiss my cheek. "You sound like Kingston and Diego."

Kingston raises an eyebrow, staying a few feet away. "Not gonna lie. Seeing you like that weirds me the hell out. You look way too natural holding that thing, Austin."

"*Thing*? Really, Kingston?" I ask.

Diego punches Kingston in the arm, clearly aware that his brother might've accidentally offended me, though I'm not bothered by Kingston's words. "Not cool. You make it sound like he's not a human." Even living in The Boxes and seeing Dougie grow, the idea of kids freaks me out because all I can ever think about is increasing the donor population, especially after the ban on contraception.

"Well, he only looks like a fraction of one. Like a lump with limbs. Not to mention the perplexing amounts of body fluid. The only one I like seeing drool is Jewel when she—"

I groan. "Kingston."

"I was going to say sleep."

"Ew. That doesn't make it any better."

Kingston flies a few feet away as Diego tries to clock him again, and he spins out of Diego's reach. Austin steps back and turns around to make sure he and Dougie don't get trapped in the crossfire if Kingston decides to retaliate.

I slide up behind Diego and hug him, wiggling my way under his arm. "It's fine, Diego. He's just teasing. At least he didn't call Dougie a future donor."

Kingston purses his lips. "I'd never...say something like that ever again. But we should think about attempting to contact Brayla again to get him out of here before you start getting unconventional and impossibly weird ideas. And if we can't, with the lockdown, we might have to go back to Haven Springs."

I laugh and frown. "Wait. Back up. Weird ideas?"

"You know. Tiny humans. Since we've...it's just better we get him home before you start experiencing desires I'm incapable of fulfilling," he says. "I don't want to be a letdown."

Holy shit balls. He did not just go there after we had sex. That was a place I knew we'd never have to go. "You don't have to worry about me ever wanting to procreate with you, dude," I tease. "One of you is enough."

"Ouch, babe."

Kingston's phone chimes from his pajama pants, and he pulls it out and mutters something about speaking of some devil. He excuses himself from the room, closing the door behind him. Worry scrunches my brows as I stare at the door, zoning in to try to hear his conversation. I fear it might be Mitchell wanting to discuss my sister.

"Where's Jewel?" Brayla's voice echoes from the hallway. "I've been waiting weeks to talk to her. Orlando was right about how some vampires are overly possessive. I didn't think you guys were like that but—"

"Did you say Jewel, Brayla?"

My heart falters, my whole body cooling at the familiar masculine voice that erupts over the line and drifts to me. Diego notices my reaction and spins me around in his arms to search my face, but all I can do is open and close my mouth. My throat locks up tight, refusing to let me even breathe.

"Hold on, Brayla," Kingston says. "Jewel will be here in a second. Is that Orlando you're talking to? Can you put him on the line? We'd like to arrange transportation and an added bonus for your heirs. There was a slight problem."

I try to step forward to get to the door, but Diego shakes his head.

Brayla huffs loudly. I can imagine her rolling her eyes with the familiar gesture. "The only problem I have right now is that my best friend called me, and you aren't putting her on the phone. I miss her terribly. Orlando promised me that he'd arrange a visit for her but you weren't interested. He said—"

"Brayla," I call, finally managing to find my voice.

I can hear Kingston leave, his footsteps disappearing along

with the whine of her voice. I don't give Diego the chance to convince me to stay with him and Austin and instead hold my finger up to him with narrowed eyes, silently daring him to stop me. He doesn't. And Austin only sets Dougie back into his crib to follow me and Diego out.

Kingston's muffled conversation sounds through his door, and he asks to speak to Orlando again, but Brayla ignores him and asks for me.

So I call her name.

"Jewel? Jewel where are you?" Brayla asks, responding to my call to her.

I hug myself for a second, gathering my nerve. It's been weeks since I've seen her, and I'm scared to see the condition Orlando keeps her in under his care. "I'll be there in a second."

I automatically grab for Austin and Diego's hands, holding one of theirs in each of mine. I've wanted this moment since Orlando took Brayla from the Blood Match Center, but I'm losing my nerve. Something makes me hesitate, and a strange noise coming through the line doesn't help. Sounding familiar but off.

"Brayla," Kingston says, taking advantage of me lingering in the hall. "Can you please just put Orlando on the line while you wait for Jewel?"

She sighs. "He's not here right now."

"So who are you with?" he asks.

Another moan sounds through the speaker to resonate through the door. "It's a surprise for Jewel."

"Brayla," a soft masculine voice says. "Please. Don't do this. I am managing fine. She doesn't need to see me."

Stepping through the doorway, I shuffle a few feet to where Kingston projects Brayla's video feed across the wall so all of us are in her view. She smiles the biggest smile, looking so pretty with perfectly styled hair, sparkling jewelry, and a dress that accentuates her cleavage.

"Jewel!" she screeches. "You look like...you've been having fun with your boy toys."

Heat burns my cheeks, but I don't let Diego and Austin go until they release me first and Kingston closes the space beside me, standing rigid and protective though Brayla would never hurt me and couldn't even do something like that through the line. "I actually just woke up, so no. Not really," I say.

She hums under her breath. "Whatever. Glad to see you're sleeping as great as me. But I'm fucking mad at you. You promised we'd stay in touch."

"Ramona never gave me your letters," I blurt. "She's got involved in..." I let my voice trail off. I don't know what to say.

"Something dangerous," Austin says for me. "Which is why we're reaching out to you. We need permission to arrange transport for your brother."

She frowns. "I was worried my mom would struggle to care for him without me. Why don't you let Jewel bring him to me when she comes."

I frown at her words. Something sounds incredibly off in her voice. "Brayla, I'm not sure when that will be. We have a lot of things to take care of right now, but as soon as I can, we'll schedule something."

She grimaces at me, slumping her shoulders. "But Jewel. I had everything arranged. Orlando promised me soon. I even have a surprise for you." Leaning forward, she messes with her camera and spins it through the room.

I was scared the voice was just a figment of my imagination, but my dad sits on a cot with a chain anchoring him to a wall. My heart picks up pace as he shifts away from me, not letting me get a good look at his face. But he looks well enough. As strong as I remember and no skinnier. His dirty clothes have seen better days, but he doesn't appear to have been hurt.

"Dad," I say. "Dad, please look at me. Tell me you're okay."

Brayla turns the camera back to herself, giving us an extra close up. She smiles at me again, something strange in her eyes I've never seen before.

I shift my gaze to look at my guys. "Do you think Orlando manipulated her mind?" I whisper too quietly for Brayla to hear.

Austin shakes his head. "Jewel, she…"

"Fuck," Kingston says, swearing next to me.

"Hang up," Diego says. "Hang up now."

Brayla smirks, tilting her head. "Oh, come on you guys. I've missed my best friend. You can't keep her from me forever."

I blink a few times, realizing she heard us at a tone no human can hear. And then I spot the glittering onyx pendant on her neck in the shape of a bird, a small vial of blood dangling from its gold beak.

"Brayla," I whisper. "A Blood Vow?"

She smiles, flashing her fangs at me. "Why do you think I was reaching out to you, Jewel? I wanted you to know so we could celebrate."

"Why would he do this?" I ask, turning to my guys.

"He loves me," Brayla says, answering a question my guys wouldn't be able to. "Our Blood Match was never about my blood. He already has a personal supply, but we agreed he could do better. And I've missed you, Jewel. I want you to join me. It'll be better than old times."

"What?"

All three of my guys growl at the same time. Kingston pulls me back, turning me from Brayla's view. She groans, calling my name again, but my head spins, my mind whirling with her words over and over again.

"This explains how Orlando managed to pull Brayla from the system," Kingston says. "I should've seen it sooner. Looked harder."

"Don't, Kingston. You know we had more to worry about," Diego murmurs.

"They can't keep us apart, Jewel!" Brayla yells, stealing my attention from my guys. "Orlando said so. He said all we had to wait on was your father. But you know what? We don't. I'm tired of waiting. I've missed you."

Panic rushes through me, and I smack my hands against Kingston until he lets me go. I snatch the phone he handed to Austin and hold it up to meet Brayla's flashing silver eyes. She grins at me again, tracing her finger over her camera in circles like she can get to me.

"Brayla, please," I say. "I've made my own Blood Vow. We can visit soon."

"To which one of your boy toys?" she asks.

I don't respond.

She raises her eyebrows. "All of them? Wow. I always knew you were tough. It's why Orlando likes you. He's going to be so happy when I make this happen."

"Brayla."

She drops the camera onto something, giving me a view of the room. "Say bye to Jewel, Mr. Jordan. None of this would have happened without you."

"Brayla!" I scream.

She glances once at me and extends her fangs. Without another word, she races to my dad and lifts him off the cot.

And then she bites him.

Snatching the phone from me, Kingston chucks it at the wall and shatters the device into pieces. All three of my guys engulf me in their arms, smothering me so tightly that I can't even gasp in a breath to cry. Numbness steals my fear and panic, leaving me in a state of shock. I can't believe this happened. I don't even know what it means.

"Beautiful, I'm so sorry," Diego says.

"I should've recognized what Orlando did immediately," Kingston adds. "If I had known, I'd have warned you."

Austin rubs his hand down his face, smoothing out the worry lines puckering his brow. He inhales a long breath, just holding my hand without saying a word. But his silence gives away everything. This is bad. Worse than bad. It's friggin' awful.

He motions for me to sit on the edge of the bed and plops down next to me. Kingston sits on my other side with Diego in front, cupping my knees.

"Jewel, I have to warn you. That bite—"

"It was a kill bite," I murmur. "You don't have to tell me. I'm no stranger to them."

"I'm sorry," Austin whispers.

I shrug. I don't even know how to feel. I'm just numb. "You don't need to apologize to me. This wasn't any of your faults. My dad—he made a decision. He accepted a blood debt, knowing that it could pass to me. I just wish I knew what he was thinking. Or what was so important. We were surviving in The Boxes. But he wanted more and the price didn't matter. *I* didn't matter. Now look at this mess."

"It's going to be okay, beautiful," Diego says. "Brayla won't get what she wants. We won't let it happen."

My lip quivers as I hear his words but know that no matter how much they don't want to let it happen, that it will happen. Because I'm afraid.

I shake my head. "I'm not letting Ramona take on the

debt."

"Jewel," all three of them say.

Tears burn my eyes. "Brayla doesn't want her. The second Ramona ends up in Orlando's hands, she's dead. She'll work through my family to get to me."

"We have time to figure this out," Kingston says. "Ramona isn't old enough to inherit it."

I sigh and rest my head on his shoulder. "But I want to be realistic. Her birthday will come before we meet with the board again about our matches. It'll come before we perform our vows. If we can even do so."

Austin gets to his feet and slams his fist into the wall. "Jewel, no. I'm not losing you. *We're* not losing you."

Tears drip down my cheeks as everything sinks in, Brayla and my dad flashing over and over again in my mind. I try my best to push it away, to think about something else, but all I can think about is how Kingston was right about everything being against us.

"I might not even have forever," I whisper. "The universe is against us."

"Fuck, babe. You think that will stop us? I've seen you in action. I know you're badass and can fight."

"And we sure as hell will fight, beautiful."

"We'll do anything for you," Austin says.

Kingston hugs me. "Always."

I nod, hugging all three of them the best I can. "Us against the universe doesn't sound so bad when you put it like that."

Their words are the only thing keeping me together when all I want to do is fall apart. But they're right. The world could be against us, but my guys are powerful. They have a lot of fight. A lot to fight for. And so do I.

We'll fight together.

Nothing will tear us apart.

EPILOGUE

THE DIVINE FUTURE

COOL AIR GUSTS OVER ME from the open door of the board room of the Blood Match Center. Dana carries Dougie in her arms, and I keep my arm around Fallon, helping her take slow steps into the last place I ever wanted them to be—in front of a table of vampires, all fang-happy and dripping with annoyance by our presences.

Ramona screeches from behind me, and Diego carries her inside with Kingston and Austin behind him. I would have preferred to keep her sedated, but the board insisted my sister be coherent and able to listen to instructions.

In other words...

The red-headed vampire, the pretty woman I hate that I

recognize immediately, glides inhumanly fast to stand in front of Ramona. She cups my sister's face, digging her nails into Ramona's cheeks deep enough to get her to freeze but not hard enough to hurt her. I tense and take a step forward, but Austin cuts me off, taking me into his arms.

He brushes his lips to my ears. "Viorica won't hurt her, Jewel. She's not Mitchell. She won't mess with her emotions."

"Ms. Jordan. Do not look away from me," the red-head commands, capturing my sister in her stare. "You will sit down on the chair over there and remain quiet. Only speak when spoken to until I say otherwise."

Ramona stops fighting, and Diego sets her on her feet. Without a word, Ramona shuffles across the grand room and sinks into the closest chair. Austin motions me to take my cousins to the same spot, and I quietly sit down and hug an arm around each of my cousins on the loveseat. Austin, Diego, and Kingston glide to the head of the long table, facing the board without asking me to join them. But this isn't about me. It's about my family and what happens next.

Mitchell materializes seemingly from thin air, but I catch sight of the now open door to a well-lit office. He flicks his gaze to mine, and I try my best to keep my face expressionless. All I want is for the board to approve my family's return to Haven Springs with a guarantee that they'll have personal protection against any Blood Rebels—but especially Hayden—if he ever tries to return to the human-only community.

"We have found and relocated thirty unruly humans from

Haven Springs," a man on the end of the table says. "Fortunately for Jewel's heirs, none of them implicated Jewel's next of kin in being involved with the revolt of our hand-selected council."

I release a deep breath, and the guy turns his attention to me for a moment before focusing on the documents in front of him.

"So, after quick consideration, we'd decided to grant the Jordan heirs permission to return to their residency under the stipulation Mitchell outlined for Ms. Ramona Jordan. They will also be under surveillance like the rest of the community," he adds, looking up from the stack of papers.

"And what of the new regulations?" Diego asks, knowing the thought was going to cross my mind before it actually did. And I'm thankful he knows me well enough to accurately predict what I'll do or say.

Viorica taps her fingers on the table. "The exemptions will remain intact but benefits may now be sanctioned, suspended, or even revoked if it's determined that an exempt is trying to use the community as anything other than how we intended."

My guys look to me to see my reaction. I nod my approval. Because it could've been worse. A lot worse. This whole situation is better than I could have ever hoped for. I was planning for the worst.

"All we need is all of your signatures for the new beneficiary contracts, and you may arrange for transportation for the Jordans," Viorica says, sliding a pen to Diego first.

Austin signs next and hands the pen to Kingston. "And

what of the Diggs' child? The Ortega file was deleted from the system without Kingston's authority."

"Kingston—all of you—were on a leave of absence, so it was passed along to the board for review. Contracts are confidential, and you three are still only on call," Mitchell says, speaking up. "But not to worry. Ms. Ortega informed us that she'd be arriving this evening."

"She's coming here?" I ask. I can't stop myself.

A light on the wall flashes on, and Viorica hits a button on the table, purposely ignoring my question. Instead, she answers the private call and turns to my guys. She motions for them to lean closer, and fear sends goosebumps sprouting across my body.

"It seems Mr. Ortega has come alone to collect the child. Will you please assure your match that he is in safe hands? Mitchell informed us of her sometimes outlandish and rash reactions."

It takes everything in me not to scream and respond to words I'm not supposed to hear. I automatically slide my arm over Dana's leg and touch my hand to Dougie's back. They're crazy if they think I'm letting this little guy go into arms that belong to someone I don't trust.

Austin closes the space to me. "Stay calm. We'll handle this."

He takes Dougie from Dana and cradles him in his arms, giving me a serious look that promises me that he'll protect Dougie no matter what.

A buzzer rings on the door, and I stiffen, hearing the low mumble of a voice that yanks out all sorts of bad shit from me. I nearly burst out crying before Orlando even enters the room. If it wasn't for Diego coming to my side to grab me and pull me into his arms, I'd have a full on melt down in front of a bunch of annoyed vampires. But I have to keep it together. None of us are supposed to know about Orlando. We've technically only formally met him once.

Orlando doesn't even glance in our direction, keeping his attention solely on the board, who welcomes him like he's as elite as they are. And he probably is. Only Mitchell shows clear dissatisfaction from his spot near the wall, overseeing but not participating more than offering an occasional nod to show his approval.

Orlando pulls an envelope from his pocket and sets it in front of Viorica and the rest of the board, finally drawing his attention in my direction. Trembles start deep in my core and work their way to the rest of me. Diego and Austin close the space to step in front of me and Kingston, blocking the vampire's view of me, one he looks like he's greatly appreciative to see.

"I'm sorry, Mr. Ortega. This cannot be processed. Participants in our Blood Match Program are exempt from all inherited blood debts."

Shit's getting real. I knew the possibility that Orlando would announce the debt to the world now that Brayla... I push the images of my dad from my mind.

Kingston growls first, cutting off all the spinning thoughts in my mind, and I snuggle into him, practically hiding myself in his jacket. I brace for a full-on vampire battle. My guys will tear Orlando apart if he even tries to come within feet of me.

"What is this about?" Kingston says, faking his astonishment.

Viorica glances our way. "It seems Mr. Ortega believes he has a right to a blood debt with the Jordans." She glances at me. "I assume you knew, Jewel, and entered the program for this reason."

I shake my head. "I—"

"It doesn't matter," Diego says.

Viorica glances at the other board members and Mitchell. "You are right. Mr. Ortega, I'm sorry. You will have to wait until the next Jordan kin comes of age, and then you can petition to nullify her exemption from Haven Springs," she says, turning to her files. "In ten months."

My breathing quickens, and Kingston holds me tighter. Diego takes my hand. I've never been more relieved in my life that they take their rules seriously as part of their way to maintain power and order. It means we still have time.

Orlando reaches into his pocket and pulls out another envelope.

What the actual hell? He smirks at me from his spot, his blue eyes crinkling in the corners to show his amusement in this emotional torture he inflicts on me. My knees wobble as I watch Viorica's annoyed face shift to confusion. She jerks her head to look at Mitchell, and he comes over and looks over the same paper.

"Ms. Divine, a word please," Viorica says.

Diego practically carries me the dozen feet to the table. The second I see the sheets of paper—especially the one with the bloody handprint—I nearly pass out. It's the petition that Hayden attempted to get me to sign in Haven Springs. The same papers that declared that my matches breached their contracts in the worst ways possible. A paper I didn't sign, but now that I look at it, someone else filled it in with my signature.

"That's not my signature," I snap, looking at Ramona. "Someone else put my name there."

Viorica hums, following my line of sight. "I see. So you confirm that you did not sign these nor have any intentions of signing them?"

I snatch the papers and tear them up, my anger giving me the bravery to throw the shreds into Orlando's face. "Yes. They are crazy allegations that Blood Rebels attempted to get me to sign by threatening my life. Their leader wanted to negotiate the release of my father to hand me in his place."

Orlando clears his throat and frowns. "I apologize, Ms. Divine. I had no idea. I'm also sorry to inform you that Noah Jordan has met his final donation."

I squeeze my eyes shut, trying not to cry. I knew Brayla took a kill bite, but a part of me was hoping it not to be true. I was hoping there was a chance that I could see my dad. Save him.

"You fucking monster," I whisper. "I'm going to—"

Kingston tugs me away, covering my mouth with his hand. I struggle for a moment until I hear Orlando say he would like my petition to be evaluated more closely.

"I'd like the board to deny Jewel Jordan's Blood Vow application," he says, shocking me. "It is still my belief that she purposely applied for a Blood Match to get out of her inherited debt. I will graciously pay for all fees and accumulated costs the Divines put toward their matching process."

"What!" I screech.

He doesn't look at me. "It is my right to collect on a blood debt."

Mitchell flies forward and slams his hands on the tabletop. "Denied! You will not come into my territory and attempt to steal the future of my sons based on loose interpretations of the law and unfounded allegations against Ms. Divine."

Orlando stiffens but doesn't react. Reaching into his jacket once more, he pulls out another envelope. "Then I'd like to petition to revoke Ramona Jordan's exemption to fulfill Jewel's place. I can assure the debt will not be paid until her eighteenth birthday but forgive me if I don't want to risk something happening to my personal blood source before the time comes where I can legally collect."

Shadows edge my vision, because no one speaks up. No one automatically denies him. They do something worse. They nod and begin to sign his document without looking at me.

"Wait!" I scream. "Wait. I'll go. I'll do it."

"No!" Kingston, Austin, and Diego all yell at the same time.

I yank myself away from them and run across the room toward Orlando. I can't let this happen. I can't let Ramona take my place. She'll be killed. I just know it. Whatever hang up Orlando has for me, he's not going to let it go so easily.

I refuse to stand by and just wait. If I go, I can figure things out. Figure out how to end this.

"Please," I cry. "If I have to breach—"

Mitchell steps between me and Orlando, covering my mouth with his hand. He shakes his head and nudges me back.

Kingston hooks his hands around my waist. "Please, Jewel. Don't say anything. It's not going to work. All it will do is jeopardize everything we have. I'm begging you."

"She's my family," I say, crying.

"We're your family too," he says.

Austin steps in closer. "We made each other a vow."

Diego leans into me. "And we swear we'll fight and get her back."

The board gets to their feet and shakes Orlando's hand. "Your petition has been approved, Mr. Ortega. We release Ms. Jordan and your match's heir to you." They turn to my guys. "Mr. Divines, we must ask that you sign to nullify the Jordan heir's contract."

Dana and Fallon remain utterly quiet on the seat behind me, and I turn to look at them. Tears burn streaks down their faces, and I rush from Kingston and hug them, whispering that everything would be okay.

"Jewel, don't blame yourself," Dana says. "This was Uncle Noah."

But it wasn't all him. It was me. I failed Ramona. I failed to see to it that she lives the life I traded away. And now? I don't even know.

Orlando crosses the room to my sister, and it takes Fallon clutching my hand to stop me from jumping onto his back to try to murder him with my bare hands. My stomach twists. Orlando bends and captures Ramona in his stare, whispering for her to remain calm, hold Dougie, and to follow him.

Ramona gets to her feet, silently takes Dougie, and turns her gaze to me.

Orlando touches her shoulder and nudges her toward me. "Anything you'd like to tell Jewel before we go?"

Ramona's eyes narrow. "I hate you! I hope they rip you apart! You f—"

Orlando covers her mouth. "That's not quite what I expected. Why don't you tell Jewel goodbye."

Ramona snarls. "Goodbye, Jewel."

With a once over to me, Orlando adds. "I'm sure we still might see each other around."

I drop to my knees, but never hit the floor. Austin picks me up and hugs me against him. Silence falls around the room, and I realize I'm alone with my cousins and my guys. The board and Mitchell have left. So has Orlando.

And Ramona.

"I'm sorry, Jewel," Austin whispers, brushing his fingers through my hair to rub my back. "It's going to be okay. Ramona is strong. We'll make sure he stays true to his contract."

"His contract," I whisper. "What I don't get is how he got mine."

"Fuck," Kingston says.

"You don't think..." Austin lets his voice trail off.

Diego grabs up the scattered pieces of the contract I tore up and threw at Orlando. "Shit. This is the exact one from Haven Springs."

"Hayden. It was Hayden," I whisper. "Orlando's a Blood Rebel."

"This isn't good," Kingston says. "If that's true..."

"He played this perfectly. He knew the board would deny him. He knew they'd relent and give him Ramona. He was probably counting on it," Diego says.

"But why me?"

Kingston groans. "Because you're going to be the next true Divine."

"Jewel," Austin says. "You're our futures."

I bring my hand up to my heart. "He's using me to get to you."

All three of my guys hug me, pulling me close. Kingston kisses my temple and says, "But you won't let him."

I bob my head, trying to wrap my mind around things. "I dare him even to try."

To be continued...

Thank you so much for reading *Blood Rebel!* To stay up-to-date on new releases, including *Blood Debt, The Divine Vampire Heirs: Book 3,* sign up for the Ginna Moran newsletter or join the Paranormal Center for Matches and Mates Facebook Group. More Vampire Heirs World fun is to be had!

OTHER SERIES BY GINNA MORAN

REVERSE HAREM

The Divine Vampire Heirs Series
The Royale Vampire Heirs Series
Academy of Vampire Heirs Series
The Pack Mates of Lunar Crest Series

PARANORMAL

Call of the Ocean Series
Demon Watcher Series
Demon Within Series
Destined for Dreams Series
Finding Nate Series
Going Ghostly Series
Spark of Life Series
When Souls Collide Series

CONTEMPORARY

Falling into Fame Series
Life After Lila

 ACKNOWLEDGMENTS

THANK YOU SO MUCH TO Sarah and Katie for all your hard work to make this happen. You two are rock stars! I appreciate everything you do from the bottom of my heart.

ABOUT GINNA MORAN

GINNA MORAN IS a writer from sunny Southern California. She started writing poetry as a teenager in a spiral notebook that she still has tucked away on her desk today. Her love of writing grew after she graduated high school, and she completed her first unpublished manuscript at age eighteen.

When she realized her love of writing was her life's passion, she studied literature at Mira Costa College in Northern San Diego. Besides writing novels, she was senior editor, content manager, and image coordinator for Crescent House Publishing Inc. for four years.

Aside from Ginna's professional life, she enjoys binge watching television shows, playing pretend with her daughter, and cuddling with her dogs. Some of her favorite things include chocolate, anything that glitters, cheesy jokes, and organizing her bookshelf.

Ginna Moran loves to hear from her readers so visit her online at www.GinnaMoran.com. You can also find her on Facebook, Twitter, and Instagram. To stay up-to-date on new releases, sign up to her newsletter. You'll not only get exclusive access to extra stories, but you'll be able to participate in monthly giveaways!

Ginna Moran is currently hard at work on her next novel.

www.ingramcontent.com/pod-product-compliance
Lightning Source LLC
Chambersburg PA
CBHW031618180726
48284CB00005B/1604